"JULIE." HE REACHED FOR MY HAND AND HELD IT. "IF YOUR FATHER DOESN'T COME, IT'S NOT GOING TO BE THE END OF THE WORLD, YOU KNOW."

He stood up and so did I, and then he kissed me and I went straight down that elevator shaft Marge had mentioned, and from the very top of the Woolworth Building. In fact it was more like falling down something like the Grand Canyon, ledge after ledge, and I clung to him until finally he pulled away.

I couldn't think of a thing to say. . . .

ABOUT THE AUTHOR

ELIZABETH BYRD is the author of twelve adult novels and many magazine articles and short stories. Like Julie, she was a teenager in New York City during the Prohibition era. She, too, researched and wrote a play about Mary, Queen of Scots, for her classmates to perform in their experimental school. Later this background helped her write *Immortal Queen,* published in 1956, which became an international best-seller.

Ms. Byrd decided to write this autobiographical novel on a rainy day in Aberdeen, Scotland. As she took shelter in the doorway of a shoe store, she heard the song "I'll Get By" on the radio. At that time, she says, she was living in a haunted castle in Scotland and her New York girlhood seemed remote. But the music revived memories, and she wrote *I'll Get By.*

I'LL GET BY

A NOVEL BY

Elizabeth Byrd

FAWCETT JUNIPER • NEW YORK

I'LL GET BY

This book contains the complete text of the original hardcover edition.

Published by Fawcett Juniper Books, CBS Educational and Professional Publishing, a division of CBS Inc., by arrangement with The Viking Press

ISBN: 0-449-70020-8

Grateful acknowledgment is made to Bourne Music Canada Limited and Cromwell Music, Inc., for permission to reprint an excerpt from "I'll Get By (As Long as I Have You)" words by Roy Turk, music by Fred E. Ahlert. TRO—© Copyright 1928 and renewed 1956 by Cromwell Music, Inc., New York, Fred Ahlert Music Corp., Los Angeles, and Pencil Mark Music, Inc., Scarsdale, New York. Used by permission.

Printed in the United States of America

First Fawcett Juniper printing: June 1982

10 9 8 7 6 5 4 3 2 1

For Barbara Starkey

One

AT WILSON, the school I attend in New York, we're denied absolutely nothing but sex and clichés; I'll explain that later. We're guinea pigs in a sort of laboratory for more timid progressive schools. Professors are forever writing papers on us: "Behavior of the Bright Child" or "Experiment in Education, 1928" or "A Study in Permissiveness." They come from all over the world to sit in on our classes and take notes. The really dedicated ones even follow you out into the corridor and ask personal questions. That's what happened to me last week.

"What's your name, young lady?" He had a German accent.

"Julie Willis."

"Age?"

"Fifteen."

He smiled, showing broken teeth through a mustache. "And what are you going to do with your life?"

"Be an actress."

"Ah. And I suppose you are encouraged to the very limit of the school's ability?"

"Yes," I said. "They let me skip Arithmetic when I

was eight, although I'm supposed to do a little Biology."

"Do you have any complaints, Miss Willis?"

"That Biology. I don't see how dissecting a frog can possibly help my future, but they call it Discipline Preparatory-something."

"I see. Perhaps this is because you will require discipline when you begin your stage career."

"I suppose so," I said.

He had started to ask another question when a bell rang. I said, "Sorry, that's English class." But he trotted along behind me to class and sat down in the back of the room to observe.

Our English instructor, Mr. Skinner, is a very tough man on clichés. We can write our compositions on any subject at all, but Heaven help us if a cliché pops up. And one did, right away, from Stewart Crandall, who read aloud a short story he had written: "He was delighted by the suggestion and nodded his head—"

"What's that again, Stewart?" Mr. Skinner pounced, and I knew why, but poor Stewart didn't.

"He was delighted *with* the sug—"

Mr. Skinner said, "That's not the point." He looked around at the twenty-four of us present. "Who detects the *terrible* writing here?"

My friend Marge raised her hand. "Of course, 'he nodded' is enough. You don't nod your toe or your shoulder, do you?"

The class giggled, but Mr. Skinner, who is more against clichés than the government is against booze, and never permits one, said, "It's a serious matter. Stewart doesn't have a bad idea here for a story, but not only does he have heads nod, on page six he has 'She shrugged her shoulders.' Would she shrug her stomach? Her ear?" His voice boomed. "She *shrugged,* that's all."

He was a short man, seeming to need to shave a lot, and rather frail looking, but he could absolutely terrify you when he projected that voice. "That's enough, Stewart. Quite enough. Sit down."

Stewart, who is terribly rich—his parents endowed the school with millions of dollars—sat down. He and I had nothing much in common because, personally, we don't share anything except a liking for history. But I feel sorry for anyone who makes Mr. Skinner erupt, so I sent Stewart a sympathetic look. He's seventeen, just a little backward, but he has to go to this school because his parents spent all that money on it.

"And you, Julie Willis."

So I'd committed a cliché too? I felt a prickle go up my spine. (Cliché.)

He picked up my manuscript and read: "She was afraid to go to bed. . ."

He looked us over, glaring. "Three dots after bed. Why, Julie? What's wrong with a period?"

We couldn't help it, we all laughed now, mainly the girls because Wilson, although coeducational, is virtually innocent about sex. The boys have their psychologist and the girls have theirs, for separate instruction. But I'm not sure the boys had gotten around to menstruation yet, if you see what I mean.

"Well, Mr. Skinner," I said when the laughter had died, "I thought that dots indicated something more to come, a sort of suspense thing."

"I do not," he said, "approve of cheap literary tricks. And we are well over the Victorian horror of calling a spade a spade or a bed a bed. And why was she afraid to go to bed?"

He paused dramatically. "You don't explain why. You're trying to be subtle. So the reader misses whatever point you may have had in mind. Of all people, Julie, you should know that you write—and act—for an audience, not for personal identification. Who on earth cares about what *you* feel? You've got to subordinate ego and remember that the reader wants to be entertained, moved, made sad or sick, or amused, but for God's sake spare us the mystery of introspective writing. Because it's—"

I shivered in my chair.

"—a bore."

I wanted to cry. Lots of us did in his class, but we had to respect him. And from age eight (me, I mean), he had encouraged me to write plays, both original ones and adaptations of the classics. That's about all I did at Wilson—write and act in plays. This made for a lot of happiness all around, for it kept the girls who liked Household Arts busy making costumes, occupied the boys in Carpentry for stage sets, and gave the Painting and Sculpture classes a lot to do, too. Everybody *creative,* although I must say Wilson had slipped a bit in the past two years, making us all take at least one science subject, or something else we hated, for that Discipline Preparatory thing. That's why poor Stewart was in English and Marge in German and me in Biology.

"Basically," said Mr. Skinner, "you are not a boring writer. Your original plays have been very good indeed, and you've a certain flair for adapting the classics."

I had adapted everything from *Macbeth* to *Jane Eyre* to *The Three Musketeers,* usually playing the meatier roles like Lady M., the Demented Wife, and Milady. Long ago I'd learned that the sweet heroines weren't the most dramatic, and I had in mind an original about Lucrezia Borgia. But with Mr. Skinner on the warpath all I could think of was the rescuing bell.

"But," he went on inexorably, "this short story"—he tapped it contemptuously—"is a bore. You don't even try to communicate, so I shan't ask you to read it because I want this class awake and alert for the next fifteen minutes."

Somehow my humiliation passed because he began to attack Vera Jordan, who is an absolute rat of a girl, always attacking everybody else. She even looks like a rat—sharp-nosed, with little yellow eyes and hands like claws. She had clawed her way to an A in English, but now it seemed she had perpetrated four clichés in one paragraph. Just for a second I felt sorry for her and even smiled at her, but I guess she took this for malice because she gave me a hostile stare. Then, mercifully for us, the bell rang.

In the corridor Marge put her arm around me. "It was awful, but that's the way he is. And probably Monday he'll be praising you to the sky about something else."

"Cliché," I said. "But thanks, anyway."

The man who had followed me in said, "Excuse me, Miss Willis, what is your next class?"

"Psychology for Girls," I told him. "Boys is across the hall there."

He thanked me and went into Boys.

Now we settled down for a session with Mrs. Curran. She's one of those elderly gray-haired women who try to be all-girls-together with us. We are supposed to have problems and tell them to her, and if we don't she is terribly frustrated, poor thing, so we generally make up problems to please her. Or else sometimes we have real questions to ask, generally dealing with sex.

There is a very curious thing about sex. You can read about it and see diagrams and understand about how dogs mate and all that, but when it comes to boys, there's a big mystery. I'm told that in public schools every child over ten knows all about everything, but my best friends and I didn't. Marge and her sister Kitty (who's in the class behind us) and I were too embarrassed about our ignorance to ask much. And Mrs. Curran wasn't telling unless somebody cornered her. Nobody did because we all pretended to one another that we knew the answers. However, we were up on our Freud about things like repression and inhibition. I thought we'd be getting on to that safe ground again when Enid Rosenblum, who is very bright, raised her hand and asked what penis-envy was.

"Penis-envy," said Mrs. Curran, "is a conception of Freud's."

"Of what?" Enid asked.

Mrs. Curran removed her glasses so as not to see us better. "You are all aware of the male penis?"

"Yes," we said in a chorus. You couldn't very well walk to school through Morningside Park without being aware—all those old men sitting on park

(11)

benches with their pants open. Only we never quite saw because we hurried past them.

"Well, some little girls envy their little brothers this —appendage."

"I don't," said Vera Jordan. "What's so great about having a penis?"

"It represents a certain power," Mrs. Curran said, "that girls don't have."

"But why should we envy it?" Enid asked. "Besides, how can we envy something we've never even seen? I haven't seen a penis. I don't have any brothers, so I don't expect I'll see one for quite a while. Am I supposed to envy it?"

"This," Mrs. Curran said, "is simply a *theory* of Freud's. It may not hold up. In future research, that is. We are rather on the threshold—you see?"

Enid has one of those logical minds. "I don't see. If I've never seen a penis, what have I got to envy? Like a savage who's never seen a can opener."

Marge said, "That's right. Why does Freud think we should envy something we've never seen?"

Poor Mrs. Curran was bombarded, because Vera Jordan said, "I've seen my brother pee, but I didn't think it was all that powerful—it just droops, that's all."

"In the process of ejaculation," Mrs. Curran said, "it does not. But you do understand about semen?"

"A girl in every port," said Jane Bliss. "My mother says never flirt with a sailor on Riverside Drive."

"Or anywhere," said Betty Scott. "You don't pick up boys."

Mrs. Curran seemed pleased. "That's right. There are plenty of nice boys right here in school." She looked over at Enid. "You understand why, of course?"

"Because they don't have our high IQs and they might have syphilis?"

"They could have your IQs," Mrs. Curran said, "but we weren't talking about that *kind* of semen. I am referring to the male discharge."

"I suppose they often are," said Marge. "The Navy is so strict. My sister Kitty met such a nice Navy boy at a party the other night, but now he's in the brig and probably he'll be fired because he's overstayed his leave."

"Girls," Mrs. Curran said, "I want you to understand precisely what semen is."

She spelled it out so that we wouldn't confuse it with the Navy, and then she went to the blackboard and drew a penis which looked quite a lot like a pickle. "This is the male organ. It generates the sperm which may or may not meet and fertilize the egg. . . ."

Coming out of class, Marge told me, "It seems such a weird chance that sperm and the egg would ever meet. All that acid—in our bodies, I mean—it's a wonder we were ever born, don't you think?"

"Yes," I said. "But do you think she had her facts straight?"

We brooded over this as we took our books to our lockers, and then we resumed conversation after we'd settled in the cafeteria with creamed chicken on toast. "The thing about sex is," Marge said, "they're trying to teach us about it at our age, but I don't think they're up on it. I mean, the way things are changing— Lindbergh flying the Atlantic. Who ever would have imagined it? I'm not so sure of anything any more, are you?"

"No." And I wasn't. But it wasn't sex that bothered me. It was something a lot more important. Something I didn't even mention much to Marge or Kitty.

After lunch I went up to Creative Arts and discussed costumes for my new play about Mary, Queen of Scots and agreed that the cast could wear ruffs made of Lily cups since pleated paper looks like linen. Stewart Crandall wanted a part badly (the casting was up to me) so I'd told him he could be Mary's executioner, and I'd thereby gained his family's permission (and money) to rent costumes from the Metropolitan Opera for those of us playing the leading roles. Not that Stewart's role was leading, but at least he was the only one left alive onstage at the end.

Miss Thain, who teaches Creative Arts—the sewing

side of it—asked me as I started out the door, "Have you talked over Stewart with Mr. Skinner? Does he—well—approve Stewart as the executioner?"

"Yes," I said. "He's got only one line to speak. So he's sure to remember it."

"Good," she said. We'd never forget the mess he'd made of Porthos in *The Three Musketeers,* not only forgetting his lines but allowing the little cushion used for padding to protrude from his doublet. "What will you need for Queen Elizabeth?"

"Besides the Met costume and the ruff," I said, "a red wig."

She nodded. "But are you sure that Elizabeth and Mary Stuart ever met, dear?"

"Who is?" I asked. "I brought up the subject in History, and Mr. Weber said it could be dramatic license, that if they didn't meet they should have, and since it was a play I could do as I liked."

"So that's settled," she said. "And will Marge need a wig for Mary?"

"A white one for Act Three. She can use her own hair up until she gets so old—forty-four. She aged terribly fast just before the execution," I added tactfully, because Miss Thain wasn't very young and there was a pleat of gray in the gold. It was rumored that she and Mr. Weber were madly in love but that he had a wife, which had thrown her hair off—I mean Miss Thain's, which had changed from blond to mousy on account of her passion for Mr. Weber. These things are said to happen overnight, but if that was so, it happened before I came to Wilson, because she'd always seemed old to me. Not wrinkly exactly, but even older than my mother, and with gray hairs in her eyebrows.

I strolled around the rest of Creative Arts—it takes up an entire floor—and admired some paintings, which would be copied as murals for the three acts of the play and serve as stage sets. I must say this for Wilson, it doesn't do things humbly, not with all those Crandall millions. We even have a huge theater, just like ones on Broadway, with stars' dressing rooms, a special room for makeup, and a prompter's box. Since I would appear, as Queen Elizabeth, in only a few scenes, I'd also be acting as prompter since naturally I knew all the lines by heart. I hadn't stolen any from anyone, because I think Schiller is dreadfully dull, and so, in fact, did Mr. Skinner, who would be our Director.

I had just started toward my locker to get my coat and leave my books when that German professor came out of Higher Math and said, "Miss Willis, might I ask you a favor?"

"Of course," I said. We were encouraged to talk freely to visiting Observers. Not that he was very attractive or young—but aside from the broken teeth and rather ratty brown mustache, he did have a scar on his cheek that could have occurred in a duel at Heidelberg. "What may I do for you?"

That sounded kind of stilted, but his precise speech affected me. I'm inclined to imitate.

"Would there be someplace we might talk in private?" he asked.

The only private place in Wilson is the gym, when it's not in use, or the swimming pool. I said, "I'm just on my way home if you'd like to walk along with me?"

He waited while I left my books, put on my coat, and closed the locker. We went down a flight of marble steps together, and he said, "Beautiful," as we passed the busts of Plato, Socrates, and President Wilson. Well, they should be beautiful. They cost enough—set in onyx niches, courtesy of the Crandall Foundation.

We came outside and he looked at his watch. "Only two-thirty. Do you not study in the afternoons?"

"If I'm in the mood," I said, "the library."

"Would you be in the mood for coffee somewhere?" he asked.

The only "where" I could think of was Freeman's drugstore, but it was sure to be full of kids, so I said, "Yes, thank you," and guided him to the very expensive drugstore four blocks away that we called the Pink Passion Palace because it had a pink front. It also had the best strawberry sundaes in New York costing twenty-five cents, so I'd been there only twice—when Dad was in town.

I ordered my sundae and he ordered coffee. "Miss Willis," he said, "I do not like to pry, but I am a psychoanalyst."

"That's quite all right," I told him. Mrs. Curran had explained them last year. "What would you like to know?"

"How you feel inside yourself about this permissive education."

"Well—aside from Biology I'm happy at Wilson—that is, as much as I could be anywhere."

"And where is anywhere?"

He sounded like a short course in Philosophy. "I mean—what's your name, Professor?"

He beamed at me. "Just 'Doctor.' Karl Gott. You mean—"

"Who is happy?" I asked. "What is happiness, really?"

It wasn't just a vague question—I actually wanted an answer. Here was somebody I'd never met before, and a psychoanalyst, who might tell me the truth.

"What do *you* think it is?" he asked.

Oh, I knew, but I wasn't going to tell him because if I did I might cry. And it was so very personal. When I'd tried to tell Marge and Kitty, they'd said I should shut up.

I put down my spoon; I couldn't finish this marvelous sundae. And I wished I hadn't come here with him.

"I'm sorry," I said, keeping the tears back. "But I think happiness is being sure of what's going to happen, not just wondering. It's okay to wonder if it's a book or a story, but in real life it's awful. Just awful."

"Something in school?" he asked.

"No. I'm sorry, Dr. Gott, but I can't tell anyone. I tried, but my best friends said, 'Shut up.' I think they think I'm dramatizing. Because I'm an actress, almost."

"But you are not acting now," he said.

"No." I slurped the strawberries around in the ice cream with my spoon.

"Do others in your school have your problem?" he asked.

If they did—and I'd guess several did—they'd learned to shut up. It was something that you lived with by yourself, and I said so. And then he said, "Who is the lady who teaches you in the Girls' Psychology? Have you not told her?"

Mrs. Curran! She'd never in this world understand. Of course, this man *might*—and even if he didn't I'd never see him again. So why not?

After all, he'd bought me this expensive sundae and surely expected something in return.

I could lie and say it was a boy. Or my mother perhaps.

"Dr. Gott," I said, and took a deep breath and held in the tears, "I love—"

If he hadn't suddenly looked as if he were about to take notes in his mind, I'd have gone on. But these Observers are all alike. To them we're just like I said—guinea pigs in a big, rich laboratory.

"—school," I said. "My trouble is Biology."

Two

WHEN I got home, there wasn't a letter from him. Mac, the nice man who serves as phone operator and mail clerk in our apartment house, looked at me and shook his head. I'm sure Mac knows, but he's the kind the Spanish Inquisition couldn't budge a word out of if he didn't feel like talking.

The lobby to our apartment house *looks* a little like the Spanish Inquisition, come to think of it. The place is new, built in 1925, but fake-antique Spanish, Aunt Celia says, and I'm sure she's right. The chairs are carved, wooden, elaborate. Torture to sit in. There is a lot of stained glass and a Moorish chandelier and tapestry and junk. Mac sort of ignores it all in his cubicle, which has the switchboard and the pigeonholes for mail. The latter are of carved wood, too, the tobacco color of Mac's face.

"Sorry, Julie," Mac said as I went toward the elevator. "Better luck tomorrow."

"Maybe," I said. "No school, anyway."

Not that I didn't like school, but in a way it was an

interruption between the eight-thirty and three o'clock mails. On Saturdays I was home for both, and you can imagine how I loathed Sundays, with nothing to even hope for. Unless he sent it special delivery, and then Mother was panting over my shoulder.

She wasn't home when I unlocked our apartment, of course. She worked at Columbia University until five in one of the filing departments. She hated it, not so much the job as the need for it. Southern ladies weren't supposed to work at anything, she said. *She* had never been trained to work. It was dee-grading, she said. I think she'd have worked under moonlight, near magnolias, to make mint juleps for a whole army of old colonels and their wives, but Columbia University didn't require that hostess touch. Poor Mother. She was caught now in 1928 when she should have been living pre-Civil War in a crinoline with white lace pantalets and a corset cover. Not that she needs the corset; she is thin as a celery stalk.

Luckily I am too. Thin, I mean. The only trouble with my figure is breasts, but we got them flattened by using heavy strips of adhesive tape. Since we started when I was thirteen, I look a lot more fashionable than poor Vera Jordan ("poor"—her parents supplied Wilson with its playground and park), whose problem was evidently ignored until she began to bulge and now it's hopeless. I could really pity her if she wasn't such an absolute rat, tattling about everybody, arrogant, and saying "Jew" instead of "Jewish," and, even worse, "Jewess," whenever Enid Rosenblum was around. So she darned well deserves those breasts, that's what. Vulgar outside and in.

Inside our apartment I hung up my coat in a closet and felt the usual depression at seeing the violet moiré dress Aunt Celia had given me. Not that it wasn't beautiful—a boatline neckline and no sleeves and a dipped hemline so that you were short in front and long behind—it was a gorgeous dress, but if he didn't come, I'd never want to wear it. And no letter for a whole week.

I took some milk from the icebox, carried it into my bedroom, and sat down and brooded. If I rightly understood my Freud, then I was a psychological mess, in love with my father! That's why no boy seemed to make an impact on me, and that's why I resented Mother so. Jealous of her? That part didn't seem to fit. But perhaps I could find the answer in Krafft-Ebing, which was being passed around school surreptitiously under the cover of *Pride and Prejudice*. Enid Rosenblum had sneaked it out of her uncle's library, and, after Marge, I was next on the list. Enid said she thought it was too advanced to share with the boys, because they mature so slowly compared to us.

Well, compared to me the rest of Wilson was as calm as Walden Pond. Not a ripple except somebody got a crush on somebody or somebody had a verbal fight in the hall. We weren't a bit like the students in the public schools, who, we'd heard, had real physical fights and sometimes even babies. For instance, nobody would dream of talking back to a teacher. Evidently our reputation had gotten around, because one day we found a message scrawled on Wilson in chalk: "A bunch of sheltared snobs." Which proves that P.S. 148 couldn't spell too well.

But we weren't snobs, really, except Vera and her clique about Jews. Nobody ever mentioned or cared about the fact that a few of us, like me, were on scholarships and had no money *at all.* When Stewart had a birthday party at the mansion on East 67th Street, our whole class was invited, and he came to our homes, too, or we picnicked on Enid Rosenblum's estate up on the Hudson, were taken there in Rolls-Royces—but the point I'm making is nobody was impressed. It was either fun or not. And when you practically grow up with millionaires from the age of eight, you never think about them that way, which is called democracy if you stop to think about it.

But now I was thinking about Dad, as usual, and got out the big box of his letters. There were a hundred and fourteen. They began "My Precious Baby" when I was little, but lately "Dearest" or "My Darling." He knew all about my girl friends and crushes—there was nothing I couldn't write him, even about how awful Mother acted sometimes. But he was mainly on her side. I had to be home at midnight on weekend dates, and I was pledged not to drive with a boy who drank. But unlike Mother he never moralized; he just told me.

I was never very clear about what he did. He was a promoter or something, and for five years he'd been traveling around Arizona and New Mexico to gold and silver mines and putting options on them—whatever that is. His letters came from hotels in Wickenburg, Phoenix, Bisbee, Nogales. I do know he's just leased (?) a mine called King Solomon's in the Superstition Mountains that he says will be worth millions. And I know the last letter by heart:

Tucson, 28 April

My darling:

The deal is almost closed, and I hope to be in New York 17 May. After your school is out we're going to Europe. I know your mother will want to shop in Paris, but I think we'll leave her there and adventure among an Alp or two and then go to Scotland. I know a lodge in the Highlands where we can fish out of our hotel windows if you are so inclined, or shoot grouse or reel to bagpipes, and I'll give you your first sip of Drambuie, which is ambrosia, tasting of peat and heather-honey, not to be confused with the damn needle beer or bathtub gin of your swains. Then we'll duck-shoot on the Borders. Hunting rights, along with castles and game-beaters, are leased quite cheaply, I hear, but money will be the least of our worries. Or would you like an African safari? I prefer things disorganized, myself, but it's up to you. It's been a long, hard path for both of you, so we'll make up for lost time.

Your devoted Dad

I didn't care where we went; I just wanted to be with him again. And now he knew he simply *had* to be here 19 May for the Father and Daughter's Dinner at Wilson. I would wear him like a bouquet, for there's not a doubt in the world that he's the handsomest man in the world, and to walk in on his arm—well, the Prince of Wales would be a measly little escort in comparison. Now, in that drugstore, for instance, Dr. Gott had just been nodded at. But how well I remembered the scurry when Dad took me there, the manager and soda clerk practically colliding in a bow, and Dad sending back my hot fudge sundae because the nuts looked stale. He'd had black coffee, to which he added a little brandy from a silver hip flask. He showed me that flask later; rather lopsided, made by an Indian friend of his in Taxco, but very beautiful, with an amethyst on its neck. He had brought Mother a necklace of amethysts and silver made by the same man, and a little ring for me.

But do you know, she *cried* when he gave her the necklace? Because he hadn't sent rent money—can you imagine anything so mundane to bring up at a time when you're being covered with jewels? I was only ten, but I remember it well, her weeping all over crepes suzette at the Waldorf where he'd taken us to dinner. In the taxi on the way home she cried some more in that soft ladylike way she has, never making a scene, just making people feel guilty. Dad was supposed to stay in New York for at least a month, but two days later he said he had business in Phoenix, and so he left.

For the next five years we lived up and down. Some summers I'd be sent to expensive camps in Maine, others we couldn't afford the subway to Coney Island. I remember a gaslit tenement on West 23rd Street and a hotel suite on Madison Avenue. Finally we came here to this big apartment house, which Mother says is a bargain because I can walk to school and she can walk to her job at Columbia University, but *I* think it's cheap because the place is so hideous.

Not inside, really. We have a long hall from the door

up to the bathroom. Off it, the living room in the middle is like the filling of a sandwich with two bedrooms like bread on either side. If Mother hadn't loved all those Kentucky antiques of hers, it wouldn't be so gloomy. Wherever we went, she carted around those Duncan Phyfes and love seats and junk. I mean, downstairs in the lobby it's spurious Spanish, but up here it's Ol' Southern. If Aunt Celia hadn't insisted on pale yellow and apricot upholstery for the chairs (and done them herself), it would be even gloomier. Anyway, it's clean. Tomorrow, Saturday, we'd be polishing up again, all the mahogany and the brass chest-pulls and the big cloud-shaped gilt-edged mirror. There's not a modern thing in the room except my victrola.

I went in there and chose a Rudy Vallee record and put it on. But "I'll Get By" always makes me cry. And there is also a sort of sacredness about Rudy. Once Marge and Kitty and I had pricked our wrists with a needle and made a solemn blood-pledge to love Rudy forever and tell him so if we ever met him. Marge laughed about it the other day and said how childish we'd been, but I notice she still plays his records and never misses his radio program.

The phone rang and I hurried to it, but it was only Mrs. Curran. "Julie?" she said. "I forgot to ask you if you're making a reservation for the Father and Daughter's Dinner."

For crying out loud, how could I tell her? "I *think* my father will be here by then," I said.

A pause. I suppose she was using gentle psychology on me. "Well, it seems such a pity to miss it again. And you know it needn't be your *own* father. What about going with Marge and Kitty's father—Professor Craig?"

They'd suggested that last year and the year before, but I didn't want an old bald-headed false-father—I wanted mine.

"I really think my father will be here."

Another pause. "You've thought so—I mean, dear, he's obviously a very busy man. Now, I've talked with

Mr. Skinner, and he's a father, you know, but his children are so young. He'd be delighted to take you."

In a way that was a compliment. Mr. Skinner was so tremendously erudite that it would make a visible impression to walk into the dinner with him. But he wasn't my father. He was only my English teacher and play director and severest critic. As I hesitated, Mrs. Curran said, "I'll put you down for the dinner anyway, Julie—with escort. How will that be?"

"Okay," I said, "thanks," and hung up.

Here we were at Wilson supposed to be "bright children," but I hadn't been able to just say I didn't want anybody to escort me but my father. Inhibition? But I did know something lurked in Mrs. Curran's mind about me or she wouldn't have made such a point of the dinner. Perhaps she didn't even believe I *had* a father. Maybe she thought he'd been killed in the war or that I was simply lying. But she had access to my case history and could certainly find out that Mother had entered me in Wilson as daughter of Emily and Ruddell Willis.

I listened to one of Rudy's records for a while, and then I wandered into Mother's room to file a jagged nail. On her marble-topped dressing table big brown hairpins slept in a cradle of hairnet. There was a little jar of fingertip rouge and a worn nail buffer with a silver handle. I found a file and worked on my nail, wishing I had a manicure set of my own, but there just wasn't money for things like that.

How to pass the time until dinner and my date with Robert? I experimented with Mother's makeup, but it was terribly old-fashioned—that white scentless powder in the cut-glass jar, the lipstick that was pale pink, the bottle of Azure that was just dregs now, probably bought before I was born.

I leaned out the window and saw the back side of Columbia campus, boys and girls dawdling back from classes. Next to Freeman's drugstore the florist was putting tubs of lilacs outside his shop. They were just the color of my evening dress, and I thought, what's wrong with a lilac corsage—*if* I went to the dinner? The other girls would wear roses or gardenias, but I might set a new style.

I wished Robert weren't coming over tonight, but it was almost obligatory to date over the weekend, whether you wanted to or not. Besides, if I didn't go out, Mother would make me a kind of servant to her bridge game. I'd be trying to read and she'd say, "Mrs. Varner needs a cigarette, dear," and I'd hop up, and then, "Pass the chocolates, Julie," and after I'd settled down again, "Open the window—it's warm," and of course I had to serve the jellied fruit salad at ten, and toast the English muffins and butter them, and make the coffee, and bring out the cake, and then wash everything when the ladies left. Bridge nights were much worse than being with Robert, and he might have enough money for a movie.

Well, I might as well get over the first chores before she came home. So I set the card table for dinner (she always used our best silver even when we were alone) and washed the lettuce and sliced the tomatoes and opened a can of salmon. It was cheap, and luckily we both liked it, and I can tell you that a diet of forever hamburger can be pretty monotonous, whether you have it in a casserole with potatoes or as meat loaf or just fried in patties. When Dad came home, it would be duckling and lamb and lobster, and in restaurants and hotels; silver pitchers of caramel sauce for ice cream; French pastry; string orchestras playing behind potted palms.

If he asked me, straight off, when he came home on the seventeenth where I wanted to go, I'd say the Villa Vallee, to see and hear Rudy in person. And I wanted to tea-dance at the Biltmore because I'd never tangoed properly, all those dips, and Dad wrote that he could dance everything except the Black Bottom, which I could teach him. That way we had two nights to practice for the Father and Daughter's Dinner, since there was dancing afterwards.

I had just taken a shower when Marge phoned. "You

scuttled off so fast with that Observer I didn't have time to ask if you want to go to the dinner with our father and us."

I liked Professor Craig and it was sweet of her, but I said, "No, thanks. If Dad is delayed I might have to go with Mr. Skinner, *if* I go."

"You mustn't miss it again, I *think* they're having Hal Kemp's orchestra. And Skinner can't dance."

"But Dad can. He said—"

"Oh, *Julie!* Whatever makes you think he's really coming this time?"

How could I say that I just knew? Marge was so disillusioned by life that she couldn't be optimistic about anything. This is because she's in love with Dick Osterman, who's a real sheik and couldn't be faithful even if married. He is terribly attractive but poison to anyone wanting permanence. Even Kitty, silly as she is, advises Marge to find somebody else, but Marge— who can't believe in my father—does believe in Dick, which is absurd. So we have a truce on these subjects. I asked if she would be ready for rehearsal of *Mary Stuart* on Tuesday.

"Yes," she said. "Miss Thain measured me for a white wig, and I hope it doesn't look too awful. Of course I'll have a black veil over it. When do we get the costumes?"

"Not until just before the performance," I told her. "We'll have to pretend we have them at the dress rehearsal—I think the Met doesn't like to hire out things for long."

"Have you figured out anything for Elizabeth's teeth?" she asked.

I insist on realism in my plays, and Queen Elizabeth had terrible dental problems, which I believe is why, basically, she was so nasty. "I tried sticking bits of brown paper in my teeth, but I couldn't talk, so I think I'll just stroke my jaw once in a while and wince, and the audience will get the point."

"You're such a good actress," Marge said (and really meant it). "Why didn't *you* play Mary?"

"Because," I said truthfully, "I'm only pretty and you're beautiful. Besides, I do character parts better than heroines. And I could never learn those Latin lines at the end where she prays,"

Wilson doesn't teach Latin or Greek—that's one reason we're progressive—but Marge has had some lessons with her father, since she intends to go on to Vassar or Smith. " 'Bye," she said suddenly, and I knew her mother had come in. Neither of us is supposed to use the phone "frivolously," so we always understood when someone hung up in a hurry.

I had dressed when Mother came in. The first thing she said was, "Any letter?" and I said no. She sort of slumped down on the couch and pulled off her hat and then kicked off her high heels. She has lovely legs and ankles, but her skirt always covers her knees. Ladylike. Marge says she is very pretty for her age, but it's hard for me to judge. Like myself, she has wavy dark-brown hair and dark-brown eyes, but our noses are different, hers long and narrow and mine tilted up. She said she was very tired and would just eat off a tray on the couch and then take a nap before the bridge game.

Halfway through her salad, she said, "I should wash those windows."

She is absolutely nagged by conscience, especially if visitors are coming. Her theme is "What will people think?" So, of course, I helped wash the windows, and then we had coffee and lady fingers. She couldn't possibly have waited for those windows until after dessert.

She was pleased that I had a date with Robert, which goes to show what a bore he is. The really snazzy boys are never approved of by parents, which is why Marge's always hover around if she dates Dick. They seem to have an inbuilt sense of danger and excitement. But Robert is welcomed everywhere by parents, even though it's obvious he is going nowhere fast. He has flunked three subjects and therefore will have a private tutor this summer. Not that he's as dumb as Stewart Crandall, but, at sixteen, he's on the way. Just the same, I like him because he's so deeply in love with me.

He didn't have any money for a movie so we walked over to Riverside Drive and sat on a park bench. We know each other so well there isn't much to say except, "What a nice night." Spring had come earlier than usual, perhaps embarrassed by all the icy slush of March. We looked up at the stars and held hands.

"Do you know what love is?" he asked.

Oh, yes, but I couldn't tell him—he'd laugh. Or if he understood Freud he'd trip me up on Dad. "What do you think it is?" I asked.

"Hopelessness," he said. "I am going to light a cigarette." He let go of my hand and poked into his pocket and brought out a pack of Camels.

This astonished me. Nobody smoked except Dick Osterman. For the first time I began to have some respect for old Robert. Could he possibly be a mystery, with a life of his own I didn't know about?

"Are you hopelessly in love?" I asked.

"Oh," he said vaguely, "why talk about it?"

Well, the truth is he couldn't talk, with all the coughing and the smoke. I waited until it had cleared a little, and then I said, "You can tell me anything, Robert."

But he simply shook his head and handed me the cigarette. "Want to try?"

I admired the way it looked in my hand.

"Puff," he said, "or it'll go out."

I puffed and coughed.

"Once in a while," he said, "you gotta flip off the ash."

I did.

"You're supposed to inhale," he said. He snatched the cigarette from me, took a deep puff and a deep breath, and off popped his necktie. It lay on my knee like a blue-striped butterfly.

"Oh, well," he said, putting the tie into his pocket, "I think we're through with this, aren't we?" and flung the cigarette over into the grass.

He looked so disgusted. If he looked like that oftener he'd be almost handsome, for his face doesn't seem so round and childish; his eyes get darker and his chin firmer. Nothing is really wrong with Robert in bits, but put him all together and he doesn't add up.

"I prefer cigars," he said. He took my hand again. "Julie, look up there. What do those stars mean to you?"

Dad, seeing them low and bright in Arizona: he'd written about how light and bright they can be. Stars meant a real star's dressing room on Broadway someday, too. I could imagine stars over Paris and over the moors of Scotland and Dad saying, "Where shall we go now? Rio?"

"I never thought much about stars," I said. But they did have a kind of magic—even with Robert. Probably it was simply because it was the first spring night of the year, and now that I was growing up I somehow knew there wouldn't be many to waste. I could see the dark, gaunt shadows of trees that showed a few leaves in the lamplight, and across the river a little boat chugged along to Piermont, lit stem to stern like a real ship.

Europe with Dad—a ship like the *Lusitania* had been, only safer. They weren't building quite such big ships any more, but they were building bigger airplanes, and Dad had written that he planned to invest in them. Perhaps I'd even be flying someday, and that brought the idea of stars as close as a heartbeat.

"I do," Robert said. "Stars. Like something to reach toward. You know?"

I knew, though I was surprised he did. That just shows that you can't judge other people even if you've known them seven years. To think that Robert even *thought* of stars was surprising. No imagination, I'd thought, no romanticism, and certainly no It. But I suppose that many persons without It can be imaginative. Just like Marge has It and isn't. If she were sitting here and being asked what she thought about stars, she'd suggest some book on astronomy and let it go at that.

"Want a soda?" Robert asked, breaking the mood, and, of course, I did, so we went to Freeman's just in time before it closed at ten. It's quite different in the daytime with the school crowd than it is at night when older people come in to have sandwiches and coffee. No schoolbags on the floor, nobody holding hands in the booths or sharing a milkshake from the same straw.

But there was Dick Osterman having a soda with a pretty girl I'd never seen before. Faithless to Marge! He saw me and looked embarrassed, and I looked back coldly. I wouldn't tell Marge, if that's what worried him, because you don't upset your best friend. Robert saw the girl, too, and whispered to me, "What a baby!"

Well, I had to admit it. But she looked like something he could have picked up from P.S. 148—"common," as Mother would have said—in a skintight dress. Not that I don't long for one myself, but it's the mark of being jazzy, and her red hair was a lot too long. In a little while Dick slunk out with her, and she wriggled as she walked to the door. I think maybe she wasn't used to high heels (you need to practice), for she nearly tripped and Dick took her arm. I knew just what was going to happen next, too. They'd get into his Stutz— he's old enough for a license—and drive way up the Drive to park and neck. Poor Marge.

"We mustn't tell Marge," I said to Robert as we walked back to my house. "About that girl."

He agreed that we shouldn't. "May I come up?" he asked as we entered that Spanish tomb of a lobby.

"No," I said, "Mother will still have her friends there."

So he gave me a peck on the cheek and went off. I went over to Dan, the night man, and asked if there was a special delivery, but he said no and looked sour. He's not nearly as nice as Mac, and I think he drinks, because he always smells of peppermint, but that lobby is so melancholy at night that I don't really blame him.

In our apartment the ladies were just about to leave, and when they did, of course, I had the dishes to do. Mother had won the bridge game (although they never played for money or anything), but she seemed depressed. We had cocoa together, and then she said, "Julie, what are you going to do about the Father and Daughter's Dinner?"

"I'm waiting to hear from Dad," I said. "Probably tomorrow—"

"Tomorrow," she said. "Even if he writes and *says* he's coming, you mustn't count on it. He's—well, so busy. You should make arrangements to go with another father."

As I started to speak, she said, "You can't miss another one. And that dress is just going to waste. After all Celia did with it."

Aunt Celia has a little dress shop in her own apartment and somehow has connections with someone in Paris who sells her very cheaply clothes that models have worn. She sells them at half price, and once in a while she's able to buy clothes from New York debutantes too. The way I got my violet moiré dress was that some deb had burned a tiny hole at the waist of it and Aunt Celia made a sash to cover it. She's Dad's sister, and clever at anything she does. She can even take hamburger and dress it up with mushrooms and herbs so you wouldn't know what it was.

"If Dad doesn't come," I told Mother, "I've a choice between Professor Craig and Mr. Skinner. But I don't want either one of them. I'd rather just stay home."

She sighed. "Year after year—you just can't, darling. I'm afraid I must insist."

Parents of Wilson students are cautioned at PTA meetings never to insist lest they obfuscate the program. It's understood when we are put into Wilson that we are free agents, subject only to Dr. Matheson, who heads the school, or Laboratory. If a parent insists too much about anything, then the student is dragged out of Wilson and put into public school.

Mother has a lovely, full mouth, but now it looked

like a seam. Our mouths are alike—my best feature—except I put on a cupid's bow with lipstick. She never sees the lipstick because I hide it in my shoe and put it on when I go to classes and rub it off before I come into our apartment. It's an orange Tangee that Marge gave me last Christmas. I gave her one, too, and she has to hide it just as I do, only she and Kitty put theirs under a big doormat before and after use.

"You can't waste your life on a—" She paused. Then abruptly she changed the subject. "Did you have a nice evening with Robert?"

"The usual," I said.

"He's such a nice boy."

Yes, but all he has is curly hair and integrity. There wasn't anyone exciting around at all, although if I weren't Marge's best friend I'd have had at least one date with Dick just to see if I could feel anything with a kiss. I'd kissed four boys and never felt anything at all, but Marge said you ought to feel like you were dropping down an elevator shaft, or from a height like the Woolworth Building. That's why I would have been interested in a date with Dick. She said he'd gotten his technique from reading *The Sheik*.

"Do you have a date for tomorrow night?" Mother asked.

I sighed. "Everett Bliss, Jane's brother. We're going to a movie, at least."

She frowned. "I wasn't blasé at your age. It's not normal. Why, I used to spend hours and hours primping for a date, and you—you just take a shower and toss on clothes and that's that."

"But I know Everett from school—he's no novelty. Anyway, there's a new Alice Terry at Loew's, and if he hasn't spent his week's allowance, maybe we'll eat Chinese later." I yawned, and so did she, and we separated to our rooms.

I was up early and ran down to see about the mail as soon as I'd dressed, but Mac just handed me a couple of letters for Mother from Kentucky. His eyes were shiny and soft, as if he were sad for me, and I think he was.

We have one of those friendships that doesn't need words, and I'm almost sure he knew it was Dad's letter I was waiting for, not a boy's, because he never teased or looked knowing like older people do when they think there's a romance going on.

Mother and I cleaned and polished, and then I went marketing without a bit of interest in things to eat. One year when we had money (I was thirteen then) I got twenty cents for every meal I cooked, so I learned how—besides having cooking courses in Household Arts. Ham was cheap today, so I bought half of one to bake, and new potatoes and peas and a new vegetable called broccoli that's very good if you're careful to peel the stems. Home again, I began the long wait for the three o'clock mail.

But there wasn't any.

That left a long, black corridor until Monday morning. The movie with Everett helped to fill it a little, only he wanted to neck and I didn't, partly because he doesn't appeal to me and partly because *Mare Nostrum* was a real work of art and I was crying at the end when only the sea survived. I didn't want Everett bothering me, but I was very tactful with him because suddenly I was hungry and I hoped to go to Chin's on 125th Street for egg rolls.

We did go, but I hadn't started on the egg roll when he said, "Julie, why are you so Victorian?"

I'd heard that one before, and I put mustard onto the egg roll. "I'm not," I said, and brought out my old line. "It's just that you're so popular—I don't want to be one of the crowd."

He puffed out what chest he had and smiled. "Golly," he said, "I hadn't thought of it that way. Suppose we date nobody else then?"

"But if I'm going to be an actress I have to mingle about."

That was a mistake. "How can you be an actress if you don't *live?*" he asked. "How can you—what's the word?—project if you don't *live?*"

Well, the truth of it is, Everett has got some acne left

over from last year, and a nose that would get in the way of a kiss. I certainly didn't want to live or project through necking with him. And I didn't think his line was especially new. I'll bet Sarah Siddons heard something similar back in 1773.

"All in good time," I said, eating. "When I feel that I may be ready to live, you'll be the very first to know."

Then the fried rice came, and we just ate and drank jasmine tea and talked about school. His Discipline was a course in Civics, and we compared that to Biology, and I got off the sex hook.

At home, in bed, I thought about sex again. Boys may mature later than we do, but they have more curiosity, and Mrs. Curran says that their function in life is to inseminate. This comes from the semen in them that has to have egress. It seems they can't help it. It is all stored until they are about thirteen or fourteen and then they try to find a way to get rid of it. I think a girl should be compassionate about this, and I can't imagine envying any of them. They've got this penis problem just like we've got the curse, only of course it's one of the things we can't talk about together. It somehow reminds me of the League of Nations and all those countries trying to understand one another but not speaking the same language. They know the facts, but they get embarrassed and upset because they're so different. And sometimes they get angry, just like Dick gets angry at Marge because she won't pet. And then they have a fight. Marge and Dick fight most of the time.

Three

I LOATHE Sundays because of no possibility of mail unless Dad writes special delivery, so I was glad when Marge phoned and asked me over to spend the day. It's a sort of second home at the Craigs'; I even have a robe and nightie there in case I stay overnight, which I generally do because we stay up late and talk so late. But I'd go home tonight so that if there was mail in the morning I'd get it before school.

Marge was alone. She said her parents and Kitty had gone to her aunt's for lunch, and she was relieved because she was in no mood for people. "That Dick," she said. "He phoned last night at the very *last* minute, so I shouldn't have gone out with him at all."

We sat down in her living room, which is nice and modern, not cluttery like ours, virtually free of antiques except for an old horn phonograph that Professor Craig is attached to. "I shouldn't have agreed to go on such short notice. Anyway, we parked up on a hill, the one near Bronxville, and he tried to soul-kiss."

"Ah," I said. It sounded almost like a proposal, but she was frowning so I knew it wasn't.

"I'd brought along some popcorn just in case, so I pretended to be hungry, and for a while that took his mind off it. Then he tried again. It's not that I'm moral," Marge added, "but going that far—what do you think?"

Now, Marge is so sophisticated that I never like to admit that I don't always know what she's talking about. So I said, "I don't know. Dick is probably full of unreleased semen, that's all."

"If I thought he was faithful—" she said, and let the sentence trail off.

I wasn't going to hurt her by mentioning that red-head I'd seen with Dick in Freeman's Friday night—I mean, why add to her worries? And I must say that Marge was lots prettier than that girl; she has a sort of classic profile and a madonna look. Jane Bliss, who is our fashion leader, thinks Marge looks passé because she still wears her hair parted in the middle with a little bun in the back. But her hair is beautiful, shiny like a chestnut, and her eyes are big and gray-green. And the way she can wear clothes! Aunt Celia said she could be a model in France even.

"Didn't Dick say a word about love?" I asked.

"He never does—you know that. And he drove me home at ten-thirty. Mad. As if he'd wasted his time. And he hasn't phoned."

I knew she was suffering. "Soul-kissing," I said carefully. "You feel it would encourage him too much?"

Kitty and Professor and Mrs. Craig came in then, and Marge and I started dinner. Professor Craig said, "How's everything, Julie?" and made himself a cocktail.

"This father and daughter's thing," he said. "You're welcome to come with us, you know."

"Thank you, but I think Dad's coming home."

"Well, you'll be taken care of, then."

Oh, and so beautifully. But aside from being bald, Professor Craig just doesn't have Dad's (the word Aunt Celia uses) panache. I mean, Professor Craig could go into that fancy drugstore and nobody would even notice him, let alone scurry for fresh nuts. But he is sweet and very protective of me, and if I'm very late going home, he either puts me into a cab or walks me ten blocks. Another thing—he isn't strict with Kitty or Marge and upholds all that Wilson stands for regarding permissiveness. He's a professor of Physics at Columbia, which is why Marge is good at Math, but he can talk about normal things, too, and I like him.

Picking up the newspaper, he got mad at Mayor Walker and our crooked city politics and how gangsters were running the country. Mrs. Craig helped him finish the drink. *I* think she's the bee's knees because, except for lipstick, she doesn't object to things and, except for Dick, never pries into Marge's private life. But Mother doesn't approve of her because of her bobbed hair and short skirts, although she concedes that she's bright. When one mother likes Mah-Jongg and the other bridge, they never meet except at school plays and PTA meetings.

After dinner the Craigs had a date somewhere, so the three of us sat in the living room, or rather Marge and I sat while Kitty leaned out of the window. She hasn't Marge's classic beauty, but she's very pretty, with loads of pale blond curly hair and violet eyes, and boys whistle at her on the street.

"Are you waiting for someone?" I asked her.

She turned for a moment. "The *cutest* boy lives across the street."

Marge said, deeply sarcastic, "His name is Jim MacNamara, he is all ears and legs, and she likes him because he never notices her."

"He does, too," Kitty said. "Once he smiled and said, 'Hello.'"

"How long has this been going on?" I asked.

"Four sordid days," Marge said. "She hasn't any pride at all, just hangs out the window. And we don't know a *thing* about him."

"We do, too," Kitty said, not turning. "He goes to Horace Mann and has two parents like anybody else."

Marge glanced at me, and I smiled and said, "It's

okay." Kitty hadn't meant to be brutal. She just never thinks much.

Marge said softly, "Do you think I should call Dick?"

"Not unless you're willing to—" I glanced at Kitty.

"It's okay," Marge said, "she's in a trance. She won't hear." But she moved over onto the couch with me. "What I didn't tell you—he tried to unfasten my brassiere."

"What?" Kitty turned. "Why?"

Well, she's the silliest fourteen there ever was and hadn't had Psychology yet, so Marge said, "He's going to be an engineer. He was interested in the hooks."

But Kitty didn't hear. She yelled, "There he comes!" and rushed for Trixie, whom she leashed in seconds and dragged to the door on her bottom and was out before we knew it.

"She uses Trixie as an excuse to walk out when he comes in," Marge said. "It's simply disgraceful. *We* never chased boys. But she's so determined. Like last year when she threw the tomato at Saul."

I remembered. It had splashed all over his jacket, and Kitty had had to have it dry-cleaned, but in a way it was a wise thing to do because he finally noticed her and even took her to the movies. But the thing didn't last long because Kitty is so fickle, and my guess is that Saul, who was planning to be a rabbi, was relieved to be rid of her. It would have been sort of like the Talmud with marshmallow sauce.

"About Dick," Marge said. "I just can't lose him."

"You could ask Mrs. Curran about soul-kissing. Maybe it causes syphilis," I suggested.

"Julie, *you* ask the question. She and the girls know that I date Dick, whereas your Robert and Everett aren't sheiks, and the question coming from you would be clinical."

"Okay," I said. "I can just say I've heard about it and want to get my facts straight. But it seems to me that his trying to unhook your brassiere—"

Kitty came in, unleashed Trixie, and dumped herself into a chair. She looked as if she were about to cry.

(40)

"Didn't he say, 'Hello'?" I asked.

She shook her head. "Just as he went into his house a girl came out. And I know he hasn't got a sister because I asked the janitor. He didn't even see me. This was a girl waiting for him, all dark and slinky. Oh, I could *die.*"

"But you don't even know him," Marge said.

"Do I have to? To be in love? What about that Francesca way back? Wasn't that the one that fell in love at first sight? Oh, neither of you understand. To think of him with that vamp, and I—I can't do a thing to break it up."

"I'll heat you some milk," Marge said, all compassion now, "and then you go to bed, and maybe tomorrow—"

"Believe me," I said, trying to help, "I live from day to day myself." But I wasn't going to mention Dad. "You'd be surprised what can happen in a few hours. You're so depressed, and then suddenly you get a let—I mean, things change." There might be a special delivery at home right now, or he might even have phoned, which he does once in a while.

"Yes," Marge said bleakly, "they do. Dick certainly has. Should I phone him?"

We talked it over and decided against it because it gave him an advantage. I had to agree with Mother that a girl should be a little mysterious and aloof; besides, though I didn't say so, I didn't want Marge put in competition with that redhead. But I thought that Dick was the type who jaded easily and would eventually return to Marge if she stayed on a pedestal, and we decided that if he did call she should be pleasant but remote. "It's funny," Marge said, "Mother and Dad never mind how late I am if I'm out with anybody else, but Dick—you can practically hear a fire alarm ring in their minds."

Kitty said, "Have you ever kissed him lying down?"

"No," Marge said. "Why?"

"Alma Wheeler and I were talking and she said you can't get pregnant from a kiss as long as you're standing up. It's when you're in bed that you get pregnant."

"I am not worried about getting pregnant," Marge said in that acid tone she uses when Kitty is especially silly. "And I certainly have enough of a baby on my hands with you. Now why don't you go to bed and let us talk?"

But she wouldn't, so after a while Marge walked me partway home. It was a beautiful night, warm and starry, and the buildings looked jeweled. We separated at 128th Street and I went on by myself, trying not to hurry in hope of a special delivery.

There wasn't one. There wasn't even any mail in the morning except what looked like the rent bill, and I left it in the pigeonhole for Mother, who goes to work a little later than I go to school. She gets so upset about bills that I was glad not to be around.

I spent most of the morning in conference about the play, and doing some rewriting in the library. Then I had History and French, and at lunch Marge reminded me to ask about syphilis. It seemed ominous to her that Dick was out sick today, but at the same time it cheered her that perhaps he had been just sick with a cold yesterday and too weak to phone her.

Mr. Skinner was especially sarcastic in English. For such a small man—about five foot six—he packed the wrath of a Jehovah. He had found no less than sixteen clichés in our essays on *Hamlet,* and there were, he said, more to discuss later. As for *Macbeth*—he said he was too embarrassed for us to even talk about what we'd written. Nobody had gotten the subtle points except Enid Rosenblum. So we would spend the last fifteen minutes in discussion of my play.

"Those of you not in the cast," he said, "may go out and skip rope or something."

Sarcasm. Nobody even laughed. Now he launched into an analysis of the leading characters—Mary Stuart, her brother James, Bothwell, Darnley, and Queen Elizabeth. "Julie has packed far too much into one play, but it does have its points. I want a rehearsal, line

(42)

perfect, tomorrow at four in the auditorium. Marge, how do you intend to play Mary? For heroics and sympathy?"

"Of course," she said.

"What did she die *for?*" he asked.

"Love," Marge said. "Her religion."

"Politics. Politics! Power politics! Don't give me any swoony stuff; she martyred herself to spite Elizabeth and the Protestants. Play it for dignity, okay, but spare us the sop. You, Julie, seem to have Elizabeth very well. Paul, your Bothwell's okay—so far. Questions?"

Stewart Crandall said, "How do you view the executioner, Mr. Skinner?"

"As a professional, that's all. He's there to do a job. And with one line, *you* should be able to . . ."

I said, "I'm cutting that line. It sounds childish. I don't think he should say anything."

"Right. Line cut."

Stewart looked terribly hurt so I said, "Anyway, he has quite a lot to do. Trying three times and finally getting her head off. He has the stage almost to himself for about four minutes."

"You've got to build suspense," Mr. Skinner told Stewart. "First you test the ax, approach Mary—then go back and sharpen it. Then you hack but it doesn't come off. You try again—and again, but taking your time."

Marge said, "Does he *have* to release catsup all over me? What will the Met think about it all over my costume?"

"We've got to simulate blood," I said.

Mr. Skinner said, "He can release the catsup on the audience's side of the block, not on her. It will take a lot of practice, Stewart, but it can be done. Any more questions?"

But just then the bell rang for Psychology, and boys and girls separated. When I came in, Mrs. Curran said, "I'd like to see you after class, dear," but that didn't worry me because I had an A. I was only curious. She's our Class Adviser as well as psychologist so I assumed she had some kind of advice.

The girls seemed mired in questions about what Freud meant by "the family romance," since they couldn't see a thing romantic about it and neither could I. My feeling about Dad certainly wasn't romantic, as if he'd been a boy. Mrs. Curran explained that it was a different kind of romance, but a pull toward one's family in preference to someone else's and a basic loyalty that endured through the years. She said, as she had about penis-envy, that it was still a theory and we mustn't take it as fact.

"Well," Enid said, "he seems to be just about all theory so far as we've gone."

"A pioneer," Mrs. Curran said. "Now, any questions?"

I brought up syphilis and I saw Marge leaning forward. "Can you get it from kissing?"

"No," said Mrs. Curran. "There has to be sexual intercourse and the germs come through the man or woman's ejection. However—"

The bell rang and the girls started drifting out, but I stayed at Mrs. Curran's desk. When we were alone she said, "Sit down, dear." She pulled some papers out of a drawer. "Now, about the Father and Daughter's Dinner. It isn't fair to ask Mr. Skinner at the last moment. Is your father really coming?"

"I told you, I'm almost sure."

"But that's happened two years in a row. We can't keep Mr. Skinner waiting to find out—"

"Then don't," I said. "*I* didn't suggest it to him. Either I come with my own father or I don't come at all."

She settled back with that let's-be-girls-together look. "Tell me about him. How long since you've seen him?"

"Five years. Five years and one month."

"Tell me about him," she said again.

I didn't know where to start. I couldn't even say for sure what he looked like because I have no photograph except that he is tall and slim and dark like an etching of Heathcliffe in *Wuthering Heights*. That's my impression, anyway, and when I wrote him about that last year he wrote back, "Dearest Cathy, thanks for the dubious compliment." There is a very blurry old picture of him and my mother on a porch of her house in Kentucky, but even with a magnifying glass you can't make out his features.

Aside from his last visit, the times he has been home were all mixed up in my mind, like a movie unreeled wrong. There was the day a long time ago when Mother had asked him to take me to Woolworth's for some pink socks, and we ended up at Best's, where he bought me a pink coat trimmed with ermine and a little ermine muff and hat to match, and she cried about the extravagance and scolded because we'd come home without the socks. Another time, we spent the morning in somebody's office on Wall Street, and I played with a typewriter and made a necklace of paper clips. Then we went to lunch at Ye Olde Chop House and had pheasant, and when we came home Mother was mad again because he had spent so much.

Mrs. Curran was still waiting for a reply, so I said, "He's great fun."

Once we picnicked in a rowboat on Central Park Lake and then moored it in the shade of trees and he recited "Kubla Khan"; he knows so many poems by heart. He took me on the roller coaster at Coney, and my stomach turned over on account of all the hot dogs and fried potatoes in it, but I didn't tell Mother I'd gotten sick because I knew he'd get scolded again. These visits of his were months, even years, apart, and Mother claimed that she missed him terribly, but when he did come she was always nagging about something, as if we were two naughty children in league against her.

I remember the smell of cinders when we saw him off at Pennsylvania Station, the smell of a lotion he sometimes used, like lemons. I remember being entrusted to put cuff links into his shirts and how he always wanted to have a shave at the same time Mother wanted a bath and his saying, "Well, come on *in,* then," and her saying it just wasn't *nice.* Mother is very modest, and maybe I'd feel funny, too, having a bath in there with a man. Certainly they quarreled— even a little girl knows, even with the bedroom door shut, no matter how quietly they do it. I think it was mostly about money. She called him "irresponsible."

Mrs. Curran was still waiting. "I'm sorry," I said. "I was in kind of a daydream. Anyway, I am sure Dad will be coming—he knows the date of the dinner and the date of the play, and he wouldn't want to miss either one."

"Well, if he does, just remember you're not the only girl who will be going to the dinner without her real father. Anne and Sylvia's parents are divorced, Lillian and—"

"My parents *aren't* divorced!" How on earth could she have such an awful idea? "It's only his business that keeps him away."

"Of course," she said soothingly, and her voice was cold-creamy soft. "I understand that. But if he doesn't come, would you prefer Mr. Skinner or Professor Craig?"

"Mr. Skinner," I said. Actress with Director. "But *must* I?"

"I very strongly advise it, Julie."

That was practically an order at Wilson. "Okay," I said, "I'll let you know as soon as I know."

"Not later than Thursday," she said. "It wouldn't be fair to upset Mr. Skinner's weekend schedule."

Out in the corridor I met Peter Vorse, who plays James Stuart, and we had a brief conference about tomorrow's rehearsal. Then I had Biology and suffered as usual—no hope of anything but a C here. I can't see how Discipline does any good to your character when it simply means boring you to death. Mr. Evert took me aside afterwards and asked if I'd prefer to have my Discipline in Chemistry. I think he wanted me off his back, but in Chemistry you can explode things so I told him I felt safer here. "Safe" is a word we students have all learned to use because we've grasped the fact that we are supposed to be made secure at Wilson and it goes straight to teachers' hearts. The key to this kind of education (I snuck it out of a pamphlet) is "to make the child feel secure in future life, which in essence is to create adaptability to all situations. Through creative action, the child learns poise and self-reliance."

Marge and Kitty and I swam in the pool, and then they wanted me to go to Freeman's for a soda, but I hurried home to see if there was a letter from Dad.

And there was. I couldn't wait to go upstairs, but sat in one of the Spanish torture chairs and read it.

Mac said as I started upstairs, "Cheer up, Julie." So he knew.

It seemed that the deal wasn't quite closed yet, but Dad hoped to be home 24 May—two days before the play—and he enclosed a ten-dollar bill. "You might want to buy something for your costume."

Once I'd gotten over my disappointment about his not being here for the dinner, I felt a little better. And *ten dollars*. I went across to Bazinet's and bought a yard of lace because those ruffs made of Lily cups tickle terribly, and Aunt Celia could make me the back-sweeping kind Queen Elizabeth sometimes wore. Then I bought a big bunch of lilacs for Mother and was putting them in a vase when Stewart Crandall phoned.

"Have you really cut out my line?" he asked piteously. "If you do, it will frustrate me terribly."

"It's my fault that the line was stupid. No executioner would say, 'Thou scoundrel,' to a queen."

"But then can't I have another line?"

I thought that perhaps if he complained to his family we wouldn't get those Metropolitan Opera costumes, so I considered giving him another one. But he'd never remember it. He was accustomed to "Thou scoundrel," so I said, "Okay, but speak it softly, just to Mary. Don't let Mr. Skinner hear it."

"Thanks," he said. "Say, are you going to the Father and Daughter's Dinner?"

"With Mr. Skinner." I explained why.

He was so grateful for his line back that he suggested a date with me after the dinner. "You'll be all dressed up and I have a tux."

I was surprised because as far as I know, Stewart doesn't date, at least not girls in school. I hesitated, because we don't have much to talk about and I wasn't sure what he had in mind.

Softly he said, "Julie, we can go to a speakeasy."

Well! That changed everything. "Are you sure?" I whispered back, as if someone could hear us.

"I've been there before."

"They'll let us in?"

"Sure. But don't tell anybody—okay?"

"Okay," I said. Not that I cared about him, but to go to a speakeasy was like being asked to Buckingham Palace or something. I wondered if even Dad had ever been to one. "The dance is over at nine," I said. "Would that be too late?"

"Just right," he said. "I'll meet you outside school. Tell your mother you're going to a dance at the Biltmore."

So it was arranged and I felt a lot better. The lace for my ruff, the lilacs for Mother, and Dad sure to be here for the play. I phoned Mrs. Curran to say I'd be glad to go to the dinner with Mr. Skinner, and then I broke my promise to Stewart because I just had to call Marge about the speakeasy. "Isn't it marvelous?"

Marge has a very strange prudent streak. "Suppose it's raided?" she asked.

"They scarcely ever are. What you read in the newspapers doesn't happen every night. But imagine old Stew being able to get into one!"

"It's money," she said. "I wouldn't be at all surprised if his family doesn't own it, like they own everything else."

"But you know that the Crandalls endow churches —"

"Probably as a front for speakeasies." I could see she was in one of her bitter moods. "But I'm glad for you and I promise not to tell anyone, not even Kitty."

"Have you talked to Dick?"

She sounded more bitter than ever. "I saw him coming out of Civics and he said, 'Hello,' and walked right on. I think he's trying to imply that I'm a prude. Anyway, he's obviously through with me."

We were talking about what she could do to get him back, when I heard Mother's key in the door and hung up. I went back into the living room, fluffed the lilacs, and told her Dad would be delayed.

Well, to make it short, she was absolutely furious about him sending me ten dollars and no rent money. "Julie! How could you? How could you buy flowers when we need necessities? You're just like him, neither of you have any idea of what it means to—to—"

"But the lilacs are for you and—"

"And I'm sick of it! *Sick!* Never to know when, what, if." She began to cry and sat down, and I went to her, but it was no use trying to comfort her—she was determined to be miserable, and make me that way too. "He says he's coming on the seventeenth, then he says the twenty-fourth, but does he ever?" She raised her head and looked at me. Then she said, "I'm sorry," and got up and went into her room, and I heard the door close quietly.

I don't like to be cynical, but I wondered if she didn't miss the rent money more than she did him. Certainly she didn't love him as I did, and none of the little things we did to try to please her seemed to work. That silver-and-amethyst necklace she had cried over. The lovely dinners we'd had ruined because she disapproved so of anything like the Waldorf or Fraunce's Tavern or Mori's. But Dad came to town so rarely it was natural to celebrate, except that she always contrived to spoil everything by peering at the bill. I guess she's about thirty-five, and she doesn't look so old but she certainly acts it. Like part of a Greek chorus murmuring "doom"—even when she doesn't say a word. It may be my imagination, but I think that pretty mouth of hers gets thinner each year, as if she were tasting vinegar.

After about half an hour she came back and said she'd had a headache, and I asked if I should start dinner, but she said no, remember Aunt Celia was coming. All I had to do was set the card table.

Then Aunt Celia came with a lot of packages, and before she said anything much at all she went into the kitchenette, which is screened off from the living room, and pretty soon there came a heavenly smell of garlic and shrimps. Then she uncapped a little bottle of wine and tossed off a gray cape and sat down and said, "May Julie have a glass?"

"An inch," Mother said, and brought glasses.

Before I go any further, I must say here and now that Aunt Celia is a witch, so if you don't believe in them you won't believe in her. First of all, she looks like a witch and would have had a short stay in Salem if she'd lived then. She has long, straight blue-black hair that she wears up, close like a helmet, and her eyes are slanty black slits. She is even thinner than Mother and I, but with a dead-white pallor, her skin like candlewax. She uses pale purple lipstick on a long, narrow mouth, and her eyebrows arch up. She designs and makes her own clothes, and tonight she was wearing a sort of medieval dress like a monk's robe—sea-green crepe de chine with huge, wide sleeves. The gray cape she'd shed was lined with the same color crepe, and now she took off a little gray cloche beaded in green.

It's not just her looks that make her seem witchy—it's what happens when she's around. She's always hearing things that turn out to be burglaries or drownings. Once when Dad was in town and we were all lunching at Entre Nous she stopped eating and said, "Hist!" and began listening. She insisted that Dad take her right home, and what do you think—a burglar had just been in her apartment and made off with her radio and some jewelry (which the police got back later).

Another time she said, at tea, "A boat is sinking off Long Island," and sure enough, next day we read about two boys drowned.

We don't like to eat with Aunt Celia in restaurants because if she isn't hearing things, she's finding them. Now, you take all the spinach ready to serve in a big hotel—all clean, maybe a ton of it—who gets the little worm? Aunt Celia, of course. Or a bug in the broccoli. Once in the Automat she put in a nickel for a piece of pie and found half a mouse in it and made such a fuss the management gave her fifty dollars to keep quiet.

She's terribly germ-conscious and never eats in a restaurant without a little chamois bag in which she carries her own sterilized knife, fork, and spoon. When the waiter isn't looking, she wipes off clean plates with a linen napkin. During the flu epidemic she wore a veil soaked with camphor over her hat.

But about her being a witch—she can read your mind. She knows exactly what you're thinking; that's why she has a sort of Mona Lisa smile. She could make a fortune by blackmailing people, but all she does with her psychic gifts is to bet on an occasional horse she dreams about. With all this she lives very well, and also gets fifty dollars a month alimony from Uncle Van, which helps support her little dress business.

"What's the matter, Emily?" she asked Mother as we sipped our wine. "Ruddell isn't coming?"

"He says he'll be delayed," Mother said.

"But in time for the play," I said. "I bought some lace for a ruff. Could you make one for me?"

I brought her the lace, and she said she would starch it, and took some measurements, and then said, "Julie dear, you could be so chic if you'd just comb back your hair."

She and Mother were always nagging me to keep the hair off my right eye, although it's the fashion and terribly seductive, like unfastened flapping galoshes and Peter Pan collars outside navy blue sweaters. "At Wilson it's smart to wear your hair like this."

"Smart?" Aunt Celia asked. "What kind of vulgarity

is that? *Smart* is mental, *chic* is physical. *Smart* is the word used in the Seventh Avenue ready-to-wear stores or by saleswomen at Klein's. I cannot bear that word misused."

I apologized. "We think hair like this is chic."

"Well, it isn't. It's an affectation, and if you want to look like a Yorkshire terrier in school, just spare us at home, will you?"

But I never mind her scoldings because she just wants me to be as elegant as she is, and when she learned that I was going to the dinner with Mr. Skinner, she offered to lend me her silver brocade cloak. It was heaven, with a white fox collar and hem, and I said, "I can wear it later when I go out with Stewart Crandall."

This created such excitement that they scarcely ate dinner for cooing. By the time we started on our French pastry they practically had me married to old Stew, to the town house and Connecticut estate and the millions. But they wanted to know why he had asked me all of a sudden. Hadn't he been dating some girl from Miss Finch's? I said I had no idea, that I really didn't care.

"You have *got* to care," Aunt Celia said. "All that wealth—the connections—"

"I doubt they have any in the theater," I said.

Mother and Aunt Celia exchanged disgusted looks. I must forget about a career if Stewart was to become serious. His family wouldn't like it.

"But Stewart likes acting," I said. "He actually begs for parts in my plays."

"And you give him the executioner," Mother said. "Really, Julie, you're carrying aloofness too far."

"It's possible that's what attracts him," Aunt Celia said, as if I weren't there. "I suppose so many girls chase him."

"Nobody chases Stew," I told them. "I'd be surprised if his IQ is much over a hundred, and he hasn't much of a chin. You know yourself he looks like an anteater or one of those tropical things. I think he's been inbred or something, and I wouldn't want to date him at all except he's taking me to a—hotel."

Now Aunt Celia's eyes began to turn dark and glowing; I might have known she would sense that speakeasy. "The Biltmore," I said hopelessly. "For dancing."

She smiled just a little, but that smile was much too knowing. "He's not the sort that would carry a hip flask, of course?"

"No," I said.

"And you'll be going in one of his limousines?" Mother asked.

"I suppose." I really didn't know. Stew comes to school in a Rolls and so does Enid and a few others who don't use cabs or can't walk.

"Well," said Aunt Celia, "when I go home I'll starch your ruff and cut it out so it flares backwards. I'm afraid I can't shorten the silver cloak, but I'll get them both here in plenty of time. And perhaps I should make a ruff for Stewart?"

"He doesn't mind Lily cups," I said. "We just cut the bottoms out."

"But it would be a gesture," Aunt Celia said, "and much nicer with his costume." She knew all about *Mary Stuart.* "I've some black lace that will do nicely. Emily, why don't we go into your room and I'll see about shortening your suit?"

This was so they could talk over Dad and Stewart in private and leave me to wash the dishes. In a way the two of them were like Marge and me—about the same age and liking their privacy. But Aunt Celia was a lot more sophisticated than Mother. Uncle Van—her ex-husband—was her second. She had left him about three years ago, I suspect because he drank a lot. At that time I was only twelve and horrified when I saw liquor at their parties because it's against the law, but Uncle Van explained that the Volstead Act was passed illegally too, when the soldiers weren't home to vote on it, and since Professor Craig seemed to think the same thing I no longer approved of Prohibition. But I am for the underdog in any situation, and that includes the

Democrats and the Russian nobility. That thought reminded me that I had some history homework, so I went into my bedroom, but my mind wasn't on it so I reread Dad's letter and was reassured. He would certainly be here for the play.

Four

OUR TEACHERS at Wilson always ask us for frank comments on the subjects they cover, so on Tuesday morning we all handed in our opinions of History. Mr. Weber gave us ten minutes study time while he read them, and then he said, "Practically none of you appreciate American history. The consensus seems to range from 'dull' to 'boring.' This is obviously my fault."

He has a boyish, rather chubby face with a perked-up nose, and I can't see what would attract even Miss Thain except that he's married and sometimes that's a challenge to a woman. "What I should have done," he said, "is to cause you to relate to your own heritage, to dramatize your pasts. For example, Stewart, what would you have been doing during the American Revolution?"

History is Stew's best subject. He said, "Fur-trapping, I guess. Beavers, I believe. In Oregon."

"And you, Julie?"

"We were Tories," I said, "so we didn't do anything during the Revolution, just sat on our plantations in the South."

"But surely during the Civil War?"

"I'm sorry," I said, "nothing."

"All Confederates fought," Vera Jordan said. "My family did."

"My family hired people to fight," I said. "They didn't go to war themselves." I realized I wasn't putting the Willises in a very good light, but it was true. "Except there was an Amos Willis who did go, only he went to sleep above the Battle of Gettysburg on a hill and woke up on top of his rifle when it was all over and got court-martialed."

That pleased Vera. "And was hanged?"

"Oh, no. He got off with a dishonorable discharge."

Before Vera could say anything nasty, Mr. Weber said, "Now you see how fascinating history can be when you relate it to yourselves. I want you all to talk to your parents, go into your genealogies, and write me an essay on the facts as you find them. Except Mikel, of course," he said, turning to a new boy who was Polish. "But Mikel can write about what his family was doing from 1775 to 1868."

"I can't understand," Jane said to me, "why the guns didn't wake your ancestor up."

Now, that's a curious thing. Violence bores some people. When Mother and I see a Western movie, she drops sound asleep at the first gunshot, no matter how well the theater is rigged for rifle pops. The same thing happens in a play when somebody fires a revolver—Mother just sits back and snoozes. Perhaps it's what Mr. Weber means by "atavistic"—she's inherited it from Amos Willis, since way back she and Dad were related.

"I'll bet he was flogged," Vera said.

I've never been able to figure out why Vera hates me so, because she doesn't want parts in plays. Perhaps it's because I'm friends with Enid and other Jewish girls and she hates *them*. And before I could defend Amos, Bernice Yellin spoke up and said, "I think you're just jealous because your ancestors didn't have the sense to stay home or go to sleep."

"And what were *yours* doing during the Civil War?" Vera asked. "In some Russian ghetto?"

Mr. Weber said, "That's quite enough, Vera." She had been a trial to him for as long as I can remember, and now he said something absolutely deadly. "Your remarks have been extraordinarily unsophisticated."

That shut her up beautifully, and he went on to give us snippets of things that he thought would interest us in American history, and a list of books to read. We were dismissed then and straggled out into the hall, where Stewart whispered, "Is it okay with your mother about the nineteenth?"

"Yes," I said. "The Biltmore, I told her."

"See you at rehearsal, then," he said, and I joined Bernice and Jane for Cooking class, where I met Marge, who looked perfectly awful.

"Dick hasn't phoned," she said as we made hollandaise, "and he's still out sick."

"Watch it doesn't curdle," said Miss Marsh, passing by.

Any edible food we prepare goes down to the cafeteria at noon, and since the Sixth Grade had done well with the asparagus we concentrated on the hollandaise until it was in a bowl, cooling. We helped the Fourth Grade with cookies, then, finally free, sat outside on a marble bench. Marge was just about to say something when Dr. Matheson came by and said, "Oh, Julie, could you take some Observers through just after lunch?"

This meant that I could skip Biology, so I said I'd be delighted, since we didn't have the play rehearsal until three. It was also a little bit of an honor to be trusted to say the right thing, but having been at Wilson for so long, I knew it all by heart. When he went on by, Marge suggested we eat early and get a table to ourselves, and we talked about Dick, of course.

"Since you've never been in love," she said, "you don't know what anguish it can be."

But I had a good imagination, I told her.

"What I think I'll do," she said, "is to use the excuse

of homework he doesn't know about. But I'll be cool," she added quickly, "as if I'm doing him a favor."

I thought that was brilliant, since no matter what he said she could keep her dignity. So we rehearsed it. And if he should break down and ask her for a date, she would say, "I'm not sure, call me back," as if she had tentative plans.

"I'll be more nervous than on opening night," she said. "Oh, you're lucky, not being in love with anyone. It's pure hell."

To take her mind off Dick, I told her about Aunt Celia lending me the silver cloak for the nineteenth; she said it was wonderful but to be very careful at the speakeasy. "Don't trust gin, Dad says, unless it's sold by someone you know or made at home. You can go blind from it."

"Then what'll I order?"

"I'll find out from Dad without telling him why I'm asking. Now," she said, getting up, "I'm going to call Dick. I'll tell you at rehearsal."

Half an hour later, I joined the Observers in the lobby. You can generally spot them at once, because they hover in a group, looking around and craning their necks, and they always have notebooks. I welcomed them and took them down to the basement, where the Third Grade was gathered for a field trip. This wasn't much of a trip—just for them to learn how the elevators work, the cables, and all that—accompanied by a teacher who'd explain about stresses and strains and technical stuff. After we'd been up to the roof and down again, the Englishman asked one of the little boys, who was about eight, "And how do you feel about the lift? Do you understand how it works?"

"Like Newton's apple," said the boy, and everybody made notes. Then we shed the Third Grade and I took the Observers on a tour of the entire building. They were so interested that I was afraid I'd be late for rehearsal, so I decided to take them with me if they wanted to go, and they all did, which in a way created a captive audience.

Mr. Skinner said, "How do you do?" and showed them to seats in second-row center. They stared up at the high blue ceiling, which is dotted with stars. They remarked that it was just like a real theater, which it is. I told them what the play was about.

Inevitably, one of them asked, "Schiller?"

"No, mine. I'm sorry we don't have costumes yet. Just try to imagine sixteenth-century clothes and sets."

Well, if ever there was a shambles of a rehearsal, that was it. Nobody but Marge and me remembered their lines. When Stewart practiced with the catsup he missed the block and got it on his feet and then slid in it trying to exit. Mr. Skinner, who never spares our feelings even if Observers are present, hopped around in a fury. "Marge," he said, "it isn't enough to know your lines. You are not a beautiful queen—you're an aging, rheumatic woman who's scared to death but trying not to be. Julie, we can't hear you beyond row three, and must you swallow what words we can hear? Not that they're immortal prose, but we'd like to hear them *if* you please. Paul, Bothwell may have been a lot of things, but he didn't scratch when he was nervous, and I find no lice in the script. *Project* your voices. All of you. And you, Peter Vorse, will you kindly tell us just what your conception of James Stuart is?"

Peter took a deep breath. "A villain. Full of intrigue."

"So you narrow your eyes and stroke your chin and glare so that we'll all know you're a villain. Even your stupid sister, Mary, would begin to be suspicious, with you acting like that. Can't you be subtle? Have you all seen too many movies?" He glanced contemptuously at the little huddle of girls who played the four ladies-in-waiting. "Why simper? You're supposed to be scared, scared out of your wits. You love your queen, and she's about to be beheaded, and you're wondering about your own heads."

I saw a tear trickle down Marge's nose. So did Mr. Skinner. "Good. Of course she cried, silently. Now let's have that Latin speech again, and when you speak it, mean it."

That was better, he said, then made us go back to Act One. I forgot about the Observers until it was all over, but there they were, asking if they could see the rest of the theater. I showed them the stars' dressing rooms and the costume rooms, and then they all thanked me and left. But Mr. Skinner remained behind.

I said, "You made Marge cry."

"If a script can't, then a director should."

"But you were cruel!"

I'd never said such a thing to a teacher before.

"In what way?" he asked.

"You said to Peter, 'Even your stupid sister, Mary,' or anyway you called her stupid."

"I was referring to Mary Stuart, not Marge Craig."

"She didn't understand it that way. That's why she cried. So, Mr. Skinner—I'm sure it will relieve you that I don't intend to go to the Father and Daughter's Dinner with you."

He looked absolutely blank.

"Didn't Mrs. Curran tell you?" I asked. "Didn't she tell you that I'm supposed to go with you? Well, I won't! Nobody could take the place of my own father anyway, and I don't care if I miss that dinner for the next thousand years. I'm not exactly starving!"

He looked just as astonished as I felt. From my earliest childhood Mother had subdued my temper to the point where I could scarcely raise it even in self-defense against Vera, and now it had burst out at a teacher. I was so stunned and embarrassed that I ran out of the auditorium and found Marge waiting, still in tears. But it seemed the tears were about Dick. He had been terribly formal on the phone, said he had bronchitis and that perhaps he would see her sometime.

We went to Freeman's and commiserated with one another, and though she thanked me for my championship, she said Mr. Skinner's remarks had just sailed over her head, but that if he wanted her to shed real tears, all she had to think of was Dick. Then Kitty came in and joined the dirge. Jim, the boy across the street, still wasn't noticing her. I wondered if he was nearsighted or something, because there wasn't a boy in Freeman's who wasn't noticing Kitty. Her curls are very loose and plump and round, the color of primroses, and there's a kind of permanent blush on her skin, like on an apricot. She needed a very tight brassiere, but she didn't look blowsy like Vera, and today she was wearing a lovely blue cotton dress that she had made herself in Household Arts, and the hem hadn't come out yet.

We loitered at Freeman's for a long time. Some of the boys in Kitty's class and in ours came over, but we didn't pay much attention to them and nobody offered to pay for our sundaes. It's funny, with almost everyone in school being so rich, the boys are all on strict allowances. Probably Stewart would have to save up quite a lot to afford the speakeasy.

Finally we separated, but I didn't feel like going home, so I sat on a bench on Columbia campus and watched the college people pass by. Some of them were smoking, and I decided that I'd better learn how to do it properly next time I saw Robert to practice for the speakeasy. I also knew I should apologize to Mr. Skinner tomorrow since he hadn't made Marge cry. But I wouldn't go to that dinner with him.

The sky darkened and people with umbrellas were raising them, so finally I went home. Mother was already there and she said, "Look! I opened the box because they're flowers, but they're yours."

Dad had wired flowers before, and I was thrilled by the single, perfect gardenia that floated in a silver bowl. Then I looked at the card. It said, "Hoping you will change your mind, R. G. Skinner."

"Now, what does that mean?" Mother asked. She has to peer and pry at everything that's none of her business. I told her that I'd told him I'd decided against the dinner, and she was furious. Not that she ranted and raved—it wouldn't be ladylike—but she has a sort of sinister coldness when she thinks I'm in error, and though I didn't bother to explain, she took up the matter as if she knew all about it.

"Phone him immediately and tell him you're delighted to go with him. At least *he* hasn't failed you."

Meaning, of course, that Dad had.

"And if I were you I wouldn't count on your father for the play, either. We can't count on him for anything."

"You haven't any faith!" Again I was astonished that I dared to talk back.

"In God, yes," she said. "But perhaps you don't know about Him?"

Now she revived a very sore point—Wilson didn't give us any religious education, and this was a severe bump for a Southern Baptist. "Your father insisted on that school," she said, "before I knew what it was all about. I was so naïve, just up North. I wanted the best for you, and since *he* said it was the best I believed him. All right, so it is the most expensive school in the world, but you got a scholarship."

As if that were my fault. I can scarcely remember the tests and that first talk with Dr. Matheson, our Principal, or all the things that went on to get me accepted. But we still have to pay a hundred dollars a year, even though it's supposed to be free for me, and though I get my books secondhand from Weiss's they cost, too, and lunches at the cafeteria can run as much as twenty-five cents.

"About God," I said, "I've had Comparative Religions, you know. But I haven't made up my mind yet, and we're not supposed to until we've matured."

"When it's too late," she said. "Children should be started early for belief in God."

"When they're too dumb to think for themselves?"

"Julie! I can't see that Comparative Religions has created anything but cynicism in you."

In a way, she was right. In the Ninth Grade, once a month, we had field trips to different churches—everything from Greek Orthodox to Jewish temples. I had liked St. Patrick's Cathedral best because we went there at Christmastime, and the altar was a mass of poinsettias, and the candles were all blazing for the saints. It was one of the times I was missing Dad the most—I always do at Christmas—so I told our teacher, Mr. Haggard, that I would like to light a candle to one of the saints, and send him a prayer.

"Which one?" he asked.

Marge, who was close by, said, "Saint Jude. Try him. He's supposed to patronize lost causes."

I don't think she meant to be sarcastic; this seemed to be a saint who took on hard labor.

The Cathedral was dim, dark, except for those white candles. And the red poinsettias, like blood against the altar. I lit a candle to Saint Jude, and it flared up higher than the others. I believe that this was the first time that I sensed God, and it was such a sacred, personal feeling that I moved away from the other students. Then Mr. Haggard came up and said I should put down ten cents for the candle, and that spoiled it all, put it on a commercial basis, and besides, Saint Jude didn't do anything to earn it, so I lost interest in the Catholics and never could perk up any with other sects.

"I'm not an atheist," I said now to Mother. "I was past that at thirteen. I'm just trying to keep an open mind. But since you've got to have faith in something —well, I have it in Dad, even if you don't."

To do her credit, Mother doesn't try to destroy my faith in him, but she makes so many blunders that it's obvious she hasn't any. Oh, she tries, like sometimes saying, "Here's the rent, a week in advance!" or "Just imagine, he sent money for the phone bill." But it's always said in surprise, and people who have real faith are never surprised. That's why people in the Bible, like the disciples, accepted miracles so calmly.

She changed the subject back to Mr. Skinner, and so I called him up and thanked him for the gardenia and apologized for being rude and said I'd love to go to the dinner with him. This wasn't quite true, but he sounded much nicer than usual, and he asked how

Marge was feeling, and I said, "She wasn't upset by you—it was something else," and he told me I was really quite good as Elizabeth but to work on my diction. So I spent the next hour in my bedroom enunciating, then heated the lamb stew while Mother made dumplings, and we ate.

Mother went upstairs to Miss Johnson's apartment for bridge, and I continued work on diction so that the words bounced and I bit them off like thread. I changed some of my words because they didn't sound right, but left ends of sentences so as not to confuse the rest of the cast. I wondered how many people would be in the audience. We were not inviting the Third and Fourth grades because of the gruesome touches like the catsup, and there was a little rough language, too, when Mary calls her brother a bastard, which of course he was.

After a few hours I wrote a long letter to Dad, stamped it, and took it down to Dan, at the desk, who smelled so strongly of peppermints that I knew he'd been drinking again. Then I went outside, just to the corner. The sky was that odd violet color that comes with spring, and a little moon had come out prematurely, and I felt suddenly terribly lonely. Maybe Duse and Bernhardt had felt that way too, but it wasn't much comfort. They had had lovers and fathers and fame. I didn't have anything except hope, and if Mother was right, I was only building on daydreams. For the first time, I wondered if Dad could be in love with someone and with her now and perhaps wanting a divorce. But we had always told each other everything, and after all these years surely he would have at least hinted?

I thought, *Nobody* can destroy my faith in him. My trouble is simply that it's spring and too beautiful, with the violet changing to pink above the rooftops and even the garbage cans along Amsterdam Avenue silvery in the twilight. And I don't know why, but something told me to remember this moment, to store it against the future, as if it would be the last spring I'd ever see.

On Sunday I had dinner with the Craigs, and then Professor Craig walked me home. On the way down Amsterdam Avenue he said, "Marge tells me you're going to some sort of party soon where you'll be expected to drink. The safest thing is a glass of sherry, if they have it, or beer. But just one."

I thanked him, and then he said, "What do you think of this Dick Osterman fella?"

"Oh," I said, loyal to Marge, "a very nice boy. Why?"

"Because we've never seen her mooning around so, and I'm not at all sure he's not a—" He paused, then said, "You can't call them cads or bounders any more, but Pearl and I think he's a lot too oily. He's more likely to end up a gigolo than an engineer."

"She can handle him," I said swiftly. "Marge is very prudent, you know. And he gets A's in Geometry."

That didn't seem to impress him. "It's very hard to play the heavy father in this day and age. We want her to have some freedom and to choose her own friends, but when she and this—this boy make up whatever quarrel they've had, we may have to forbid her dating him."

Even if I hadn't loved Marge, I am, as I said, always for the underdog. "If you do that you'll just push her further toward him. What you and Mrs. Craig should do is trust her completely."

"But what about him?"

"A good woman," I said, "can always reform—"

"Nuts," said Professor Craig, lighting a cigarette. We had come to my house now, and he hesitated, then patted my shoulder. "This is just between us, Julie, okay?"

"Word of honor," I said, waiting.

But he didn't say anything more than "Good night," so I guess he meant that I should keep our conversation secret, which, of course, I would. But poor Marge,

even if she got Dick back, there would probably be bar-
riers. The more I was hearing about people in love the
gladder I was that I wasn't. Aunt Celia and two hus-
bands. Mother with no faith in Dad. Marge and Dick.
Kitty pining after Jim. Miss Thain's hopeless craving
for Mr. Weber (if that was true). It seemed to me, as I
went into the apartment lobby, that the wisest thing
was never to get into it at all.

Mac was at the switchboard—each week he and Dan
alternated—and he said, "Nice evening?"

"Just with girl friends," I said, "and their parents."

"Thought you'd be out for a real date," he said.

"I've just decided that romance is not for me. All it
causes is heartbreak."

"Julie," he said, "you want to go through life just
safe? That's not living. If I'd wanted to be just safe, I'd
still be in Mississippi waiting for the train to go by,
watching the people get off. But one night I heard that
train whistle, going north, and I was waiting with a
little bag of clothes, and I climbed on and hid in the
gentleman's and then sneaked off in Washington and
hitched a ride here. Suppose I hadn't? I'd never have
met Odessa and had my kids and a nice job like this.
You've got to dare, Julie."

"But—"

"No buts about it. So maybe you get a broken
heart—at least you know you got a heart, and it
mends. It's a muscle, you know."

He was so darling, always had been. "But, Mac, all I
really care about is my father."

"For now," he said. "You just wait and see how
things change. Somebody said, I don't know who, that
all you can trust in this world is change. So you go
upstairs and have some cocoa and sleep and stop trying
to stop life, you understand? Just be waiting, that's all,
ready to pack and take that train."

It was the first time I'd ever thought that I might go
to Dad if he didn't come to me.

Five

WE HAD a much better rehearsal on Tuesday, but it was decided to transfer the catsup into a wide-mouthed bottle since Stew had such a hard time shaking it out, and when it did come, it flooded. There was, as a matter of fact, quite a controversy going on in the letter column of the *Graphic* about catsup bottles, readers agreeing that you have to work too hard to get the catsup out of those narrow necks. I'm not supposed to read the *Graphic* because it is sensational yellow journalism, but you do pick up some little items in it that are helpful. For instance, about how girls are selected for the white slave trade and what to do if you are approached by a motherly woman who is their front. And I often store up information that I wouldn't get anywhere else that I might use for plays—like a person in the electric chair sizzles before he dies and that choir singers aren't always safe from ministers. Maybe I'll never use any of this knowledge, but, as Mrs. Curran says, no memory is ever wasted. The girls at school leave a *Graphic* on top of the second toilet bowl in the girls' room, and whoever leaves last sticks it into the trash.

Dick had recovered and was back in school, but he avoided Marge, and naturally she was merely coldly polite when they met. She said she even thought she was getting over him, but that was just bravado, because much as she loves macaroni and cheese she put down her fork when he passed by our table in the cafeteria and wouldn't eat. Well, he is good-looking—if you like that blond Scandinavian type—but not lithe and pantherish, which is my ideal in men. Being an athlete, he bulges in the wrong places, too, and by the time he's twenty he'll have a thickening waist. But there's no accounting for tastes, and it's probably true that love is blindly chemical.

Enid brought up that point in Psychology. "Why is it," she asked Mrs. Curran, "that sometimes the prettiest girls fall for the ugliest boys?"

"Unattractive people often make up for lack of looks by being charming," she said. "A matter of courtesy and tact, and it is vitally important to be a good listener. Do you have any special problem?" she asked Enid hopefully. "You may see me after class if you do."

Mrs. Curran wanted so desperately for us to confide in her it was pitiful. Here she was our Class Adviser as well as psychologist and nobody asked her advice. Not that we didn't trust her, but she was so old.

This was my day for Music Appreciation and you're not really supposed to do anything but sit in a semi-darkened room and listen to classical records, and then there's a little lecture by Mr. Tate, introducing the next record. Shortly after the music started, Dick came in and slid into the chair next to me. Marge was up in German, and I felt disloyal that he was sitting so close to me that I could smell his hair pomade.

"I think Beethoven did okay, considering he was so deaf," Dick said. "Only I like the Fifth better."

I said, "Shush." As long as Marge was being cold to him, that was my role, too.

We had endured some Elgar when he whispered again. "Want a soda at the Passion Palace?"

Oh, the betrayer! And how crude to pick on Marge's best friend. "No, thanks," I said.

"But I want to talk to you."

I said nothing more until the lights came on and Mr. Tate dismissed us. Then I said, "You can talk right out in the hall."

He picked a secluded bench where the potted plants were and said, "I'm worried about Marge. I think she's frigid."

"*What?*"

"She won't kiss properly."

I was about to hop up and leave him in a fury, for telling me such intimate things, then I said, "You're evidently not using a sophisticated technique. None of us like small boys slobbering. And besides, your reputation isn't too good."

The blank face flushed. "What do you mean?"

"Oh, anyone can have you," I said wearily. "I haven't mentioned to Marge that I saw you with that cheap little redhead in Freeman's, but she's not stupid. If you want her back—not that I think she's interested—you'll have to stop dating other people and start being courtly."

"Courtly?"

"Sending flowers. Treating her as someone special. And not trying to double-cross her with every vamp that comes along. She's above all that, you see."

He was still awfully red and began to chew on his lower lip. He looked a little like a melancholy Viking, but I was pitiless. "G'bye," I said, and walked away, hoping I'd done some good.

Kitty met me at the lockers. "Look," she said, "Mother called me at lunchtime and said she'd had to take Trixie to the vet—some ear trouble. Could you pick up Trixie on 120th Street—you know the place—at two-thirty and I'll come by your house at four?"

She knew I had no more classes, so I said of course I

would and decided to go home first and check the mail. But there wasn't any, so I left my books with Mac and went to the vet's and got Trixie and turned west to walk along Riverside Drive, Trixie trotting along, sniffing things.

There was a forsythia bush in bloom by the Claremont Inn, and someone had put a bunch of pink laurel on the tomb of the Amiable Child. But there weren't any spring smells. I couldn't smell anything but new paint on a trash basket and gasoline fumes from the Fifth Avenue buses.

I sat down on a bench near Grant's Tomb, wondering why spring can hurt so much just by the way it looks. The wet buds on the trees and the pale yellow of the sky and those fat clouds that somehow look so innocent. If I'd been younger I'd have wanted to write a poem, but it wouldn't have been a happy one. It seemed to me that spring promised a lot more than it delivered. Unless Dad came, it would mean only another sizzling New York summer, with your clothes sticking to you and two showers a day and never feeling clean. Your friends away for the summer and maybe no money to go visit them. Last year when the Craigs rented a cottage at Cape Cod, I couldn't afford the train fare up because Dad hadn't completed a deal. But surely this summer would be different, in Europe.

A boy came along, and though I try never to stare at them, this one made it practically impossible not to. For one thing, he was carrying a small couch on his shoulders. It was upholstered in red velvet, and tasseled, but its bottom had springs showing through. Even bent over as he was I figured he was about six feet, and I admired the fact that he wasn't staggering under its weight. As he came closer I heard him whistling.

When he was near my bench he lowered the couch to the pavement and I saw that it was a love seat. For a minute he stretched like a big cat, took cigarettes from his pocket, and lit one. Then he turned around, and I saw his face.

It was strong and full-lipped, like the etching of Heathcliffe, with scowly black brows. His eyes were big and black and shiny, and I had to make a real effort to look away from them.

He sat down on the love seat and saw me. "Hello," he said.

Of course, I didn't answer, pretending to look at Grant's Tomb.

"I wonder if they buried him with his cigar?" he asked.

Still I said nothing, but Trixie took advantage of my limp hand and broke away, trailing the leash, to jump up beside him. I'm afraid the two of them on that love seat plunk on Riverside Drive made me giggle, and he said, "How old is your dog?"

"Three," I said.

"Doesn't look it," he said politely.

"But she's not mine. She belongs to a friend. I'm just walking her."

He nodded, told Trixie to stay, and came over to offer me a cigarette. Well, I had to learn, didn't I? And it was terribly exciting, the way he took that Camel out of its pack and bent toward me and lit it. Elinor Glyn wrote somewhere about her heroine sinking into the "black wells of his eyes," and now I knew what she meant because I sank.

"Wouldn't you be more comfortable on the love seat, Miss—?"

"Willis," I said. Well, it was like being in someone's living room. "Julie Willis."

He escorted me over to the love seat, Trixie between us, and told me that his name was Ricci Innocente. He pronounced it Ree-chee Inno-chente and I thought it was beautiful. "People call me Rick."

"Italian?" I asked.

"My parents are. I was born here." He looked at me worriedly. "Don't you know how to smoke?"

Well, since he was eighteen or nineteen, I said, "I want to learn for a speakeasy I'm going to," knowing he wouldn't be shocked.

But I think he was. "You, at a speakeasy?"

"Oh, it will be all right," I said. "I'm going with an old friend. It's only the cigarette that's a problem."

"What you do," he said, "is pull on it. No, like this." He demonstrated. "Try again. Now inhale. No, no, draw in. Got it?"

Enough to mimic the way he did it, enough to feel fairly secure about it. I tossed the cigarette into a bush and realized, suddenly, that I'd picked someone up.

This is exactly what Mother calls "cheap behavior." And it shows the boy that you are so desperate that you need people you don't know. In a way it's like saying, "I'm not popular, I haven't enough friends of my own, so I'm reaching." In other words, it's an admission of being lonely.

So I got up and pulled Trixie after me and said, "Thank you for the cigarette."

"Must you go?"

I certainly didn't want to, but I couldn't think of an excuse to linger so I said I had to go home. So he picked up the love seat and said he was going in the same direction.

Certainly he had a lot of poise; somehow I didn't think he was an errand boy for some antique shop or auction room. And being an actress—almost—I'm conscious of accents, and his sounded educated.

People passing us smiled as they almost always do when they see other people carrying something preposterous, and this love seat was.

"Where are you taking that?" I asked.

"To 114th Street. My sister's having it fixed up. Isn't it awful?"

"Awful," I agreed. With its gilt frame and carved gilt legs it looked like something you might see in the Renaissance Room at the Metropolitan Museum.

"Rosa goes around buying this old junk for three or four dollars and then spends twenty or thirty having it fixed up. Joe—that's her husband—goes wild. But he'll agree to anything she wants because she's pregnant."

I said that Joe sounded nice.

"He's scared. He's afraid not to humor her. My family's full of these old superstitions." He paused a moment and caught his breath. Then he shifted the love seat and went on. "They think if Rosa doesn't have everything she wants, junk like this or whatever crazy food in the middle of the night, that the baby will be disfigured."

"Why?" I asked, fascinated.

"Just superstition. They even believe in the Evil Eye and when the kid's born it will wear a charm against *stregas.*"

"What are they?"

"Witches."

We crossed the Drive, and then I told him about Aunt Celia being a witch, and he said that was nonsense. He was almost a scientist and had no patience with that kind of thing; he was studying medicine at Columbia. Then we came to a drugstore, and he lowered the love seat and said, "Boy, it's hot—want a soda or something?"

I said yes, but when I started to follow him in he said just to sit on the love seat and he'd bring me what I wanted, which was a frosted chocolate.

So Trixie and I sat and waited for him, people staring, but you couldn't very well take furniture into a drugstore or leave it unattended, and it was pleasant here in the shade of an awning. And when he came back with our frosteds, he also had a little package of cookies and gave one to Trixie.

Mrs. Curran had told us to be good listeners, so I asked what kind of doctor he planned to be, and he said he might go into obstetrics and practice on Bleecker Street, which was way downtown where he lived. He said that even now he was disseminating birth-control information, but it would be a long, tough fight. He said he was still a Catholic but a liberal one, and he couldn't stand seeing poor families having dozens of children they couldn't afford and didn't even want.

"But how do you manage to control birth?" I asked him.

He looked astonished. "Why—how old are you, Julie?"

"Fifteen," I said, wishing I weren't. But I've a feeling that if I'd lied he'd have known. Those black eyes went right through you. "It's okay, I go to Wilson and we have very frank talks in Psychology, but we haven't gotten on how to control birth."

Well, it seems that birth control is a sort of science plan, but he was being very vague for fear of shocking me, I guess, and he said it was a matter of economics. Just use that word, and I'm lost. Certain words create a kind of mental deafness in me: Civics. Biology. Baseball. Finance and Wall Street, which go together like hot dogs and buns. Not that he bored me, but I didn't want to show my ignorance, so I said I really had to get home to give Trixie to a girl friend who would be waiting at my apartment house on 120th Street. Subtly, I added, so that he'd remember, "It has such a silly name—the Alhambra." Even more subtly I added, "I've left my books with the switchboard operator."

So he knew how and where to phone me. That is, if he remembered that my last name was Willis.

He rose from the love seat, and I thanked him for the frosted, and I had the terrible feeling that he might not remember anything but Julie. So I said, and this was *really* subtle, "That love seat would appeal to my mother. The Willis family has collected antiques for longer than I like to remember," and then I waved good-bye and went home.

Kitty was waiting in the lobby, but she wouldn't come upstairs because she wanted to get back about the same time Jim came home from school, so she dashed off with Trixie. I said "Hi!" to Mac and was about to climb the steps when he said, "Julie, there's a letter for you."

Special delivery, from Bisbee, Arizona. Mac looked pleased, as though he knew it was good news, and I thanked him and took it upstairs, and sure enough—

Dad said the deal was almost closed, he was almost sure to be here May twenty-fourth, and he even enclosed a rent check for Mother.

But was she thrilled when she came in? Oh, no. She just said, "And about time. I've been worried *frantic,*" and slumped down like she usually did after work, pulling off her hat and fluffing up her hair. Sometimes when she's happy she looks almost young because she doesn't have any real wrinkles. But then she's never really happy. If Dad doesn't send money she's depressed, and when he finally does she complains because it's late. I said that I still had most of the ten dollars left and why didn't we go and see *Glorious Betsy*?

I always want to do something that's fun when I feel wonderful, and meeting Rick and hearing from Dad within just an hour and a half was more than I could have hoped for. Of course, I couldn't tell her about Rick in her present mood, but I'd think of a way if he phoned me. She is *hopelessly* provincial. If I said he was Italian, she'd want to know what pushcart he pushed or where he had his shoe-shine box. She'd forget all about Caruso and Marconi and Dante and the Caesars. So I decided not to say anything about Rick until—unless—I heard from him.

"You'd better save your money for necessities," she said.

But I wasn't going to let her spoil things, because I had a lot to think about that was happy. I creamed some leftover ham as I'd seen Aunt Celia do, with parsley, and served it on a bed of rice, and then, mercifully, Mother decided to go to bed early so I was left alone to think.

Dad came first, of course. The daydreams about Dad being at the play and, if he had enough money, the Villa Vallee later that night. But now Rick was in the dream, too. I wanted him to come to the play and see Dad bringing up flowers at the end of Act Three, and I was sure if Rick didn't have any money Dad would contrive a way to make him feel that it didn't matter at all. Dancing with either of them would be so wonderful if Mother didn't sulk. Then I enlarged the canvas to include Marge and Dick in the nightclub, and Kitty if we could get a boy for her. That Jim seemed to be hopeless.

Being so happy, getting ready for bed, I wondered why something bothered me in the back of my mind. It wasn't Mother. What, then? Freud says that your subconscious mind is cleverer than your conscious one and likes to hide things from itself. Things you don't want to face.

Then I remembered that when Rick and I had said good-bye he had been casual—imitating me—but he might at least have stared after me; instead he had just hoisted that love seat again. That was what bothered me. He wouldn't think of me again. He wouldn't call. Probably he thought I was too young for him.

I never could fool myself very well.

Six

I TOLD Marge about him next day, but she still hadn't had a phone call from Dick and was just generally bitter.

"What can you expect from a pickup?" she asked.

"But he's so nice, and oh, Marge, those eyes!"

"You're such a romantic."

That was a label she liked to pin on me when she was in a bad mood. And since all she had was Professor Craig, she couldn't understand the appeal of my kind of father. Sometimes I wondered why we were such close friends when we were so different.

Two more days went by, one good rehearsal, and then came Saturday and Aunt Celia invited me down to her apartment for lunch. It's not a bit like our place, although it, too, is full of antiques. These are French—what she calls "a mélange" of small brocaded chairs with gilt backs, little sofas, a chandelier in the living room, and lots of dove-gray wallpaper. Beyond is the larger room lined with closets and a big mirror where her clients try on clothes. I tried on the evening cloak, which was a little too long, but she showed me how to wrap it around me so it wouldn't trail. She wouldn't shorten it because of the white fox hem. I felt like a movie star.

She had my ruff ready, too, and a black one for Stew. She said I shouldn't call him that, but Stewart, and asked all kinds of questions during lunch as to whether I had properly thanked him for asking me out, if I wasn't surprised at his asking, and was I sure he wasn't dating a girl from Miss Finch's? The way she went on and on. Then finally over coffee she lit a Turkish cigarette and said, "You did say the Biltmore, didn't you, Julie?"

Did I dare to lie when I knew she knew it wouldn't be?

"Yes," I said.

Either her psychic sense wasn't working or she didn't even care that I was going to a speakeasy with him. "I've advised your mother that, considering it's such an important date, you needn't be home until one."

Heaven! And when Aunt Celia advised something, Mother always agreed. I was actually beginning to look forward to the date with old Stew.

She looked at my hair and sighed. "I think you should have a marcel the day before, dear. You can't trust it not to wave in a funny way. I'll give you a dollar—"

"I have about eight left from what Dad sent."

"Take it anyway and take a cab home now." She certainly had Dad's flair. "You'll have the two ruffs and the evening cloak to carry, and I've made a *gâteau* for your mother's bridge game tonight."

But when I left and she followed me outside, the first cabdriver wouldn't do—she sent him off because she said he looked "unsafe." The second one was too young, and when the third came up she nodded but took down his number and even his license plate in an elegant little notebook. Alone in the back seat, I asked him to go through Central Park, which was full of flowering trees, and nurses, and babies in carriages, and couples stretched out getting suntans.

The people lying in the park looked nice, lazy and sleepy on the grass. I wondered where Rick was this Saturday afternoon and if he had to study. Perhaps he had called me. But when I got home, all Mother said was, "Everett called and asked if you'd like to go to a movie."

Glorious Betsy. But I decided to stick around just in case Rick phoned. So I phoned Everett and said I was busy, and later I sure was, with Mother's bridge game. You wouldn't think four women would need so much attention when they were supposed to be learning Contract. Peanuts. Ice water. Window up. Window down a little. Matches for Miss Werner, who smoked. An ashtray. By ten o'clock when I percolated the coffee and served the cake, I knew it was too late for Rick to call.

I sleep late on Sundays, not because I'm especially tired but because I hate Sundays. No regular mail. And Mother home all day, sometimes dragging me to church. But even if I were marooned on a desert island, I'd somehow know it was Sunday. Everything lively and lovely on tiptoe, scared to express itself. I'll bet monkeys don't gossip in palm trees on Sunday, that coconuts are afraid to fall because of being noisy, that cannibals reject missionaries. And here in New York there was this deadness—muffled traffic and nobody's phone ringing.

Mother had that old-fashioned Kentucky idea that Sunday dinner should be at 1 P.M. instead of at night. How can anybody be hungry at 1 P.M. except people on farms, who've been up since dawn? But we had the ham again, glazed with orange marmalade and simmered in milk, and peas and potatoes and what was left of the *gâteau.* Then, since she loved making lists, she made one out for shopping on my way home from school: Hamburger. Carrots. Beef bones for soup. Macaroni. Strawberries (if cheap).

If some people are night people, then some people

are list people. Whenever Mother traveled, even to spend the night with her friend Miss Rebeck in Plainfield, New Jersey, she made a list two days before of what would go into her old overnight bag. When I sometimes spent a weekend with the Craigs, I just dumped what I needed into that bag, and she was always appalled, saying if I didn't make a list and cross off everything I'd packed, I'd forget something. I never did. And that annoyed her. I could just imagine the lists she would make before Dad took us to Europe this summer; she'd probably start well over a week ahead. And at the last minute he and I would just toss our things into our suitcases and be ready to go before she was.

It's painful waiting for a boy to call who doesn't, so when Marge phoned and asked me to dinner—they have it in a civilized way, at eight—I was glad to go. She and Kitty were alone. Neither had had any luck with her boy. Kitty said morosely, "There must be something wrong with us."

"Me, too," I said. "I'd hoped to hear from Rick."

Every six months or so we held a Fault and Flatter session. This can be very dangerous if girls are prone to be catty, but with us it never was. We were just honestly clinical about one another's good and bad points, and the nice things we said weren't really flattering but true. Kitty brought some ginger ale and cookies, and we sat down in their bedroom.

Marge began on Kitty. "You have a beautiful complexion and hair, but if you don't cut out sodas and sundaes you're going to be curvy."

Kitty gave her cookies to Trixie. "What else?" she asked.

I said, "I think you need to be a little subtler with boys. You shouldn't throw tomatoes or anything or chase Jim like you do. Next time you see him why not cross the street?"

"But he's like a magnet," Kitty said. "He draws me so."

"Resist it," Marge said. "Look how I'm resisting Dick, I mean not phoning or even seeming to notice him in class."

"That's gotten you nowhere," Kitty said.

"But it's dignified," I said. "I haven't even allowed myself to see if Rick's family has a telephone on Bleecker Street for fear I'd be tempted to call."

"Go on," said Kitty.

But she was so terribly pretty I couldn't see any faults except general silliness, and she'd outgrow that. "Just be a little more mysterious," I said. "My Aunt Celia, even at her age, is lethal to men because she has a sort of Mona Lisa smile. They don't know what she's thinking."

"You want to be a challenge," Marge added.

Then it was my turn. Marge said, "I've noticed that you're apt to giggle when you say 'Hello' on the phone. That's nerves, I think—anyway it was today because you were hoping to hear from Rick. But you want to have poise on the phone, as if you were so busy with some fabulous man in the living room that you don't *care* who calls."

I wasn't aware I had that mannerism, and I was grateful. "I'll stop it. What else?"

"I think you take wider steps than you should, and when you wear high heels you should sort of glide."

I nodded. High heels had been a problem for six months, mainly because I had only one pair and never wore them except on a date.

"You have a beautiful figure," Kitty said, "and legs. But you should buff your fingernails oftener and push back the cuticle. It's an awful bore but you owe it to your hands."

Now came Marge's turn. We both said the same thing, that she should cut her hair. That little bun at the back was vintage 1918. "You can still have that madonna look," I said, "by parting it in the middle."

"Well," Marge said. "But I read somewhere that boys just adore being able to take your hair down in private. Dick did."

"It wasn't enough to hold him," Kitty said. "Cut it. And think what you'd save on hairpins."

"Five cents every six months," Marge said. I could tell she wasn't going to change her hair. "What else?"

Maybe I was treading on thin ice, but I said, "You have such a sweet, serene look—classic beauty—but you're apt to be sarcastic and it's like a nun turning nasty."

"Yes," Kitty said.

I said hastily, but not flattering, "You have those big gray-green eyes, so soft—and then you say something cutting and it doesn't go together."

"I don't mean to be cutting," Marge said, surprisingly humble. "Maybe it's my love-hate for Dick that comes out on other people. I'll try to control it."

It had been a successful session; we'd all learned something—except I knew Marge wouldn't cut her hair and Kitty pretended that Trixie needed a walk. Marge slid Krafft-Ebing over to me in its cover of *Pride and Prejudice* and said I could have it for a week, then it went to Bernice Yellin.

"Did you learn anything from it?" I asked.

She lowered her voice even though Kitty was out in the street. "A man and a goose can have an affair."

"Really?"

"I mean, a real goose."

"How, Marge?"

"Well, it was a case history like the rest of the book. The doctor didn't seem to like the idea, but the man said, 'What's wrong with a goose?' I expect he fell in love with it like Leda with a swan. Probably it's just a myth."

"Does it say anything about boys?"

"Nothing I could find to help. I wouldn't call it very practical. Oh!"

For the phone rang. I admired the way she wanted to rush to it but let it ring three times. Then, by her expression, I knew it was Dick, and since I hate people listening in on conversations I went into the living room and looked out the window.

Kitty had parked Trixie at a flowering bush, but at least she wasn't watching for Jim. She was looking at her shoe. She looked as if she really was walking a dog, and the sun caught those fat, bright curls that were like little golden hoops you could almost see through.

But I didn't want to spy on her any more than I wanted to eavesdrop on Marge, so I picked up *Vanity Fair* and looked at the clothes. Aunt Celia had things just as advanced as these, and my violet moiré was long-in-back-short-in-front, too, which wouldn't reach America until autumn, Aunt Celia said.

Kitty came in. I knew from the way she dragged up the stairs that she hadn't seen Jim. She unloosed Trixie's leash and sat down, and I said, "I think Dick's called. She's on the phone."

"Do you like him, Julie?" She knew I didn't much. She just wanted reinforcement.

"I don't see him as he is but the way he will be—fat around the middle and a double chin. And a betrayer."

"He can betray while he's still thin," she said, "but if he gets fat he won't be able to any more. If they're still friends, I think she should decide which way she wants him. If I were Marge, I'd bake a whole lot of cookies and feed him whipped cream if I wanted to keep him from other girls, only then I wouldn't want him myself."

Marge came in. "It was Dick! Honestly, he's so *adorable*. He asked me for a soda after school tomorrow."

"At the Passion Palace?" I asked, hoping he'd decided to be courtly.

"Freeman's." She sounded defensive. "But he wants me to drive up the Drive afterwards."

She looked so happy. I didn't want to spoil it, and Kitty didn't either. "I'll ask Mother if she'll let him come for dinner tomorrow night."

Just for once Kitty was subtle. "Let's have spaghetti and ice cream and chocolate cake. Boys love it."

But Marge wanted something suave like Aunt Celia's lemon veal and shredded string beans and mushrooms. We were talking about that when the phone rang again. Marge maintained that clever, leisurely walk to it. Then she said, "Julie, it's for you."

Golly, if it wasn't Rick! "Your mother said—she gave me this number. I hope I'm not interrupting."

It was difficult to talk with my heart up there in my throat, but I said, "Oh, no, Rick."

Later I thought of things I could have said, like, "I was just finishing a tango lesson with a boy from Rio," or "It's okay, we were just having a drink," or, deliberately, stumbling, "We were only reading sonnets." Why did I have to say just, "Oh, no, Rick," as if he were God?

"What have you been doing?" he asked.

This time I managed to be more intriguing. "Rehearsing for a play I wrote. I'm playing Queen Elizabeth."

He said that was great. "Have you been to that speakeasy yet?"

"No," I said. "That's for the nineteenth."

"I read about a raid last night," he said. "I looked for your name." I had to giggle at that, and then he said, "But the main thing is, bootleg booze can be dangerous. You be careful, stick to near-beer."

So he actually *worried* about me! Then he said, "Are you free for dinner Wednesday night? I've told my sister about you."

It took all my will power to pause and pretend to think. Finally I said, "Why, yes, I am free Wednesday," and he told me he'd pick me up at six, and we hung up.

Marge and I, both so happy, tried not to bubble over in front of poor Kitty. But Marge didn't bubble very long. When her parents came in, they said that she could go to Freeman's with Dick but they didn't want her driving with him even in the daytime, and how did she know he really had a license? And she couldn't ask him to dinner. At Freeman's she was to tell him that she couldn't date him again.

For such sophisticated people, the Craigs were surely stupid psychologically, and I was astonished. "We don't even have to agree to the date at Freeman's," Mrs. Craig said, "but you can explain it all there better than in school. You're due that privacy, at least."

"*Thank* you," Marge said grimly. "I do appreciate that. Giving me half an hour in which to ruin my life." She poked at a piece of fried eggplant on her plate. "And what am I to explain? That I've got medieval parents?"

"Blame it on us if you like," Professor Craig said. It seemed to me that he was eating heartlessly, taking second helpings while she suffered. I'd stopped eating out of respect for her, and so had Kitty. Besides, I was too excited about seeing Rick.

I left early and Marge walked me home in the soft twilight. She didn't want to talk, and I was afraid to. Finally, as we came to Columbia campus she sat down on a bench and said, "People lie. They say time heals and all that junk, but it doesn't. I still haven't even gotten over Mischief's death."

That was a puppy they'd had three years ago that had gotten run over. "My feelings go deeper than most people's. I'll never, ever get over him. If even somebody like Richard Barthelmess came along, I wouldn't care. My life is literally over."

There was no way to comfort her. I just said I'd be home from school early tomorrow and to call and tell me all about it, and then we kissed good-bye and I watched her walk forlornly up Amsterdam Avenue.

Parents! Mother wanted to know right off what boy named Rick had called me, and I told her that we'd been introduced on the Drive by Marge—it was the safest excuse I could think of. Then she wanted his full name, and then, of course, she said, "Italian, dear? I really don't want you involved with foreigners."

That's an ugly word she loves to use. Involved. It took every bit of my persuasion for her to agree to my having dinner at his sister's, though she was a little impressed that he was a medical student. But some of Aunt Celia's suspicion has rubbed off on her, and she said, "Is Marge sure he's got a sister?"

Well, we got that over with. I said she could ask Rick all about his sister and his studies when he called for me, and she said, "So at least he's not afraid to come upstairs?" and I said he was a gentleman. I never use that word, or even think it, but it gets Mother right in the magnolia mood, so finally she said, "All right."

Marge was superb in rehearsal next day, but I knew she wasn't acting tragically—she was feeling tragic herself. Grief over Dick and their imminent parting at Freeman's had given her a sort of noble dignity. When Mr. Skinner complimented her, she said, "I've decided if Julie doesn't mind the script change that I won't cry. Mary wouldn't have. At the block she'd have been way beyond tears."

We all agreed. And it was the best rehearsal we'd had. Stew had learned how to release the catsup, Paul as Bothwell had stopped scratching, and Peter had become wonderfully sly as James Stuart. My diction had been okay, too.

After Biology and a swim I went right home. There was a letter for Mother from Dad, and it made me nervous. Perhaps he wasn't coming. I propped it up against the powder jar on her bureau and looked out of the window toward Freeman's. Just a drugstore to anybody without imagination. But this was where Marge and Dick would be parting forever, and I could imagine her not wanting anything but maybe a Coke.

I realized that all the great tragedies of life aren't played out in castles or hospitals or on romantic beaches. Freeman's was just an ordinary place with six booths, chairs and tables and a long white counter where cakes were displayed under glass covers to keep flies off. A row of stools there, and a calendar with a picture of a bathing beauty holding roses.

It was nearly five when Marge phoned me. She said bleakly, "Well, it's over."

"What did Dick say?"

"Nothing much. What could he say?"

"Nothing about running away?"

"Oh, for Heaven's sake, Julie, he hasn't any money

of his own. He just said, 'I'm sorry, I liked you a lot,' and finished his banana split and then a lot of kids came in and we left and he walked to his car and I walked home."

"It's simply terrible."

"Yes. I'm going to bed now. I don't want to eat or think."

Then Mother came in, and I told her a letter from Dad was in the bedroom. She went there, and after a while she came out and said, "This daydream about Europe! Don't believe in it, Julie. I wrote to him to send six months' rent ahead instead, but he didn't even mention that—he just said for me to try to book on the *Mauretania* for June."

"Well, that proves he has the money—"

"I want the rent first," she said. "I want assurance that we can pay the gas and electric. That we'll have a roof over our heads."

If she'd been in English, Mr. Skinner would have had a field day for clichés. But I couldn't help but feel sorry for her because she lacked faith.

"So you won't book passage?" I asked.

"No. He sent a hundred dollars for that, but I'm saving it. *If* he comes, he can book. If he has any money left by then."

I just hate cynicism. Maybe she caught it from Aunt Celia, who mistrusts men so. Maybe that's why they were such good friends, sharing it. Anyway she called Aunt Celia, who came and cooked dinner, and they went into Mother's bedroom afterwards and talked a long time, but evidently the subject of Rick didn't come up, and I was grateful because Aunt Celia mistrusts foreigners more than anybody.

Back with me in the living room, they talked about Stew and the play, and then Aunt Celia said she had to go; she had an engagement and had to dress. At the door I heard her say, "Toothpicks," and that seemed peculiar, since I knew she wouldn't be caught dead using one.

Then Mother came back into the living room. "Can

you get an extra ticket for the play, dear? Celia wants to bring along a friend."

There were a few tickets left. "Who?" I asked.

"A gentleman friend. She thought it might am—I mean, interest him."

"Anything for an audience," I said.

"Julie!"

"Well, it's not supposed to be an amusing play. And it's pretty well booked up, but I'll try."

There's one cliché you can't avoid: her eyes narrowed. Well, that's what eyes do, and there's no way around it. "After all Celia has done for you, the cloak and ruffs! You can certainly get a ticket for a friend."

"I'll try," I said. "Like you'll try for the ship."

It was the first outright rebellion I'd ever shown and I don't know why except that perhaps Marge's situation had affected me. It's all in the subconscious, as Freud says. Family romance! She stood there and we hated each other, and then she said, slowly and tiredly, "If you can't get an extra one, I'm sure Mr. Forster can use the one you've reserved for your father."

"I'm not so sure," I said, "that Mr. Forster is coming. He only wants to be amused. And," I mimicked, "just what do we know about him?"

That was what she was always saying about boys even when they were my schoolmates.

"He is a very wealthy man," she said sullenly. "He's made a fortune in toothpicks."

"How could he?" I asked. "One box of toothpicks costs five cents and lasts for ages. How could he sell enough to make any money?"

"That is not your problem, Julie," she said frigidly.

Well, I was glad it wasn't. I suppose a lot of people spilled toothpicks, and when Aunt Celia gave parties she used them for spearing little sausages and cheese. But that wouldn't account for many unless, with no competition, he had a dynasty.

"You will get Mr. Forster a ticket," she said.

And the way she said it—I was a child again, scared to cross her about the slightest thing. I don't remember ever being spanked; her look and her voice had been enough to seep every ounce of courage from me. It did now. I said, "Yes, Mother," and realized that she still had the power to make me miserable. In my bedroom, in bed with the light on, I couldn't even look forward to Dad or Rick with any happiness.

I tried to read Krafft-Ebing, but it bored me. Then I thought of what Mrs. Curran had said about word association, about how revealing it is, and I took a pad and pencil from the night table, wrote a word and then the very next one that came into my head—no pausing to think.

And this is the way it came out: Dad—love. Rick—kiss. Marge—Juliet. Mother—wastebasket.

It all made sense, except it seemed I wanted to throw Mother away.

Seven

WHEN RICK came to the door, I whispered to him, "I had to tell Mother we were introduced by my friend Marge Craig on the Drive. She's in my class," and he nodded and followed me down the hall into the living room.

He looked so handsome in his dark blue suit, and I always love broad, loosely knotted ties instead of narrow ones. Certainly Mother couldn't criticize his manners. After they'd shaken hands and she was seated, he offered her a cigarette. To my surprise, she accepted it. I sat beside him on the couch.

"So you're studying medicine?" she asked.

He was marvelous all through the cross-examination. Yes, his married sister Rosa lived on 114th Street near the Drive. No, he and his parents and two brothers lived on Bleecker Street. True, medicine was a very demanding career. No, his father had not been a doctor. "When he came from Italy in 1901, he worked in a little Italian grocery. Now he owns it."

I wriggled uncomfortably. This was awfully close to

pushcart peddling. But he must have had a decided impact on her, because she asked if they sold provolone and green noodles, and he said yes, and they had sixty varieties of pasta. Suddenly she turned actually coy—with all that prudishness, she does like good-looking males—and became embarrassingly Southern Belle about not knowing how to cook exotic foods; ol' Mammy jus' beat up hot biscuits and chicken fricassee without a recipe, and corn puddin'. "Why, I didn't even know a thing about cooking until just a few years ago."

Bragging—and lying, too. Rick said if he might visit us again he would bring her some provolone and other things she might like, and then I said we'd better go, and I left them to put on my hat.

It was a pale green cloche that Aunt Celia had "whipped up" to match my green-and-yellow print dress that had a flared skirt and short sleeves. I'd hated Rick to see me without my lipstick on, so I ran down to my room and put it on and then into my purse. Mother would never notice it in the darkish hall when she let us out.

Outside, Rick said, as we walked toward 114th Street, "Your mother is very pretty."

Not "very nice." When you've studied psychology you notice things like that. Then, hesitantly, "Your father is—"

"In Arizona," I said, "on business," and as best I could, I explained that he was a sort of promoter of mines and things and that he was coming home soon and that we were going to Europe. I had hoped Rick would say something like "Not for long?" but he said instead, "I envy you," as if the separation wouldn't mean anything to him.

Well, his sister's apartment was what Mother would have adored, full of old antique junk, gilt and crimson, cloud-shaped mirrors—the works. Rosa was a darling but very fat, being so pregnant, dark like Rick, but her heavy black hair swirled up on top of her head, and she was blue-eyed, so they didn't look alike. She wore tiny gold earrings and an enormous apron and after she had greeted me, her husband, Joe, came in, and I liked him, too, and they asked if I'd like a glass of Chianti, which was red wine they'd made themselves, and after we'd talked about the weather and stuff, she said she had to see to the dinner and would Rick please come into the kitchen and open something or other.

Joe, who was apparently the kind of Italian husband who never does a thing but support the household, had another glass of wine, while I sipped mine, and we got onto the subject of antiques, which he said Rosa loved but he didn't. I could see we were kindred spirits (cliché), and I could also see why Rosa loved him, because although he must have been nearly thirty he was still good-looking and rather masterful, despite what Rick had told me about his catering to Rosa's every whim on account of witches. *I* think he catered simply to please her. But for some reason—perhaps the wine—I needed to go to the bathroom, and he told me where it was. And as I passed the kitchen, I heard Rosa say to Rick, "I never can keep track of them. What's her name again?"

"Julie. Julie Willis."

So he had brought so many girls here. I was obviously one of a dozen or more. My first impulse was to be angry, then I realized how foolish I'd be to stalk out. I guess the only thing I'd learned from Mother was dignity, but I felt bleak. All I could think of was getting home to bed and trying to forget Rick, who was as bad a Casanova as Dick, only millions of times more attractive.

So I went back in, and Joe led me into the dining room, and there was more food than all the starving Armenians could have coped with. Under tall yellow candles, there was a silver bowl of daffodils and a lace tablecloth and on top of that covered dishes that held what Rosa called antipasto. Cold eggplant in oil, pimientos, salami. A big loaf of Italian bread. Then came spaghetti in clam sauce, roast chicken, green beans, and a bottle of wine that they all drank but I didn't. I forced myself to nibble, I even managed to laugh when they said something funny, but it was absolute hell, and then more food—salad and cheese puffs and a cherry-and-nut ice-cream cake. Every once in a while Rick looked at me as if he were worried, but only because I wasn't eating much.

"Dieting?" Joe asked, smiling, and what could I say but "Yes," which naturally was an obvious lie. But I was past the point of even pretending to eat, and they didn't nag me. Perhaps they thought I had become suddenly shy. Anyway, after we'd had very black coffee in the living room, I said to Rosa, "It was lovely," and got up. "I'm afraid I have an exam tomorrow. I must go home and study."

"So early?" she asked.

"Yes," I said. "My school is awful on exams."

Well, the truth is, Wilson doesn't have them, or even tests. We just get report cards every two months. Rick put on the act of Must-You-Go-So-Soon, and I insisted I must. So after I thanked Rosa and Joe again, we left.

"What happened?" Rick asked as we walked home. "Was the food too rich?"

"Oh, no," I said. "It was very good."

"Julie, something happened. You're upset."

"Just the exams," I lied.

"Why didn't you tell me before, then? We could have made it another night."

The sky wasn't quite dark yet, and a scent of new-mown grass came along over the Columbia campus, and I imagined I could smell violets and clover borne downwind from places like Peekskill and Tarrytown and villages on the Hudson.

"I'm sorry," I said.

I walked fast so he had to. Then he said, "Did Rosa or Joe say anything to offend you?"

"Of course not," I said.

"But *something* happened."

"Don't be silly." We were nearly at my house then. "Please tell Rosa how much I hope she has a lovely baby."

"You can tell her that yourself."

"But I'll be in Europe all summer."

Outside the apartment house he faced me, those enormous black eyes looking into mine. "You've got to tell me what's wrong," he said.

But I saw Mac going in to relieve Dan at the desk, and I said, "Hey, Mac!" and then to Rick, "I have to see him about mail," and then I said, "Thank you," again and was safe inside the Spanish Inquisition lobby.

I sat down in one of the torture chairs, realizing it was far too early for me to go upstairs and face Mother's question of "Why are you home at this hour? I thought it would be ten at least." So I waited until Mac had finished with some switchboard calls, and then I said, "I have to stay here awhile. Do you have a book I could read?"

He always had a small library hidden in back of a desk, and he said, "Sure," and I went over and looked through the selection. There was H. G. Wells and Cervantes and Conrad and Emily Brontë and Wordsworth. I picked the Conrad and went back to my chair and tried to read, but it was no use; I couldn't have grasped so much as a First Grade primer.

Mac said finally, "Why don't you go on up, Julie? Your mother went out somewhere."

Bless him. He always seemed to understand without words. He knew I wanted to be alone, and he also knew I didn't want any questions asked. So I took the book back to him and we said good night, and within twenty minutes I was in bed, the hall light on to show Mother that I was in, but my bedroom light off.

I knew there would be questions the next day. All about Rick and his family and the dinner. So I prepared myself, as you do for rehearsal. It would be so easy to say, "They were so nice, but I was bored and don't want to see him again." Or, "They're so foreign," but I wouldn't lie to please *her*. Certainly I couldn't tell her the truth, which was that I had fallen in love with a boy who had so many girls that his sister couldn't keep track of them.

I wasn't going to be hurt, like Marge. I wasn't in so

deep that I couldn't pull out in time. Besides, it wasn't love, I told myself. It was only the way he looked and talked and behaved and all mixed up with spring.

At breakfast, of course, the questions came. "You couldn't have been out long, dear, because I was in at quarter to eleven."

"Rick has exams," I said. "He's cramming."

"And what was his sister like?"

Oh, gosh. "Pretty," I said. "Pregnant."

She doesn't like that word and looked tut-tutty; I should have said, "She's going to have a baby," and then she would have taken on a sympathetic simper for Rosa. I gulped down my orange juice and coffee, said I had to get to the school library early, and was off before she could ask what we'd had for dinner.

Dan was sorting mail at the desk, but I couldn't wait to see if there was anything for me in case Mother came down, so I went to school. Practically nobody was there yet but the janitor, who'd just opened the huge marble doors. These came from some Roman castle and have friezes with nymphs and things on them and have bars on them at night to keep them from being stolen. A woman was dusting Plato and Wilson as I went up to my locker. Then I heard footsteps, and there was Marge looking like I felt—only I hadn't been able to cry and her eyes were tight and reddish.

"How did it go?" she asked.

I don't know why I wanted to defend Rick because I knew I would never see him again. I just said, "Tell you later," for other girls were coming in now and I needed a chance to think. If I told Marge he was a Casanova like Dick, then if I *did* decide to see him again she'd be armed with ammunition against him.

So maybe I was going to be stupid and hope he'd phone me?

That was an awful day: another frog came up in Biology; Mr. Skinner said my diction had relapsed; I made a mess of French grammar, and my soufflé fell flat in Household Arts. As if that weren't enough, I almost got into a brawl with Vera Jordan in the girls' room because she made a pointed remark about Jewesses in front of Enid. Anyway, I was glad to slide into the pool at three and float on my back and look up at the terra-cotta cupids on the ceiling and just let my thoughts drift in the blue light.

Then Marge swam over. "Tell me," she said.

"If you promise not to preach," I said.

"Since when have I ever?" She lowered her voice. "You didn't *soul-kiss?*"

"No." I told her all about it.

To my surprise, she defended him. "So suppose he does bring girls to his sister's? It just shows he's popular. I think you've treated him badly, I really do."

"But I don't want to get hurt."

"Better than to have nothing at all," she said, "like me. At least if you see him again you'd be living, not existing."

A giggle of Ninth Graders dove into the pool then, and we climbed out and went to the showers. After we had dressed, I asked if she wanted a soda at Freeman's and then apologized for the blunder. It would be exactly like asking a widow back to the graveside. So we pooled our money and went to the Passion Palace and had Cokes.

"I think you should call Rick tonight," she said. "Tell him you were worried to death about exams but now they're over, and please to forgive you for being so abrupt."

"But all those other girls—"

"You have a chance, at least. Faint heart never won—" She stopped the cliché fast. "You know what I mean. And this is the first time I've ever known you to be really stuck on a boy."

I said I'd think it over.

There wasn't any mail. Or any call from Rick that night, and that didn't surprise me. I was torn between Marge's advice to phone him, and my pride. But I was almost about to go to the phone book and look up his number on Bleecker Street, since Mother was upstairs for bridge, when the doorbell rang. And there he was.

Well, wouldn't you know I was caught in an old kimono and wearing horrid pom-pom bedroom slippers with the soles nearly off, and no lipstick. But I was so glad to see him that I didn't care, and I led him into the living room, where he sat down beside the window.

"Julie," he said, as I curled up on the couch with my slippers under me, "I was talking to a boy who used to go to Wilson and he said they never have exams."

He had almost a perfect profile, like John Barrymore, but he wasn't *pretty* like John, and now he looked terribly stern. "I want to know why you rushed off last night. Don't you like me? Were you bored? Rosa thought the food might have upset you."

That gave me a cue and I took it, although all I'd seemed to do lately was lie. "The truth is," I said, "I am rehearsing this very formidable part as Queen Elizabeth."

He nodded encouragingly.

"It was on my mind. I was worried about my diction, and when I saw all that food I got more and more upset. My friend Marge plays Mary Stuart, but since I wrote the play an awful lot depends on me and I feel guilty—and today's rehearsal went horribly, all because of me."

Looking back, I realize that was kind of lame. But Rick either believed me or pretended to. He came over and sat down beside me and took one of my hands and said, "You must always confide in me. I'd have understood even if you'd broken the date. But not knowing, I worried."

Those shiny black eyes had me almost hypnotized. And he was so close. He leaned toward me, and I knew he was going to kiss me, probably far backwards like Valentino does, in a dip like a tango step. I wanted it but also I didn't. It wouldn't be just flirting, as if he were Robert or Everett. I was afraid I'd slide down that elevator shaft or high building with no way to get up again.

So I managed to wobble to my feet and say, "Would you like some coffee or something?"

It's lucky I did because I heard a key in the door and Mother came in. She certainly got down that hall fast, and at first she didn't see Rick and said, "We've finished up a score pad," and then she saw him.

"Oh," she said, and then glanced at me in my kimono.

Rick rose and said, "I just dropped in, Mrs. Willis. I tried to phone but the switchboard was busy."

"I see," she said, but still looked at my kimono. "Julie, you had better go change."

I certainly wanted to, but I didn't like that cold disapproval. In my room I dressed hastily, hoping Mother would go back up to her bridge game, but when I came out I heard her saying, on the phone, "Sorry, something has come up—we have a guest," and I knew she was settled here for the rest of the evening. Her friends would just have to play three-handed without a score pad while she sat and chaperoned.

She doesn't do that with boys like Robert and Everett because I suppose the general dullness and acne lend an aura of safety, and besides, I've known them so long. But now I was sure what went through her mind: Italian. Older. Too good-looking. And of course, in italics, *What do we know about him?*

In a way, she was rather clever. She decided to bore him out of there and trotted out an old photograph album full of relatives I'd never even known—cousins twice-removed, grandfather with a beard, and lots of children in long clothes, none of which, thank Heaven, was me. Then pictures of houses in Kentucky: "That was Great-Aunt Sallie's—she died of yellow fever in N' Orleans. Now this one, I remember playing on the porch—see the wisteria vine? I think it was Uncle Edmund's—or was it Uncle Richard's? I should have them labeled. Oh, that's a yard dog—I think his name was Blackie."

I decided then and there that Rick would make a

wonderful doctor. He took it all—an hour of it—without even the anesthesia of coffee. Finally came a picture of her in her wedding dress, all bustle and puffed sleeves, and he said, "What a beautiful bride," and then she went all coy and said, "Guess who?" and giggled.

"And where's the groom?" Rick asked.

"Well, Mr. Willis never did like to be photographed. Besides, he always moved at the last minute and came out a blur." She looked up at me. "Julie, why don't you fix some orangeade or something?"

But Rick had had enough. "I must go," he said. "Heavy classes tomorrow."

"And what kind of doctor are you going to be?" she asked as they both got up.

I hoped he wouldn't tell her. For I just happen to know that obstetrics is poking about women's insides, and if *she* didn't know he'd have to explain. Fortunately, he must have noticed my warning look. "I'm not certain yet," he said, and thanked her for showing him the album, and we escaped together down the hall to the door.

"I'm so sorry," I said, whispering.

But he ignored that. "Julie, may I see you Saturday night?"

But that was the Father and Daughter's Dinner and the speakeasy afterwards. "Sunday?" I asked.

He agreed to meet me at Grant's Tomb at three. And we were just leaning toward each other again when Mother came down the hall, and I said, "Good night, Rick," and closed the door behind him.

I wanted to go into my room and undress and close the door and think about Rick in private. But she came in and sat on my bed and said, as I took off my dress, "He *seems* very nice."

I knew a "but" was coming, and it did. "But he's just a little too—I can't put my finger on it—sophisticated. I'm not at all sure he's to be trusted."

She gets this from Aunt Celia. Women and girls are forever being "abandoned" or "deserted," and I've heard them talk for hours about how men can't be trusted. It's morbid and unfair, and if they had their way there wouldn't be any sex in the world, just marriage and babies without it. When I wriggled out of my bra and step-ins, Mother turned her head so as not to see me until I had my nightgown on.

"He's a perfect gentleman," I said, using that word again.

"On the surface."

"For crying out loud, you've only met him twice! How can you expect to get to know a person, seeing him twice?"

"Don't you raise your voice to me like that!"

So she reduced me to a child again, just by that look of hers. And, of course, when she left my room, I couldn't start daydreaming about him without suspicion to spoil something that was pretty fragile at best. I *knew* he had a lot of girls, but I'd been trying to forget that. And now she made me wonder if all he wanted to do was go the limit, which is way beyond soul-kissing.

Restless, I turned over, toward the window. Across the court Mr. and Mrs. Goldenstein still had their lights on, and the lights shone on some pink and white hyacinths in pots on the fire escape. Mrs. Goldenstein always put them there at night to get air and perhaps a little rainwater. In the morning she had their mattress out to air, too.

I don't know why the idea of the Goldensteins pleased me so, except that he was never away and nobody could say she was abandoned, and she and her daughter, who was about my age, were always laughing together and cooking together. Erna went to P.S. 148, so I didn't know her very well, but it seemed to me she had everything I didn't. Maybe not such freedom in school, or the loan of a brocade evening cloak or a date for a speakeasy. But I pictured her sleeping without a care in the world, being trusted, and not having to lie. Having faith in those candles they lit every Friday night and being able to believe in God.

But then, she doesn't have Dad or Rick—and if I

didn't either, at least they weren't entirely remote.

I remembered, half asleep, what Robert had said once—that the only way to pray is to forget He's managing the universe and all that, and to talk to Him naturally as you would your own father. So I raised partway up on the pillow and said, "Look, will You please send Dad home before the play and rid Mother of all that suspicion of Rick and fix a happy ending?

"Thank you," I added, and then a wind must have come up, because my curtains blew, and one of Mrs. Goldenstein's hyacinth pots fell and crashed in the alley, and a cat yowled. I wondered if it was an omen.

Nothing unusual happened in school next day except our costumes came from the Metropolitan Opera ahead of time, so we were able to have a dress rehearsal. Marge, of course, had to wear black, but mine was a deep red burgundy with that V waist and stiff sleeves that ladies wore in the sixteenth century. Doublets, hose, capes, everything—but it took the cast so long to dress that we were able to get through only part of Act One before the bell rang for Psychology. This was a very interesting session because Bernice Yellin brought up birth control.

"Well," said Mrs. Curran, "there are means of controlling birth. Have you been reading about it, Bernice?"

"No," Bernice said. "It just sort of came up in conversation. You see, I know two girls—" She hesitated. "Not very well. They're sisters, twins. They live with their parents in a house way out in New Jersey."

Mrs. Curran seemed a little impatient. "Please stick to the facts."

Bernice has very pale skin, and it began to flush. "It's a nice house," she said. I could sort of see her mind skipping ahead to what she didn't want to say any more. "Very nice girls, sixteen. They made the organdy curtains themselves all ruffled—"

"Will you please get to the facts, Bernice?"

Bernice swallowed, then took a deep breath. "Their

parents went to spend the night with a sick uncle. My friends—I don't know them very well—asked two boys to come and listen to records. They brought a whole bottle of gin and wanted to neck. Of course, these friends I don't know very well wouldn't drink, but one of the boys brought out nine things from his pocket and said they would prevent babies. They seemed to be made of rubber, much too big to swallow, not like pills at all. It's very confusing to my acquaintances, who wonder what kind of plan they could've had?"

"What did they do?" Mrs. Curran asked.

"Why, nothing. They didn't want to drink or neck— my acquaintances, I mean—and told the boys to go home, pretending some old cousin was due to arrive any time. So the boys left in a hurry. But the girls want to know what these rubber things are that can prevent babies."

"They can't," Mrs. Curran said firmly. "That is, they can't be trusted. They are called contraceptives and are sheathed onto the male penis but are very much inclined to break and thus release the sperm into the female. Highly dangerous."

"And not be swallowed?"

"Certainly *not!* They are worn externally by the male but are absolutely no certain protection against the possibility of pregnancy."

"Then what is?" Enid asked.

I had an idea that Mrs. Curran knew almost as much as Rick but wasn't going to tell us. "Various experiments are being made," she said, "in laboratories all over the world. But thus far I believe I may say that contraception is still in the experimental stage and that any girl who indulges in sexual intercourse may well find herself pregnant." She paused, then said, "Now, I'd like your opinions on Jung's split with Freud."

The bell rang and we all swarmed out into the corridor. Vera Jordan looked at Bernice right in the stomach and said, "Well, well—is it too soon for us to knit bootees?"

"Shut up!" said Enid Rosenblum. "You've got the dirtiest mind!"

"Dirty?" Vera purred. "But sex is so pure and beautiful. *You* should know, dating that Polack."

"Mikel is not a Polack, he's *Polish.*" She's a little taller than Vera and she looked down at her and said, "You know what your trouble is?"

"B. O.," Bernice said.

"Halitosis," said Jane.

"No," Enid said, supremely haughty. "Anyone who is anti-Jewish and anti-Polish and all that suffers from the vulgarity of insecurity."

It was a kind of reverse snobbery, and it was so magnificent that Vera actually shriveled. We left her and strolled to the water fountain, and I said, "Gee, I'd never have thought of that!"

"I didn't," Enid said. "I swiped it from a *Times* editorial."

Mr. Skinner passed by and broke it up by taking me aside and asking what color dress I'd be wearing to the dinner. So he was sending flowers! "Another gardenia?" he asked.

I'd heard the girls discuss orchids, gardenias, roses. But I said, "Maybe it's unconventional, but I'd love a spray of purple lilacs or violets," and he nodded and smiled and said he'd send them late Saturday afternoon and call for me at six.

That night I had dinner with Marge and Kitty. After their parents left, I told them all about Rick, and they both had advice. When I met him at the Tomb on Sunday, I should be careful not to walk anywhere where he could kiss me; the longer I didn't kiss him, the quicker he might fall in love.

"Let's face it," Marge said, "you haven't had much practice. But once he really likes you he can forgive anything."

"She could always say it was her first kiss," Kitty said.

Marge had that pained look that Kitty sometimes

engenders. "Don't be silly. That would be admitting to outright juvenilism."

Kitty looked offended and went to take Trixie for a walk. "She won't give up on Jim," Marge said, sighing. "Even that dark girl that he seems to be dating hasn't brought her to face facts. I'm afraid she and I are alike in a way—when we love, it's forever."

Even in just the week since she had relinquished Dick, she'd gotten thinner, and though it's old-fashioned to think that people can die of broken hearts, I wasn't so sure. I wondered if maybe Rick's younger brother might be a possibility for her. He was seventeen, but that's all I knew about him, except he planned to be a doctor, too. And Mr. and Mrs. Craig wouldn't be prejudiced against Italians. But I decided not to say anything until I'd met him—if I did.

Poor Kitty came in. Her lot seems to be infallible failure. Poor Marge, too. Our lives were like a seesaw, one up, then one down. We never seemed to be happy all at once. At the moment I was the luckiest, with Rick, and Dad coming home.

But when I got home, I had to shed my friends' troubles and get into my own. Mother wanted to know if Rick had asked for another date, and I could see the mistrust spread a mile wide, so I lied and said, "No." I would meet him secretly so she couldn't spoil the very beginnings of something.

Eight

EVEN THOUGH we lived very close to Wilson, Mr. Skinner took me there in a cab. It couldn't have been a more dramatic entrance, all those limousines drawn up and us walking toward the big marble door, he in a tux, me in that gorgeous cloak, violets pinned to my little evening purse. Enid, who had just gotten out of her Rolls with her father, looked at me and said, "Wow!" and Vera glared so I knew I was a success. But nobody will ever know, not even Marge, how sad it was not to have my own father.

The cafeteria had been made into a dining room, and I'd never have recognized it except I knew the way there past the cloakrooms, where I checked my wrap. The tile ceiling had been covered with some filmy yellow material that also draped the walls. The tables had leaf-green cloths, jonquils, and the whole room was a glow of candlelight. Near the counter, which was normally used for sliding down trays of food, an orchestra played behind big pots of ferns. It was a waltz from *Maytime.*

Mr. Skinner peered around and found our table with place cards. When he seated me, I realized I was in enemy territory. There was Vera, her friends Betty Scott and Mabel Darrow, and their fathers. Betty and Mabel resented me because I hadn't given them parts in plays, which was simply because they couldn't act. The fathers looked stiff. I was grateful for Mr. Skinner. He had shaved quite carefully, and slim and small as he was, he had a kind of air about him. I could see that the other men at our table were something dull, like bankers or lawyers.

Waiters brought tomato juice, and then Dr. Matheson stood up and rapped for silence. He asked us all to rise and drink a toast to this special evening, but he had the sense not to go into a long speech about fathers and daughters since some of us, like me, had substitutes. Then we all sat down and waiters passed soup.

I can't say there was much general conversation, except that the fathers got onto U.S. Steel. They asked Mr. Skinner's opinion, and he said he preferred poker, but nobody laughed except me. Then Vera told Betty that she was going to Westhampton for the summer vacation, and Betty said she was going to Nantucket, and Mabel's father said they always went to Maine. I couldn't resist saying, "My father is taking us to Europe."

It wasn't that I wanted to outdo them; I just wanted them to know that I really had a father, with plans for me. "Oh," Vera said, "I thought your parents were divorced."

How it hurt. "No," I said, but I couldn't say anything else. The words wouldn't come. Mr. Skinner suddenly began talking about what an education Europe was at any age, but particularly when one was young and not jaded yet, and how wise he thought my father was to take me there. I began to relax a little but could only nibble at the roast beef and asparagus because my stomach felt funny.

And I knew what else it was: fear that Dad wouldn't

come, that it was all a fairy tale. Not that I cared about Europe so much—I'd have gladly spent the summer on the Staten Island ferry if he was along. And looking around the room, I didn't see a single handsome father except maybe Susan Ward's, and he was an actor and I think he had false hair. How smug they all were, those daughters with fathers. I wondered what the other girls without fathers were thinking—Lillian and Connie, Sylvia and Anne—but they were way across the room.

Cake came, and ice cream and strawberries, and the waltz music resumed. But I didn't feel any better, and I think Mr. Skinner knew why I couldn't eat, because he patted my hand under the table. You wouldn't think, his being so cynical and sardonic in school, that he could be so kind out of it. Just loud enough for the others to hear, he told me what a great Queen Elizabeth I was creating and what he expected next week when we were all accustomed to the costumes. Then, very softly, he asked, "Is your father coming, Julie?"

"I think so."

Finally coffee was over and we all moved out into the wide corridor while the tables were cleared and removed for dancing. Mr. Skinner and I went over to talk to Marge and Kitty and Professor Craig. Then Marge and I went into the girls' room and I put on more lipstick.

"You look absolutely catsy," she said.

It was a wonder, the way I felt. What food I'd had was wanting to come up, and I rushed into a toilet to see if it would, but it didn't. When I came out, Marge said, "It's missing your father, isn't it?" and was suddenly very sympathetic, which she usually isn't on that old subject, so that I began to cry. Since some girls were coming, we both ducked into the same toilet, and I dabbed at my eyes, and then I really got sick, with Marge flushing the toilet so nobody would hear, and patting me.

"I just don't see how I can go out there and dance," I

said, "and as for Stew and that speakeasy—"

"You've got to do both," she said. "You're an actress, aren't you? Well, prove it."

One thing was sure, there was nothing more to come up. So we left the toilet, and I primped again, and Marge was so wonderful that I realized Dad would never have to be a taboo subject again. She said she knew now that I hadn't been dramatizing or romanticizing him, and to forgive her for past sarcasms, and we kissed, which we almost never do except at good-byes for summer vacation, and went in to dance.

Wouldn't you know that the very first dance was "I'll Get By"? That's the absolute shatterer when I'm unhappy, but Mr. Skinner danced so badly that I had to keep thinking of my feet and how to keep them out of the way of his. Then Professor Craig cut in on us, and then there was a waltz with Enid's father, who was great, and finally I saw that the clock pointed at five to nine, and I told Mr. Skinner I had a date with Stew.

He seemed grateful to go, paused while I put on that sumptuous cloak, and then accompanied me downstairs and outside. Stew hadn't come yet, so Mr. Skinner and I stood by the door and he lit a cigarette.

"Were you awfully bored?" I asked him. The fresh air was bringing me back to normal.

"Of course not," he said. "I thought you were."

In a rush of confidence I said, "You see, I miss my father, and tonight it was worse than usual. If he's not here in time for the play, I'll simply die."

"Not before Mary Stuart does," he said, "or you'll twist up history," and that made me laugh. Then he said, "I'm sorry the play is running only one night. I tried for a matinee, too, but Matheson said no, the auditorium will be full of Observers watching films."

Films made since the school started, I knew. The "bright child" in class, at play, all subtitled, and then eminent educators lecturing on our aims, our failures, but mostly, I suspected, our successes. Marge said probably the Crandall endowment wouldn't last forever and more and more money would be needed.

Then a cab pulled up and there was Stew, all tuxed-up, and I thanked Mr. Skinner for bringing me, and he said, "Not at all," and I waved good-bye and got into the cab, pulling up the white fox hem of the cloak.

"Golly," Stew said as the cab turned down Amsterdam Avenue. "You don't look a bit like you."

I suppose that was meant as a compliment. Even though he wore a tux, he was the same old Stew, small-eyed and big-nosed and with chapped lips which at least weren't as cracked as they were in winter. I have learned at Wilson that no amount of wealth can make up for good looks if they aren't born in. In fact, when I saw my mother and Mrs. Crandall sharing a table at a school tea, I realized that all those sables couldn't make Mrs. Crandall as pretty as Mother in a wool coat. I believe that, at ten, it was my first deep thought, although, of course, it sounds very trite in later years.

"What speakeasy are we going to?" I asked, as if I'd been to lots.

"The Aquarium Club. It's the best."

"But how do you get in? I mean, even lots of older people can't."

"You'll see," he said, and put his arm around me. But I squirmed away.

"What's wrong?" he asked. "Don't you like me?"

I used the old line about his being too popular and poor little me had to know him much better before I risked getting a crush.

"But you *could?*" he asked.

"I'm afraid so," I said wistfully. "But I heard that you date a girl at Miss Finch's."

Evidently he did because this put him on the defensive. By the time we'd passed the Plaza, he was still explaining that she was really a friend of the family, and forced on him, while he was so bored by her he'd gone to sleep during *Parsifal*. Of course, he would have anyway; as I said, Stew is a little retarded intellectually.

I wasn't noticing just where we were going except

west from Fifth Avenue in the fifties, and then the cab pulled up and Stew helped me out. While he paid the driver, I stared at a row of old brownstone houses where nobody seemed to be home because not a light showed. My guess was the club had been raided and closed, but Stew went ahead, and I followed down a few steps toward a basement entrance. He rang a bell four times.

A little grilled window opened and a man's voice said, "Name?"

"Benjamin Miller," said Stew.

"Birthday?"

"August 16, 1911."

"Wait," said the voice.

I was really proud of Stew for remembering his line, "Benjamin Miller." But we waited about five minutes before a door opened and a man in a black suit, like an undertaker, led us into a small room behind a staircase. It was full of metal file cases, and the man said, "Mr. Miller, we must have the young lady's name and birth date."

Before old Stew could speak, I said, "Vera Jordan, December 8, 1911." I didn't want to seem merely fifteen.

The man took out a white card and wrote me down and filed it and then said, "Go on up," and we climbed a carpeted staircase in very dim light. At the top a maid took my cloak and gave me a metal token with a number on it. Then we went through another dimly lit hall that led into a huge room that looked like somebody's living room with a lot of people sitting in upholstered chairs at small tables.

I think this house must have been a mansion once; they'd kept the heavy red damask draperies, the Oriental rug, and all the chairs were big, overstuffed things upholstered in red. At the far end was a kind of counter (Stew called it a bar) that ran the whole width of the room, and it was based on a long tank, with goldfish swimming around. About two dozen men in tuxedos stood there drinking, but there were a good

(112)

many women and girls sitting with men at the tables, some of them about my age and all of them dressed up. The wall lights were shaded with red, so the whole atmosphere was rosy.

A waiter came to our small table, and I ordered beer, but Stew asked for a Manhattan cocktail. While we waited for our drinks, Stew explained that there was a very elaborate arrangement at the bar. There was a pulley, or dumbwaiter on ropes, that brought the booze up from a cellar, although near-beer was kept on the counter and alcohol put in just before serving. He said that if cops came and raided, all the illegal booze would be dropped down a secret shaft after it hit the cellar. No glasses were in sight; everybody drank out of teacups with saucers underneath.

It was terribly exciting. "Don't the cops ever find the bottles that are dropped into the shaft?" I asked.

He smiled. "Of course. They're supposed to confiscate them, but they don't. It's more like the bottles are held in ransom because the cops and Mayor Walker and the gangsters who own these places are all in the same league."

"Was that a gangster who let us in?" I asked, thrilled.

He shrugged. He was enjoying being sophisticated. "Probably. Sometimes there's an honest cop who tips off some honest police station about a club like this and it's a real raid, but mostly it's all understood *before* there's a raid and a lot of money changes hands. Anyway, even clubs that are closed reopen if they have enough money to bribe higher-ups."

Our drinks came, and I thought the beer tasted terrible, but Stew said his cocktail was great. It was a dark amber color, and he gave me the cherry in it. I listened to the talk around us—everyone spoke softly except a woman near us in a glittery sequin dress who kept calling her date "Daddy," though it was obvious they were about the same age. Then Stew pointed out some celebrities: Helen Morgan in a tight black dress and pink feather boa and one of the Happy Wonder Bakers from

(113)

radio. There was a piano in a corner, and a tiny little dwarf-like man went to it and played "S'Wonderful."

And it was. My drink began to taste a little better. The woman in the sequin dress got up and said, "Daddy, dance," but a waiter came over and said the club had no license for dancing, and everybody who heard laughed, and Daddy ordered lamb chops for her which came with little paper frills.

"Stew," I said as he ordered another Manhattan, "I'm hungry."

Now, remember his family had all those millions, but he said he couldn't afford any food and that even my beer cost a whole dollar.

"Isn't there a sandwich or something I could have instead of another beer?" I asked.

But he said sandwiches were $2.50. If I wanted to stay on, I'd have to order another beer, or ginger ale. So I ordered ginger ale, but I was getting hungrier by the minute. Some men at a nearby table were having steak sandwiches, and smelling them, all charcoaly, was sheer torture.

Stew sipped his cocktail, and I don't think it was my imagination that his skin, which is rather fair, was beginning to turn a peculiar green. His eyes, small to begin with, were backing in on each other, and what chin he had wobbled.

"Shtay here," he said, and suddenly he was up and away.

Well, I knew what it was to be sick, and I felt sorry for him and a little guilty that I was so hungry. All I could think of was that when Stew came back I'd ask to go home. I'd make a hamburger and there was some rhubarb in the icebox and milk and things. Meanwhile I just had to wait.

I waited and waited. So did the waiter, watching me. The room began to fill up so that all the tables were occupied and a line of people waited in the hall.

The waiter, who was old, came to me and said, "Where's your boyfriend?" and I said in the men's room, I thought. He left me for a while and then he came back and said, "He's not in there—he's skipped the bill. You'd better pay up."

But I had only fifty cents in my evening purse. Even the violets pinned there were wilting.

"But I haven't any money. And he's probably just walking around the block to get some air."

"Well, you're not staying here, taking up a table."

Suddenly a big, heavyset man in a tux loomed up beside us and nodded curtly to the waiter and said, "What's the trouble, miss? Boyfriend ditch you?"

"I think he got sick," I said.

The man sat down and told the waiter to scram. "I been watching you," he said, "and wondering what a nice little girl like you was doing in a place like this."

And then he tutted, just like Mother. "Boys that can't hold their liquor got no right to bring girls here. Does your parents know?"

I shook my head. "I lied to my mother."

"And what about your father?"

"He's in Arizona."

This time he clucked; in fact, he looked really shocked. And he started to lecture me about lying and deception. But when he saw how miserable I looked, he called the waiter and ordered steak sandwiches and milk for me and "the usual" for himself, which came in a teacup. But all the time he went on and on about the danger to a young girl of going out with a boy like Stew, and had he driven me here?

"No, a taxi."

He approved of this, at least. No boy should have a car who couldn't be trusted with booze. "Now you stay here," he said, "and I'll take a look for him outside, and if he ain't there I'll personally take you home."

So since Stew had apparently vanished, this man paid the bill and tipped the girl for my coat and we walked partway down the block and got into the biggest black car I ever saw. It had a bar in the back and was upholstered in tiger skin and had the kind of windows you can look out of but not into. I sat beside him in the front seat and he went on lecturing me all the way through Central Park and up Amsterdam Avenue. He said he didn't know what youth was coming to, he really didn't. Hadn't I no church education? I told him about Comparative Religions, but he snorted. The thing was, I should have been started in a good Catholic school, and by the age of ten my morals would have been set. As we waited for a green light at 115th Street, he asked me to promise I would never go to a speakeasy again, and since by now I really didn't want to, I promised.

When we parked in front of my house, I asked his name, but he said, "That don't matter. What matters is, you are only a baby and it's lucky for you I'm a guy with principles."

I thanked him for paying the bill and my sandwich and everything and hopped out and then watched the great car speed off through a mist that was coming in from the Hudson. And then I went inside the lobby, and Mac said, "Hello," from the switchboard and put down a book.

"You look real lovely," he said.

I sat down on the chair nearest him. "Thanks. But what time is it?"

He looked at a clock. "Twenty to twelve."

"Oh, goodness," I said. "I'm in too early. I'll have to stay here until one."

The wonderful thing about Mac is, he never asks questions. He just said did I want a book to read? But I wanted to talk, and I told him everything about the evening, but he didn't lecture me at all—he said it was just too bad. "Sometimes you have adventures that just don't come off right," he said, "and other times you set out on just a little walk or something that turns out to be wonderful. I don't think you can plan on anything, Julie."

He had a thermos of coffee and poured me some in a Lily cup, and for a while we were quiet, drinking our coffee. Once or twice he had to plug in a call, and two or three people came home through the lobby, but I had the fox collar turned up around my face and was curled into the chair just in case a neighbor noticed me, which wasn't likely because the Alhambra has light bulbs about ten watts.

"Mac," I said, and it was true, "you're the nicest older person I know. You see, my biggest problem is my father," and I burst out with absolutely everything, and how I felt about Mother and Rick. I must have talked a full twenty minutes, and he didn't interrupt.

"I think Rick is the most exciting boy I ever met, but in a funny way I can forget about him for hours, worrying that Dad may not come home, so it can't be real love, can it?"

He shook his dark head. "There's all kinds of love. All different. I loved my pal who got killed in the war—we were in the Argonne—better 'n I loved my own brother. Odessa and the kids—that's other different ways of loving. We got a little neighbor man, half-blind—I love him, too, and not just pity. What I don't see is why people make love just one kind of thing that's mixed up with hearts and flowers and valentines. Or respect, like for parents." He paused and lit a pipe, which takes quite a while. When he finally had it going, he said, "Some parents, like mine, don't deserve respect, so you're lucky."

"But Mother hasn't any faith in Dad at all."

"Is that your business? Let her not have it, but you keep it. You keep it, hear? She's a nice lady in her way, but what right does she have to smear him? She sees him one way, you see him another, just like you listen to the same music and get different feelings. Who's right? Nobody."

We talked some more, and then, feeling a lot better about everything, I went upstairs.

Mother was waiting in her room with the light on, of course, sitting up in bed with a dozen questions waiting. She even wanted to know what music we'd danced to at the Biltmore. Then when I was about to escape, she said, "Don't plan to go anywhere tomorrow afternoon—Miss Jeans is coming for tea."

Now this Marie Jeans is possibly the worst bore

Mother knows, and that's taking in a lot of territory. She's a retired schoolteacher about sixty, doesn't approve of Wilson or me, but likes Mother because they met in an antique shop and kept on meeting through the years to talk against Yankees and about Kentucky. One of the close friendships that grew out of a rosewood chair or something, and when Mother speaks of her she goes all respectful and hushed, and I notice when they're together—about once a month— Mother's southern accent gets twice as molasses as it usually is. Even if I hadn't had a date with Rick, I'd have found an excuse not to be here.

"I'm sorry," I said on the way to the door. "Marge and I have to rehearse the play—"

"You can do it Monday night."

"Marge is busy all week. Besides, Miss Jeans really wants to see you, not me."

"She loves seeing you, dear."

Well, as waitress to serve angel food cake and tea from the silver pot. To look down on. When I was about twelve and was telling them about my script for *The Three Musketeers* and that I was playing Milady, Miss Jeans had turned to Mother with a sneer and said, "The child is so dramatic, isn't she?" and I'd hated her from then on.

"If you don't realize that this rehearsal is important," I said, "you just call up Mr. Skinner."

The bluff worked; Mother is afraid of authority even if she doesn't approve of Wilson. So I went to bed knowing that everything was okay for the next day.

Nine

I CALLED Marge from Freeman's booth on my way over to the Tomb, to ask her to cover up in case Mother phoned. Marge said they were all going to her grandmother's for the day in Greenwich, pure hell, but if Mother called I could say we hadn't answered the phone because we were in the midst of rehearsal. I told her about Stew, and she said, "Aren't you worried about him?" and I said, "Not a bit," which she thought was cold, considering that he was a classmate and had spent a lot of money on me.

"Money? It was that nice man who paid the bill, not Stew! All he paid for was the cab. That man must have spent about six or seven dollars."

But she said she still worried about Stew, even if I hadn't a glimmer of compassion, because he wasn't too bright even sober. And then she said her mother was lurking, so we hung up.

That mist I'd seen last night was heavier now as I approached Riverside Drive, but pearly, not gray, so you could see the laurel bushes and forsythia through it like a soft impressionist painting. Rick was sitting on the steps of the Tomb and got up as I came near and said, "I was afraid you wouldn't come."

"Weather never bothers me," I said.

"You okay from that speakeasy?" he asked.

So he had remembered. I said, "Oh, yes," very casually.

"How long can you stay out?"

I guess he understood that I lived in a sort of prison. "Until about six," I told him.

It began to rain, not just sparkles of it but sheets of it, and there was no shelter except the Tomb. I suppose it was open to visitors, but Rick took my hand and we made a dash for a Fifth Avenue bus and climbed to the top. My dress was wet and my hair and the little bandana that I wore as a hat. He took out a handkerchief and sponged me very gently, then took off his blazer and put it around my shoulders.

"Where are we going?" I asked, although, of course, I could see it was downtown, past all the Columbia fraternity houses, toward 110th Street.

"To a friend of mine's," he said.

I was disappointed; I wanted to be alone with him. We got off at 102nd Street and walked a few blocks east to an old Victorian house that had pepperpot towers and iron balconies, and he let us in with a key. He said the electricity wasn't working because his friend and family were in England. When we got through the hall, the living room was shrouded, all the chairs and the sofa covered with white sheets.

The rain hammered the big bay window. "It's creepy," I said, and sat down on a little hassock that wasn't sheeted.

"It won't be when I make a fire," he said. There was coal in a copper scuttle, and logs, and pretty soon he had a blaze going. Then he said he'd get us something to drink, and I looked around.

A big radio took up about six feet of the floor space, and it was all draped in muslin. There were rubber plants at the windows, and a little rock garden of cactus laid out on the sill, and another that was Japanese. I'd have liked to have seen how that room looked when it was normal, but now it seemed to be waiting for people who might never come home.

Rick came back with a tray that had two glasses on it. "It's Dubonnet," he said, "but I couldn't find any cookies."

He sat down on the heavy brown hearth rug at my feet and we sipped our drinks. It tasted queer to me at first but a lot nicer than beer, and then I asked about his friends, and he said Sandy was his best friend who had gone to England with his parents to look over Oxford for next year. Imagine, all that money just for a boy to go and look over a school! But Rick said Sandy was terribly bright and that if he chose Oxford it would be lucky to get him.

"And when will you become a doctor?" I asked.

He said it would take ages yet. What he hoped for was to intern at Bellevue, where you got amounts of practical experience you couldn't get anywhere else; besides, no matter what people said about its being a charity hospital, it was the best in New York, never mind its being shabby; if he were a millionaire able to afford the fanciest he would still want to be treated at Bellevue. "I can see myself about forty, with the gout—no, I wouldn't be that stupid—with a broken leg lying in a Bellevue ward with it stretched up on a diamond pulley and the nurse bringing orchids in *if* she had the time."

"And who'd be sending you the orchids?" I asked.

"A very great actress named Julie Willis. Not that she'd bought them—the orchids were left over from baskets of flowers she'd received on opening night."

I liked being put into the dream. "I'd want you to be there on opening night. And why should you break a leg?"

"Trying to get past the crowds to your dressing room."

Well, I knew it was all a line. Just the same, he made me halfway believe in it. "You don't have to be forty to come to my opening night," I said. "It's next Saturday night at eight, at Wilson, if you'd like me to get you a ticket."

He said, "Swell," and then asked more about the play, and I told him all about it.

"What are you doing afterwards?" he asked.

If he could dream ahead, so could I, and probably I was in better practice. "I'm almost sure my father is coming, so afterwards he'll take you and me and my friends Marge and Kitty and Aunt Celia and her friend Mr. Forster to the Villa Vallee to dance."

Then I told him all about Dad. "He's just *got* to be there."

"He sounds great," Rick said. "But I don't think your mother likes me. Won't she be along?"

"Oh, I suppose. Did I forget to mention her?"

"Yes."

I hesitated. "I'm sure she likes you, but she has a funny thing about any boy who isn't dull. In fact, I didn't tell her I was coming out to meet you this afternoon."

"So it's that way," he said.

He got up and poked at the fire, and I wished I hadn't told him. It made me feel so childish, being dominated by Mother. Now I was afraid he'd ask why she didn't like him—that would have been clear enough—and I couldn't say because he was Italian. And worse, because his father had a store.

He turned and looked up at me from the hearth rug and said, "I'd like to come to the play, Julie, but I haven't enough money to go to the Villa Vallee. So we'd better not plan on that. I'll just come to the play, that's all."

"Dad would insist—"

"Julie." He reached for my hand and held it. "If he doesn't come, it's not going to be the end of the world, you know."

The rain kept on drumming the bay window. I finished my Dubonnet. Then I said, "I know, but my mother—being alone with her all summer and having her say, 'I told you so.' He just *has* to come."

He let my hand drop, and then he said, "I don't like skulking around keeping clear of your mother. And she doesn't object to me because I'm not dull, but because I'm Italian and older and she doesn't trust me, so let's get that clear right now."

He stood up and so did I, and then he kissed me and I went straight down that elevator shaft Marge had mentioned, and from the very top of the Woolworth Building. In fact it was more like falling down something like the Grand Canyon, ledge after ledge, and I clung to him until finally he pulled away and I was back on the hassock.

I couldn't think of a thing to say except "I love you," but, of course, I didn't. I was just one of all those girls his sister couldn't keep track of, and I was furious with myself for not being the one who had broken from him. So when I'd caught my breath I said, "I wonder what time it is?" and he looked at his watch and said, "Ten after five."

"I should be going."

"I'll take you home," he said.

He could have begged me to stay or said it was still early, but he didn't. He simply made that fire go out, first with a poker and then by stamping his boot in it. Then he took away the glasses and, I guess, washed them while I waited.

We didn't say anything on the way to the bus stop except "It's stopped raining," and "Yes, it has."

That silence was so dreadful that I had to break it. "Tell me," I said, "are Italian green noodles made of real spinach or green tinted stuff?"

"Spinach," he said. "No dye."

The bus lumbered along, puffing up a little hill on the Drive, and now we could see a few boats on the river.

"Do you like shad?" he asked.

"Yes," I said. "Why?"

"Those are shad boats."

"It's very expensive boned."

"I read that shad boners get four dollars an hour," he said. "It's such a short season for it."

"Bones like little wires, aren't they?"

"Yes."

We got off the bus and walked to my house, and then I said, "Thank you for—"

"But I'm coming in."

"You can't! I told her I was with Marge this afternoon."

"So we happened to meet on your way home. I won't go through any more lies, though. If she doesn't like it, she can say so."

I was scared to death. "Miss Jeans will be there. She's awful."

But he didn't even ask who Miss Jeans was, and we went past Dan, who was at the switchboard, and on up the steps. I opened my door.

I usually rub off my lipstick before I come in, but then I realized it had been kissed off. "Go on in," I said, and closed the door and then led the way up the hall.

Mother and Miss Jeans were sitting on the couch next to an old cracked Limoges tea service on the table. This is what Mother brings down for very special visitors, using a stepladder to the top cupboard. And although she's constantly complaining about how we can't afford this and that, she'd snuck over to the bakery, which is open on Sundays, and bought a chocolate cream roll, which costs forty cents. All to impress Miss Jeans.

"Hello," I said to Miss Jeans. "This is Rick Innocente." Then to Mother, "I met him coming home from Marge's."

Miss Jeans extended her hand and Rick shook it, and then we sat down in opposite chairs and were looked at. Miss Jeans always has an invisible lorgnette. She also has a weird way of doing her hair, which is very long and thick. The blond part of it is twisted onto the outside and the gray onto the scalp in loops, so the blond—faded as it is—manages to predominate. Mother says it is very clever, as one day she will emerge all silvery as though it were overnight. But her being tied to a railroad track would be more profitable to the human race. Not that I think she ought to be run over, but a scare would do her good. And she has a very evil influence on Mother, bringing out that "southern belle" not in small doses but in concentrate, so that she says "y'all," and "mah gracious," and "kin" instead of relatives.

I won't go into that terrible dialect as she said, "Julie was practicing a little play with a girl friend—about Mary Queen of Scots."

"From what I hear," Rick said, crossing his legs masterfully, "it's an epic."

Miss Jeans tittered. "Are you in it?" Missing what he'd said.

"He's not in my school," I said. "He's in Columbia."

"It used to be very good," Miss Jeans said, "before it turned progressive."

"Rick's in medicine. It should be progressive," I said.

It was the first time I'd ever dared correct her or argue, and I suppose it was because having Rick there gave me courage. So much so that I turned to Mother and said, "Rick's coming to the play."

For just a moment I felt sorry for her; she couldn't say no in front of Miss Jeans—we sort of had her trapped. Then I stopped feeling guilty because Mother said, "Julie thinks Mr. Willis will be home by then."

It was never "my husband" or "Julie's father" to Miss Jeans, but "Mr. Willis." She always liked to brag to people that Grandmother referred to Grandfather as "Mr." even with the family. As Queen Victoria might have said at table, "Prince Albert, please pass the salt."

"And what makes you think so, dear?" Miss Jeans asked. "As I recall, he's been promising things for years, but, of course, his business must take precedence, mustn't it?"

As always, when people said that kind of thing, I had

no answer. It always crushes me, and Miss Jeans knew it, so she got up on that lovely exit line and said she must be going home.

"Perhaps Rick will walk you to the subway," Mother said.

"And come back for dinner," I said to Rick.

To do Mother credit, she didn't wince. But when they had gone she said, "You know we have practically nothing for supper."

"I'll curry some eggs, and there's rice—"

"I'm not very hungry," she said, and started to wash the tea things. No wonder she wasn't hungry—there was about an inch of chocolate roll left. "And I do think you should consult me before asking people."

I wished I hadn't asked him. She'd sulk. I could see that Rick was in for a deadly hour or two.

But she wasn't cool—oh, no, she was charming. But, boy, after we'd eaten, did she make him work! She asked him to climb up to the top shelf with the Limoges china. Then after the ladder was down, she remembered the teapot had to be washed and after that he had to climb up again. He had to put a new bulb in her bedlight, mend the hook on the kitchen wall, force some thumbtacks into linoleum, see why the bathroom lock didn't work, and then fuss around with a fuse.

"Men are so handy," she said when he crawled out from under the couch where she thought the wiring was defective. "Now, I wonder if you'd see why that window doesn't open."

When she couldn't think of another chore, she said, "Well, I expect you both have a lot of studying to do tonight," and so, of course, he had to go.

I was hoping that he would kiss me good-bye, but she went down the hall with us and turned on the light there, and I said, "Call me about Saturday," and he said, "Okay," and thanked Mother for the dinner and left.

I wanted to get into bed and think about that kiss, but she followed me into my room and said, "Since you've asked him to the play, I suppose there's nothing

I can do. But I don't want you involved after that."

Involved. How I loathed that word. "Why don't you come right out and say you're afraid of sex?"

She gave a shrill little squeal. "How dare you speak to me like that?"

I don't know where I got the courage. "Because you've got a dirty mind, that's why. I am not 'involved' or pregnant or anything but in love!"

She stared at me for a moment, and then she asked, "With *that*?" as if Rick were something lower than an amoeba.

"Yes. And when Dad comes, I'm going to tell him all about it. You wouldn't understand."

"When Dad comes," she said, mocking. "Oh, that'll be the day! Oh, that's really funny," and she did a kind of imitation laugh. "You, you're all I have in the world, and you leave me out of everything just as he does—you go your own way, just like your father. And now you say you're in love with that Italian, and I suppose you think he's in love, too—you build on nothing but dreams. A nice steady boy like Stewart"—who hadn't even called to apologize for last night—"but you get involved with an Italian and use foul language to me—*pregnant*—and then pretend your father's coming home."

So finally she'd said it—right out. She didn't believe Dad would ever come. Oh, she had dropped hints before, but never like this.

"Has he written that he's not coming?" I asked, scared to death.

"Of course not—it's fun for him to keep us on the hook. Only I'm just a little past that—I seem to have heard it before. And it's high time you learned not to believe in dreams."

Now I knew she hated him. It was in her face. It was such a shock, hearing her say this, that I was afraid to say a word. My old fear of her was back and with it a worse fear—that she was telling the truth. About Dad. About my supposing that Rick loved me. After all, what's a kiss to a boy whose sister can't keep track?

Mother left my room and I went in and took a shower and put on clean pajamas. When I came out, there was no light on under her door. In bed I thought about faith, but I wasn't a saint. It's very hard to keep faith up when it's always being knocked down. There wasn't a single person in all the world who believed in Dad except Mac and me. As I finally fell toward sleep, I imagined I could feel Rick's kiss, but then I knew it was only the pillowcase touching my mouth.

Ten

AT LUNCH in the cafeteria, Stew came by my table and said he had been very sick on Saturday night from some lobster he'd had at dinner and was sorry if I'd had to take the subway home. But I told him about the wonderful man, and I think he was quite pleased about not having to pay the bill. After he left, Marge came along, carrying a tray with nothing on it but milk and an apple, so I didn't need to ask her state of mind about Dick. I told her all about the weekend, and she said, "Well, at least your father isn't against Rick. When he comes, he'll probably tell your mother to jump in the lake."

It was the most beautiful thing she'd ever said to me—I mean, this reversal from cynicism to belief. And she said one happy thing had happened over the weekend: Kitty had walked Trixie all the way to Inwood Park in a fit of melancholy and had met a girl who introduced her brother, Bob. "It was a pickup in a way, but with the sister along, and they offered Kitty tuna sandwiches and cream soda, so she's made the transference from Jim, and he's coming tonight to take her to a movie."

That was wonderful, and I hoped that if he was a lounge lizard, it wouldn't show up to the Craigs. It's the really smooth kind like Dick that makes parents nervous. I didn't think Rick, who was so forthright, should make Mother nervous, but Marge had a thought about that. "If he's as good-looking as you say, then she's probably jealous. And she wants you all to herself. But when your father comes—"

"Excuse me." It was Mr. Skinner. "I'm going to ask the cast to stay over the usual hour and a half. The sets are ready, and I want you all accustomed to them *and* the costumes. Okay?"

We said it was, and then an Observer came over and sat down and interrupted us again. She introduced herself as Dr. Crawford from Smith College, and Marge perked up because that or Vassar was where she wanted to go. Dr. Crawford asked the usual questions— what did we like and object to about Wilson, what were our aims. She was a nice rolypoly woman of about forty and took notes as we replied. Then she said, "I heard the cutest thing in the Third Grade."

The women Observers adored the Third Grade, who this year all seemed to be plump children with horn-rimmed spectacles. "It was a history class," Dr. Crawford said. "The children were asked what their ideas of the sixteenth century were, and a little boy named Peter said, 'It was a time when the men went out and stocked the larders with food and every day killed something or someone.'"

We're a little weary of cute Third Graders. I think they put it on and rehearse before Observers come. But since I knew it might benefit Marge to get into Smith, I told Dr. Crawford that Marge was playing Mary Stuart Saturday night and then subtly added, "She prays in Latin at the end," and Dr. Crawford asked if she could get a ticket, and I said I'd try. The fact is, we had about six hundred people coming—the largest audience we'd ever had, except when President Harding opened the school officially. So I left them and whisked up to Mr. Skinner's little office, got a ticket for her, reserved one in Rick's name, and then whisked back to give Dr. Crawford hers.

I was glad about the longer rehearsal since we needed it, and also because it kept my mind off Rick and what he might be thinking. He might have found Mother too much trouble; he might have been just polite, saying he'd come to the play. I thought of the very sophisticated girls he probably met at Columbia, studying to be nurses or even doctors, with permissive parents and brand-new radios and their own cars. After all, he was nineteen, and I wouldn't be sixteen until August.

Mac was at the desk when I got home, and he waved a letter at me, and I went over to the chair nearest him and read it while he read a book.

Tucson, 17 May

My dearest:

I am much more disappointed than you will be, but it may be June before I'm able—

That's all I read just then.

"Oh, now," Mac said, "it can't be that bad, Julie."

"But it is. It is. He won't be coming to the play."

"You haven't finished it. Go on and finish it."

But there wasn't anything I could depend on. He hoped we could sail for Europe in July, and he would be sending Mother a rent check as soon as he could. Suddenly I knew just how she felt—not about the rent—after all, she'd taken that hundred dollars for it instead of booking passage—but about always being disappointed. "If he doesn't want to come back, why doesn't he *say* so?"

"He just doesn't know," Mac said. "If I was in his shoes, I'd feel worse, as a man, than you do. These deals he's got—he's waiting on them like you're waiting on him. Only the deals I'd get wouldn't be gold mines and things that could make a fortune, so looking at it his way, he's out to get the real big money, any day, and so he has to wait." He took a phone call and then said, "How long since he's been here?"

"Five years."

"It doesn't seem that long to me. Oh, I remember him, handing your mother down those steps like she was a queen, and a white carnation in his buttonhole —they were going to some party and you were spending the night at your aunt's. I remember that because he asked me to put you and your aunt into a taxi, and he gave me a dollar. *A dollar.*"

The switchboard got awfully busy then, so I went upstairs and reread the letter, and then because I'd have to tell her sooner or later, I left it propped up on Mother's dressing table. That's where we left messages for each other, and I saw a marketing list and two dollars and remembered we didn't have much in the house to eat, so I went out again. This time it would be beef stew and skirt steaks for later in the week; you have to argue with the butcher to get them as they're so good and cheap and scarce. But when I got home and started the stew, I knew I'd be eating alone because Mother would have one of those headaches—partly sulking, partly angry at Dad and me for simply existing.

When Mother came home, in just the mood I knew she'd be in, she read Dad's letter and then said, "Well, so that proves it, doesn't it? Now you know," and she said she wouldn't be eating and stayed in her room.

Dad—well, I'd just keep on waiting. At about nine Rick called, and I was so relieved I felt tears in my eyes.

He said, "Is your mother still disapproving of me?"

"She disapproves of everything. But she can't stop you from coming to the play."

"And your father?"

To my astonishment, I hadn't even thought to tell Rick that Dad would be delayed. "He won't be coming. So there won't be any Villa Vallee. No celebration afterwards."

(132)

"Julie," Rick said, "I don't want to cause any trouble between you and your mother."

"It's already there."

"What's the best time to call you?"

"Four or five o'clock."

"I'll call," he said, and we said good-bye.

Love came up in Psychology, and Jane Bliss wanted to know if some of the movie stars like Conrad Nagel were father images.

"I'm afraid I'm not especially acquainted with movie stars," Mrs. Curran said. I'd noticed that it was very fashionable for adults not to notice movie stars except Charlie Chaplin, whom they considered a genius and we all felt was a bore. "But it's not unusual for young girls to admire older men."

Betty Scott said, "I think I have a mental block about all boys on account of Valentino. Nobody can measure up to him. That was two years ago and I still can't get over him, I stood in line at Campbell's Funeral Home for eleven blocks and cried every inch of the way."

"I used to have a crush on him, too," Marge said, "until a boy told me he was all pockmarks."

"Girls!" said Mrs. Curran. "We are not here to discuss personal preferences in movie stars. Jane raised a point about father images that is perfectly valid. The young girl worships her father and then generally transfers this love to a young man who is very apt to have the same strengths as the father."

As Rick had. And the same dark good looks, too.

Mrs. Curran asked the usual hopeless question: Did we have any personal problems to consult her about after class? And, as usual, no one had. If I were Principal of Wilson, I'd choose a young woman for Class Adviser and have a separate psychologist.

Marge and I had a brief conversation at the lockers. Kitty had had a wonderful evening with this new boy, Bob Lee, who had made a very good impression on their parents, and she was to be allowed to see him again on Friday night.

"Dad isn't coming," I said. "Maybe in June."

It was really strange that I hadn't told her immediately. I think it was the combination of having Rick on my mind and putting up that mental block against anything too hurtful. She looked at me for a moment and then patted my shoulder and said, "You're okay, though?"

"Yes."

"And your mother?"

"What would you expect?"

"Come and stay all night with us, then."

My first thought was no, because Rick might call. Then I remembered that Mac was on night duty and could give Rick the Craigs' phone number. So I said yes, I'd be there for dinner.

Mother was absolutely frigid as I dressed to go to the Craigs'. I think she had always been jealous of them because she knew I admired Mrs. Craig, and so, of course, she sniped at her (to me) for still liking Mah-Jongg, for having shingled hair, and for not wearing her skirts below the knee. But the worst was, Mrs. Craig had written a letter to *The New York Times* saying it was high time the Bolshevik scare was over and that we shouldn't be seeing anarchists under every bed, and that letter—with a denunciation of the Ku Klux Klan—was printed. Mother said that Mrs. Craig was all wrong, especially about the Klan. What did Mrs. Craig know about the South?

"I hope *you* have a pleasant evening," Mother said.

I got out of there fast, telling Mac where I'd be.

The nicest thing of all about Professor and Mrs. Craig is that they're so popular they're hardly ever in, so Marge and Kitty and I could talk freely and have the kind of food we liked. Marge said it was as if we were all pregnant at the same time. Two years ago we'd all had a mad passion for liver and bacon. Then it was fried-egg sandwiches. Then it was jellied pineapple salad. Now we were back to eggs again, only in a way we'd learned from a French recipe. You fry a piece of toast in butter and then lower the gas and pour in milk and egg, and it comes out a sort of omelette with the toast in the middle.

After that we had strawberries.

We talked a long time after we'd eaten. Rick didn't phone. Around ten o'clock I began to have hiccups, which Marge said were simply nerves, and she brought me a little glass with some of her father's gin in it mixed with water. That stopped the hiccups but I had a terribly bleak feeling and said so. "If Dad doesn't come, I'll be spending the whole summer with Mother, who'll try to insult Rick out of my life. And there's not a hope of meeting him secretly because he wouldn't go for that. After all, why should he? I'm sure there are plenty of other mothers who see him as maybe a future son-in-law."

Out on the Hudson a boat horn tooted. I remembered what Mac had said about listening to train whistles and finally getting on a train going North and making a new life. But men can do that kind of thing without money. Girls can't. Women's suffrage hasn't done a thing except give us the vote.

"I think you should write your father the whole thing," Marge said, "and get *his* permission to date Rick."

"In writing," Kitty said.

But I knew that was useless. Mother would write him all kinds of exaggerations about Rick, and they had always sided on things like how late I should be out. They even might on foreigners.

Then the boat whistle tooted again, faint and far-off, but it was like a summons: I would get to Arizona—somehow. And I said so.

"And leave Rick?" Marge asked.

Leave everything. Once I had really talked to Dad, everything was sure to straighten out. He would come back with me, and whether we went to Europe or not, it would all be sane and normal and lovely. I could see the summer beckoning ahead like a long, pink, blossomy road. And I knew it wasn't the gin or my imagination. It would be real.

The next day I walked to school with Marge and Kitty.

"Oh!" Kitty said as we got to 120th Street. "Look at that boy!"

He was standing on the corner, the wind ruffling his trousers and his hair.

"Don't stare," Marge said, staring.

It was Rick. He came up and said, "I'm sorry I couldn't phone last night, Julie. But I thought I might see you here."

Golly! To think he'd waited around! I tried to play it suavely and introduced Marge and Kitty. He looked embarrassed, probably because they were still staring at him. I knew just what was going through their minds. How could anybody so handsome care about Julie?

Not that I minded; I'd been surprised myself. It was like winning in a lottery—not that I'd actually won, of course. He hadn't said he loved me or asked me not to date anyone else. It was a miracle to me that he hadn't been discouraged by Mother and just oozed away with a "See you sometime, baby." But here he was—practically at the crack of dawn. And he had had to come all the way up from Bleecker Street to a subway stop past Columbia.

Marge and Kitty tactfully walked ahead of us. He asked, "May I see you after the play?"

I told him that Aunt Celia and Mr. Forster and Mother would probably contrive some kind of after-theater celebration. In a way I was glad he was foreign because he had a kind of Old World understanding about how families can be.

"Would anything change your mother's attitude?" he asked. "Suppose my parents invite you both for dinner?"

There was the remotest possibility that Mother would agree. I didn't want to tell him how remote. He said he would phone and suggest next Thursday. "Swell," I said. "Do your parents know about me?"

"Of course," he said.

I wondered if, like Rosa, they had trouble keeping track of all the girls he brought there.

Later that afternoon, when Marge and I got out of rehearsal and the pool and had a chance to talk at Freeman's, she said, "I can see just why you're so crazy about Rick—so can Kitty—but if ever there was a boy designed to make a mother frantic, it would be Rick. You're too blind to see."

"But—"

"*It* is all over him. He can't help it. He doesn't even dress like a sheik, but it's a kind of aura. When you can get that without slicked-down hair and Turkish cigarettes, it's just natural, elemental sex appeal."

"And you think my mother catches on?"

"She's not a dumbbell. She has eyes. Why, even a nun would sense that *It*. Compared to him, Dick was just a cub scout."

I'd never have thought she could have spoken of Dick in the past tense and so calmly. She even asked Mr. Freeman for another scoop of ice cream in her soda. In a way, it was chilling to realize how quickly a great love can die.

"I never told anyone this," she said with contempt, "but the hip flask Dick had wasn't even gin. It was just Coke. To think I could have been so *childish.*"

I almost felt like defending him. "But his necking?"

"He was pretty good at that. Only now I feel that I was an experiment, someone to practice on." She took the straw from her soda, crumpled it, and threw it back into the glass. Then she reached for the paper casing, poured a drop or two of melting ice cream on it, and made it wriggle along the table like a caterpillar. Nerves, I thought. Marge hadn't made a caterpillar since we were about ten.

"I am definitely through with boys," Marge said. "I'm glad for you and Kitty, but I wouldn't be in love for anything. I'm going to concentrate on studying and devote my life to a career after college."

She'd never been very clear as to what career, but perhaps she would be now. "What'll you be?" I asked.

"Anything but a wife and mother," she said. "I might get into politics. Mother says it's about time we had a woman president to stop wars and things. Only I suppose I'd have to study law, and that would bore me to death."

Well, I at least was sure about my career. But when I got home, I realized that it was going to be difficult because I didn't like my voice. Standing speaking into a corner, like you're supposed to, I could hear the way it sounded, echoing back from the wall. It was too high. And I didn't want to play cute little juveniles. I'd have to ask Mr. Skinner what to do.

About the same time Mother came in, Rick phoned. I heard her say very coldly, "How nice of you. But I'm afraid Julie must help me here next Thursday—we're having a few people in. But thank you just the same."

Back in the living room she said, "I must say he's persistent. He asked us both to dinner at his house, but I told him we were having guests."

"And are we?" I felt about ten years old, the decision made for me.

"My bridge night."

"Look," I said, "do you mean that you won't let me see Rick any more?"

"I should think that's clear enough, Julie. He's too old for you, and after all, you have other boyfriends: Everett and Robert and Stewart Crandall. Why don't you ask Stewart here some evening, dear?"

"For tiddlywinks?"

"Don't be sarcastic. He's a fine boy, from a fine old family."

With fine old oil wells and fine old mansions and most of upper New York State as property. But as far as brains go, as I said, he's semimoronic. And though I couldn't say so, of course, a moral leper, letting me down as he did in that speakeasy, glad to have a stranger pay the bill.

But I couldn't argue with her. I went into my room

and wrote Dad a long letter about how wonderful Rick was, and please to intercede in this situation and write Mother that as head of the family *he* gave permission for me to date Rick. I took the letter down and bought stamps from Mac and then put it through the mail slot, which is the open mouth of a Spanish carved goat or something.

I brought Mac up-to-date about Rick and everything. "Well," he said, "what I'd do if I was you is get to your father, no matter what. Or how. He'll settle it all. He's man of the family."

"But maybe he'll come in June."

"If he doesn't come," Mac said, "you go. I'm telling you, it's gotten to the point where a young lady needs her father or else—"

"Or else what?"

He got busy on the switchboard then, and I went upstairs.

That afternoon at four Rick phoned, and I had to tell him that Mother wouldn't let me see him. "She thinks you're too old for me. It isn't *your* fault you're nineteen, but there it is."

"I see." Oh, he saw a lot more than that.

"I've written my father. If I can get permission from him to see you, may I phone you?"

"Yes," he said. He was silent for about a minute, and then he said, "I'd better not come to the play, then?"

He wouldn't know anybody in the audience but Kitty. "I guess not—it might seem very juvenile to you. But there's a ticket reserved if you want it."

Again he was silent, and I hoped he was going to suggest that we have a secret date or defy my mother together, but all he said was, "I'm sure it won't be juvenile. Good luck, Julie."

And we hung up.

The fact that he could take it so calmly was terrible, for he must have realized there was scant hope of Dad's being able to convince Mother about a boy sight unseen. He hadn't even tried to fight for me. He just accepted authority. What a Romeo! All this you hear about hot-blooded Italians—ha! Now, even if Dad wrote that I *did* have permission to date him, I wouldn't phone Rick. And when I became a great star and he paid for standing room and then went around to my dressing room, I'd raise an eyebrow and say, "I'm sorry, I didn't catch your name."

Oh, I'd forget him in a hurry.

Maybe even in a year or two.

One thing I wasn't going to take—the Thursday bridge night. I told Mother I had the cramps and went to bed about seven-thirty with two aspirin and *Photoplay* and *Theatre Arts* and a quarter pound of caramels hidden in my bedroom slipper. The walls are quite thin, which shows you that the Alhambra isn't exactly built like a fortress. I could hear Miss Johnson and the other ladies calling out spades and clubs and hearts and then arguing about rules from the Contract book. But they gossiped as much as they played. "Before I bid this hand I *must* tell you," or "Emily dear, Macy's has a sale on vests, really nice rayon," and then finally the game was over and I heard the rattles of cups and plates and "Oh!" and I knew it was squeals of delight over strawberry shortcake. Except for Mother, they were all old maids, and it didn't take much to create whoopee, poor things. And then I heard Miss Norton ask, "What's wrong with Julie? A cold?"

"No," Mother said. And I could imagine the archness and the blush. "It's one of those *times.*"

And then Mother said, "I want her to save her strength for the school play. She really is an extraordinary actress."

Not "for her age." An extraordinary actress. Just that.

Perhaps she was bragging to her friends or just making conversation. But nobody in all my life had ever said that about me, and for a few minutes I forgot about Dad and Rick, love and hate. Mother wasn't exactly a drama critic, but then she wasn't a liar, either. Whatever she said she believed.

The light off, I began to think about Mother and wonder if perhaps she wasn't basically a very fine person, with areas of retardation she couldn't help. I almost felt that I could begin to love her, in a way.

Eleven

MOTHER LOOKED absolutely marvelous the night of
the play. It seemed that Aunt Celia's toothpick tycoon
was taking us somewhere afterwards, and Mother
wore a dress Aunt Celia had gotten from Paris. It was
made of very thin black crepe with long, tight sleeves
that came to a point. A panel of the same material
draped down in the back over one shoulder, and it was
tight—the dress, I mean—so her figure was lovely, like
a stalk, and there was a matching coat lined in coral
silk. She'd had a marcel and even spit curls on the side,
and when Mr. Forster came for us he looked kind of
goggle-eyed.

But then he *was* goggle-eyed. Those unfortunate
eyes that protrude, perhaps from goiter. His stomach
protruded, too, but he had a nice smile and was tall and
looked very well with Aunt Celia. She looked like
something out of *Vogue,* in a short white sheath, belted
very low in rhinestones. These are called cocktail
dresses, and the Woman's Christian Temperance
Union is against the name because they are so against

liquor. But Mr. Forster had brought a bottle of chilled champagne, and we sat around our apartment and had it, with nuts, before we went to Wilson.

I didn't want any, really—I took just a sip to be polite—because I knew what a job I had ahead of me. The role of Queen Elizabeth is very exhausting, and as Mr. Skinner had said, I could not play her as a villainess because she and her subjects thought she was right in her attitude toward Mary Stuart. I had to be a nervous, frustrated, jealous, brilliant woman of about fifty-three, and I would have to spend at least forty minutes on makeup. I couldn't wait to get to the star's dressing room and out of my violet moiré and into my costume to begin aging myself.

Mr. Forster had a long, sleek car outside, and the chauffeur opened the door for us, and we drove to school. Marge was already in her dressing room, next to mine, and said she was having awful jitters. So was I. Alone, I put on greasepaint—very white—and then Miss Thain came in and aged my eyes and cheeks with some brown stuff and wrinkled my throat with it. I put on the costume and then sat while Miss Thain arranged my red wig and attached the ruff with tiny safety pins.

"No lipstick," she said. "The paler the better. You have come to offer Mary help in Act One—and in a hurry. In Act Two you are too upset to bother about looking beautiful. In the last act you are bloodless, almost ghostly. It is Mary who, in bravado, wears"—she consulted the script—"lip paint and rouge and scarlet undergarments to be beautiful in death."

I sure was no beauty. Staring into the mirror, I could see myself in middle age, throat all crepey and wrinkled. When Miss Thain left to make up the rest of the cast, Peter Vorse ducked in, looking great as James Stuart, but worried that his beard might come off. I sent him to look for Miss Thain, and then Mr. Skinner appeared.

"Julie!" he said. "Just fine. Remember to exhibit

your hands—Elizabeth was very proud of her hands and accustomed to showing them, even under stress. Now put your rings on. Good." Then he smiled at me. "A capacity house. There are even some people standing."

"Really?" I found that I'd almost lost my voice and was terrified. It came out a croak.

"Stand up," he said.

I did, the velvet gown heavy. A cloak covered it in Act One, and a kind of lace thing in Act Two, so it didn't seem to be the same dress, and in the third act I didn't wear anything over it.

He put his hand on my stomach. "Now breathe in—out. No, the opposite way. Stomach out, deep breath, then in. Right. Talk."

"I have not wanted to harm you, but thou hast harmed me."

It was amazing. I had my voice back, and projected. And it seemed low-pitched.

"You've got to practice those exercises more," he said, and left me.

The whole play, now that I think of it, was a blur. Except near the very end, when I made my exit and left Marge and old Stew together. I stood in the wings as prompter in case I was needed. There was Marge being led to the block by Stew, and about a dozen of the cast, witnesses to the execution. Marge, superb in red silk vest and petticoat, knelt. Calm, regal. She prayed aloud in Latin.

Stew raised the rubber ax. I hoped he'd speak his one line softly—"Thou scoundrel." But for a long while he didn't say a word—building suspense? He never had in rehearsal.

Then he looked toward me in the wings, ax still raised. Marge wriggled uncomfortably. Then Stew said, hopelessly, "Thou scallion?" He let the ax fall and released the catsup from his left hand.

But apparently nobody had heard him, and when the curtain fell, there was tremendous applause. Then the curtain was raised and we all took a bow, and by gosh if there weren't flowers for Marge and me. Hers, I learned later, were from her parents. Mine were a long box of red roses from Dad and an orchid from Aunt Celia and Mr. Forster, and lilacs from Rick, with a card just signed with his name.

Marge and I had a brief hug in the hall outside our dressing rooms, and then I went into mine. Dad's card said, "I'm here, baby." He meant in spirit, of course. And then to think that Rick had bothered!—it was almost too much. I cried a little, being so happy, and then took off my makeup and costume and put on the violet moiré and pinned on the orchid. I was just putting on a little cape when Peter Vorse knocked and came in and said, "Julie, my aunt wants to see you. Miss Vorse, this is Julie Willis—I mean, anyway, meet me outside, Aunt Mae, okay." And he wiped blue off his face, and I stood facing this very tall lady.

I will say for Wilson, even the stars' dressing rooms are comfortable. Miss Vorse sat down on a little blue-padded stool and smiled at me. She had a very wide mouth, so a very wide smile, and if it was a little buck-toothed, it was friendly. I'd think she was about forty, but as Aunt Celia would have said, she was chic—short skirt over long legs, all of her encased in a blue crepe de chine thing and matching turban, so I don't know what color her hair was.

"Julie," she said, "you were superb!"

Mr. Skinner doesn't approve of exclamation points, but that's the way she said that sentence. I said, "So was Peter," but she shrugged that off.

"What roles have you played before this one?" she asked.

It took me about ten minutes to tell her. Milady in *The Three Musketeers*, the mad wife in *Jane Eyre*, Roxanne, Lady Macbeth, Becky Sharp, and loads of witches and evil princesses I'd made up in my youth. "Either I adapted the classics or wrote my own original plays."

"But aside from Roxanne, I notice that you have preferred the character parts—the meatier ones?"

"Yes."

"Even if they were small, like Mrs. Rochester."

"Yes, Miss Vorse. Jane Eyre was just a heroine."

"That's true dedication," she said. "Most girls want to play the pretty-pretty parts. Where did you get your training?"

"Why," I said, "just here. With Mr. Skinner, our English teacher."

"No drama school?"

I shook my head, and she seemed astonished. "Then you're a natural-born actress. Have you considered dramatic school?"

"I'd love it. But aren't they terribly expensive?"

"Not for you," she said. "Why do you think I came here to talk with you?"

I'd no idea.

"Let me tell you a little about myself."

It seems that, in school, she was a girl just like me, only in Cincinnati. She ran away to New York at seventeen to go on the stage, but found she hadn't any real talent. "Now," she said, "I'm on the board of the Young Theatre Guild, and my job is to look for promising young people. And, my dear, I've found you."

I was so excited that I didn't get it all straight, but it seemed that I could study at the Guild on a scholarship next fall and still continue at Wilson. Then, when I graduated from Wilson, I could study with the Guild full time if I proved worthy. After three years' training I was guaranteed small parts in the Guild plays on Broadway. It was their way of developing new stars like Alfred Lunt and Lynn Fontanne, who were also teachers there.

I stammered out how hard I'd study. Oh, I'd do *anything*. But then I'd have to get my mother's permission.

She waved that aside. "When I explain, she will see all the advantages."

"She's probably right out there in the corridor now," I said. "You could talk to her—"

"Not now," she said, rising. "Give me your phone number, dear, and I'll call her Monday, and perhaps we can meet."

I didn't have a pencil and neither did she, so I scrawled the number and my address in lipstick on a bit of the cardboard from Dad's flower box. Hands trembling are supposed to be a cliché, but mine really did. Then I said, as she went to the door, "Didn't you think Marge Craig was good as Mary, too? Couldn't she—"

"No, dear. She was charming, of course, but she didn't really project. Now you talk to your mother and to your principal, and I'll call you."

I'll never forget that moment, alone there by the mirror, with Dad's roses and Rick's lilacs and the orchid pinned on; I almost felt beautiful. I wanted to hold it, to keep it, but people were waiting for me. So I hung up my costume, pulled my hair over one eye, put on just enough lipstick so Mother wouldn't notice, and went out through the wings, past the empty seats and into the corridor, where little groups of people were still standing, including Marge and Kitty and her parents.

But this was no time to tell Marge; for one thing, she looked so happy, with a lot of boys around congratulating her, so I just waved and blew her a kiss and joined Mother and Aunt Celia and Mr. Forster.

"Thank you for the orchid," I said, holding the other flowers in my arms, and then Mr. Skinner came up and said, "Bravo, Julie," and some classmates piled up— but all this time nobody could have guessed what a tremendous secret I had. It would just have to wait until we got where we were going in Mr. Forster's big Rolls-Royce.

Well, to make the evening complete, we went to the Villa Vallee. It was all golden and shimmery, and we had a table next to the dance floor where, for the very first time, I saw Rudy in person. When he sang, the spotlight on that wonderful wavy hair of his, it all seemed too sacred to dance to. After Mr. Forster had danced with Mother and Aunt Celia, he asked me to—and, of course, it had to be "I'll Get By," reminding me of Dad. But I was in no mood to cry, and besides, he danced quite well, not hopping about like most older men do. All this time, I'd been dying to tell them about Miss Vorse and the Theatre Guild, but there hadn't been a chance. And when we got back to our table, there was a blond young man in a tux, about eighteen, whom Aunt Celia introduced as Marvin Adams. He apologized for being late and then asked me to dance, and I realized this is what the underworld calls a con.

Not that he was; he was just getting out of prep school, not a prison. But I knew exactly why he was here—to take my mind off Rick. Mother had told Aunt Celia, who had told Mr. Forster, and so this son of a partner of Mr. Forster's had turned up. He was quite good-looking, too, if you like very pale blonds. He was also a good dancer—the number was a test of coordination since the tempo was so slow that you could end up, in the wrong hands, just shuffling.

But was he conceited. He told me he was late because he'd had to go to a debutante dinner at the Ritz. He bragged about getting a Stutz Bearcat as a graduation present from his parents. Then he talked about entering Princeton in the autumn and being faced with the awful decision of which eating club to join, as if he'd already had offers. And then he said, condescendingly, "A.B."—that was Mr. Forster—"said you were in some sort of little play tonight?"

I opened my mouth to say, "I'm going to study dramatics with the Young Theatre Guild," then closed it. I wasn't going to waste my glory on him. So I just said yes, I'd been in a play, and let him prattle on about himself while I listened to Rudy's music. Then, while we were still dancing, the room darkened, and the music softened, and Rudy, in the spotlight, sang "Lover Come Back to Me."

It was sort of understood that you didn't dance. You just got closer to the bandstand and listened. I think even Marvin was moved by that throbbing voice because his arms tightened around me. For about seven minutes I pretended he was Rick, but it was no use. I have learned that you can't take substitutes for anybody.

Back at the table, we looked at enormous menus, and I ordered lobster Newburg. While we waited for the food, Mr. Forster ducked under the table and poured whiskey into the setups of club soda for everybody but me. Marvin had one. I must say he handled it better than poor Stew, but then he'd probably practiced at loads of wild parties.

Do you know when you have a secret stored up that doesn't have to be one you simply itch to tell it? I was waiting for a lull in the conversation, but then the food came. Afterwards the music started up again and Mr. Forster asked me to dance (he was even better this time than before), but he wasn't the one I wanted to tell. Besides, he wanted to talk about Aunt Celia and how they had met. A year ago his wife had learned about these fabulous French clothes and how she didn't have to take the ones already worn but could order new ones through Aunt Celia, and then his wife had suddenly died and his sister had quite as suddenly needed a mourning veil, and together they had gone to Aunt Celia's. They found something suitable, too, all black.

"You aunt is so charming," he said. "She was a great comfort to Dorothy and me. She came to the funeral, all in white. She said it was a French custom. She said she had revived it from the sixteenth century. What I like," Mr. Forster said, "is enterprise."

That got him onto toothpicks. He said he was planning to manufacture colored ones for spearing food with. He also had a sideline of white and colored ruffles for the ends of lamb and pork chops, and little metal things to hold corn on the cob. He manufactured Lily cups, too, and I told him half the cast of the play had used them for ruffs, which he said was very gratifying but that, if he'd known, we could have had them free.

We returned to the table for ice cream, and Marvin,

who was sitting beside me, whispered that he'd like to see me again. Did I like the theater? Now, there was a dopey question, but I said yes. Opera? Some of them. How did I feel about Isadora Duncan and The Dance? I didn't see why we had to whisper about that.

"Sexy?" he said, meaning Isadora.

This always gets my goat. Just because she doesn't want to get married—I mean, what's sexy about that? And those big, bare feet. I said I thought Clara Bow was a lot sexier with all her clothes on, and I'd bet Isadora couldn't even Charleston—probably she had fallen arches and couldn't wear high heels. Evidently she was one of his idols because he retaliated against Rudy, who, he said, sang through his nose. That was enough to convince me that Marvin and I had better not date, so I became very vague about summer plans, and then Mr. Forster took us home, dropping Marvin off on Central Park South.

At last, as we drove uptown, I had a chance to tell them about Miss Vorse and the Theatre Guild. I didn't think Mother would pull one of her you-can't-do-thats in front of them. This is her immediate reaction to anything new or exciting, but she didn't have a chance to say much, what with Aunt Celia asking questions and Mr. Forster saying, "What an opportunity!" But trust Aunt Celia to be suspicious, as always. How did I know the training would be free? How was I so sure of a scholarship? I said I supposed after Miss Vorse introduced me to the rest of the board, I'd have to audition before things were signed. All Mother said was it would take a great deal of thinking over.

At my house we thanked Mr. Forster for the lovely evening, and he kissed us both on the cheek and drove off with Aunt Celia. Upstairs, Mother said, "I'm not at all sure that I want you in the jungle of the theater."

She *would* call it that. I could see that I'd have an argument all day tomorrow, for I was determined to get permission before I went in to Dr. Matheson on Monday. Anyway, we both went to bed. Probably she fell asleep, but I couldn't. I had put the roses and the lilacs in vases near my bed, and their fragrance was heavenly. It occurred to me only then that Mother hadn't remarked on either gift. She was probably angry that Dad had spent so much and that Rick had "presumed."

But she couldn't take away what they'd given.

Luckily, she and Miss Johnson had a date to go to church next morning that I refused to be dragged into. So I had a chance to call Rick and thank him and tell him my wonderful news. He said, "Great." Then he asked if I'd written Dad about him, and I said yes, but that I didn't expect a reply until the end of the week, so he said to be sure to let him know. He still didn't suggest dating secretly.

But I had a feeling that everything was going to be all right, and when I phoned Marge, she did, too. I knew I could trust her not to be jealous about the Theatre Guild chance—after all, she didn't want an acting career herself—but she warned me that I had better butter up Mother to the hilt. So I had the card table prettily laid when Mother came in, and food ready, and then, over coffee, she said, "There is no point in discussing this Theatre Guild thing until I talk to this lady—"

"Miss Vorse."

"—and I doubt that Dr. Matheson will want you to devote any time except to your regular studies."

I kept quiet. I knew I could convince Dr. Matheson. Hadn't I made him realize the absurdity of Arithmetic (for me) at the age of eight? Of Chemistry? Then I thought, I'll have Mr. Skinner on my side, too. I'd see him first thing in the morning, after his early class.

When I got to school, Marge was already there. She'd told Enid and Bernice the good news, and they were thrilled, though I told them nothing was settled. By ten-thirty it was all over school—our class, I mean—and everybody was congratulating me, except, of course, Vera Jordan. Robert and Everett both asked for dates ahead, though I evaded anything definite, and finally I got Mr. Skinner alone and burst out with the whole thing.

He was a darling, perhaps a little flattered that his protégée had been singled out. He said that, if I got Mother's and Dr. Matheson's permission, he would do all he could to help but that he was in no position to interfere with authority. However, I must face some hard facts. Pretty girls were a dime a hundred. Only ability would count, and very hard work. I couldn't neglect my studies at Wilson, and I would be taking on an extra burden.

Oh, I knew that. But did he have any idea what the Guild training would be like?

"Every facet of the theater," he said, "from proper breathing for voice placement to tedious diction lessons, to fencing before you get even a tiny part as a maid without a line to speak." He looked up at the big clock above his desk. "Now scamper."

I really felt like a star at lunch in the cafeteria, with even seniors coming up to congratulate me. Robert and Stew wrangled over my check—twenty-five cents— which was delightful, although it turned out that they both forgot to pick it up, so I paid the cashier myself. And on the way out, two girls from the Tenth Grade asked for my autograph.

It was during History that Dr. Matheson's secretary came in, asking if Julie Willis would please go to his office. Usually when this happened, it meant we were in trouble, but I couldn't think of anything but that he wanted to discuss the Guild. It was years since I'd been in his big oak-paneled room that faced Morningside Park. It suits him because he looks rather Olde English, like Mr. Pickwick, with a fringe of cobwebby brown hair and a cozy kind of plumpness.

To my surprise, Mr. Skinner was with him. Both of them got up, and Mr. Skinner motioned me to a big leather chair near the window. They lit pipes. Well, of course, they looked grave—my chance for the Guild wasn't a frivolous matter.

"Julie," Dr. Matheson said, "you're in First Term Psychology, aren't you?"

"Yes," I said, bewildered. No bad marks thus far.

"So I assume you don't know much about abnormal psychology?"

"No, sir."

"Do you have any understanding of what it means to be mentally ill?"

"Oh, yes."

"And you have pity for people like that?"

"Yes." I couldn't imagine what he was getting at. It worried me that his voice was gentle as a dentist's when he says, "This won't hurt."

"You realize the compulsive nature of the diseased mind, Julie—that such people can't help what they do?"

"Yes, sir."

"Have you ever known a mentally unbalanced person?"

I thought a moment. Then I mentioned the moron who used to work at Stuhmer's Bakery—the son of the owner—who used to just sit in a corner and count pennies over and over again.

"And of course you felt compassion for him."

I nodded. Some of the kids used to jeer at him, but I always felt too sad to look at him.

"Julie, I'm sorry to tell you that Miss Vorse—Peter's aunt—is mentally ill. She's never been on the board of the Theatre Guild or had any part in it. What she told you was all in her imagination."

It took a while to penetrate. "You mean, she's craz—"

"Mentally ill," Dr. Matheson said. "She was only recently released from an institution. I'm afraid that nothing she has told you is true."

"Except," Mr. Skinner said, coming around to stand by my chair, "that you're a fine little actress."

Suddenly the whole room seemed out of focus. I watched the sun sliding down the casement windows and turned away from it, blinking.

"We know it's very hard on you," Dr. Matheson said.

I managed a kind of croak. "How do you know she is—"

"Apparently she went home and told her family that she was getting you into the Guild. So Peter's father came in just an hour ago to talk to me and explain how sorry he was."

"And does Peter know?" I asked.

"No. No one must know. Unless you tell your mother in strict confidence."

One thing I was damned if I'd do—cry. But it was all I wanted to do. I hung on by clenching my nails into my hands so that the pain helped me forget the disappointment for a moment.

Mr. Skinner put his hand on my shoulder. "You've got to do a *real* acting job, Julie. You've got to walk out of here and pretend to be angry because Dr. Matheson feels you're too young to accept this offer."

"That's right," Dr. Matheson said. "Make me out the villain in the script. Pile it on all you like. Tell your friends I insist that you concentrate on your studies here."

I thought, I had three little worlds. Dad, Rick, this chance. Now the chance was gone—in fact, it had never existed. Dad might have to stay in Arizona, and it was up to him if I ever saw Rick again.

"Go ahead, cry," Mr. Skinner said, very gently. "That's what you *would* do, wouldn't you?"

But not in front of them, and I wasn't going to bawl like a baby in public, either. If only I hadn't bragged to Marge before it was all settled, half the school wouldn't know about it. That's the terrible ego of the actress, I guess.

Dr. Matheson's phone rang, so I got up and said, "Thank you for trying to make it easier," and then Mr. Skinner opened the door for me and followed me out into the corridor.

"There will be real chances someday," he said. "I'm sure of it."

We went to the water fountain, and I pushed the

little button and drank. Coming up for air, I said, "What seems to make it even worse is that a *madwoman* was the one who thought I could act."

"Am I mad? I think you can. Now how about coming out for a soda with me and let's discuss plays for next term?"

I said okay. I'd meet him outside. And I was prepared with a very angry expression just in case I met any questioning friends, but there wasn't a soul in the lockers and the only people I met on the way out were Third and Fourth graders. I think I was mostly in a daze. I believe if someone had pinched me—hard—I wouldn't have felt it.

In the Passion Palace Mr. Skinner said he wasn't surprised that I wanted only an orangeade. He had coffee and relit his pipe, and then he said, "Are you going to Europe this summer?"

"I don't know yet."

"Well, if you've any spare time, I hope you'll write a new play that we can schedule for October. And another for early winter."

Oh, I knew enough about Wilson techniques to realize what he was doing: therapy. *If the bright child is deprived or depressed, fill the void.* But how do you fill something completely empty of ideas or ambition or hope?

And then the sunlight fell on him in a peculiar way, on the lank, rather lifeless dark hair, the slender face, the mouth like a thick inverted U—and he reminded me of someone. Someone gangly, only on horseback. Someone sad and funny but not a clown. It wasn't anyone I'd ever met, but it was a schoolmaster.

Perhaps the word "October" had brought it to mind. Pumpkins, yes, and "jolly autumn" in the Hudson Valley. Of course, now I knew. And what a play it would make.

"Would you ever take part in a play?" I asked.

"Depends," he said.

"Would you play Ichabod Crane in *The Legend of Sleepy Hollow?* None of the boys could."

"Well. And would you play Katrina Van Tassel?"

To look pretty for a change. To be a flirt. Comedy. "Yes."

He took a fountain pen from his pocket and unfolded a paper napkin and said, "How about this for the first set?"

Haystacks in fields and Ichabod getting off his off-stage horse and looking around, scared at the sound of a rabbit. We talked and we talked, and suddenly the play was almost real—we even figured out how to do the chase by the Headless Horseman.

"I think Stew Crandall is just enough of a dumbbell to play one of the rustics," I said, "and what about Peter Vorse as Brom?"

It was nearly five when we went outside, and it had begun to rain, and I decided to cry when I got home. But I didn't have a chance. Because, in the lobby, Mac handed me an airmail letter from Dad that said not a word about Rick, but "Enclosed is a check for your train and expenses." I was to arrive in Tucson June eleventh.

I read and reread it. All the details, the arrangements, everything clear. Dad didn't say how long I was to stay, but he had a house for us.

Mac pretended to be busy reading a book, but I knew he was interested and curious, so I said, "I don't have to hop a freight! Dad is sending for me," and I told him all about it.

Mac was so pleased that dimples came and his eyes got shinier. "Now that's what I call luck."

Then I thought about Rick, and Mac said, "What's the matter?" and I told him. "He'll probably forget all about me during the summer."

"You can write."

Of course, I could. Mother couldn't prevent that. I would write him marvelous, very artistic letters so that he would come to realize how important to him I could be, and Dad was sure to agree to our dating when I returned.

"I'd better run upstairs and phone Rick before

(157)

Mother comes in," I said, and Mac said, sure, I'd better do that right away.

I must say Rick took it a little too well. I mean, I'd hoped he'd be wistful or grieved, but he just said, "Have a good time. And do write me."

I almost said, "Every day." Instead, I said, "I will," and I gave him Dad's address and then waited for him to say how very desperately he would miss me. But he said, "Be sure to use a lot of suntan oil," and then I heard Mother's key in the door and said, "Bye."

First I told her that Dr. Matheson had refused to let me enter the Guild, and she was so relieved that she had a terrible time not smiling. Then I showed her Dad's letter, really feeling sorry for her because she wasn't even mentioned. But in her way, I guess she was an actress, too, because she simply took a deep breath and swallowed and smiled. Not a word about the rent, the gas and electric. But I believed I knew the reason for her calmness—she was sure I'd forget Rick once I left New York.

She said, "We must make a list of things to pack," although I wouldn't even be leaving for nine days.

She got on the phone and asked Aunt Celia if she had any cheap little cotton dresses, which, of course, we both knew she didn't. But Aunt Celia always seems to manage a tiny burn or some defect in the fabric, and she said, "Tell Julie to come here for lunch Saturday and we'll see."

I felt so sorry for Mother that night, making her lists. So that when I kissed her good night, I meant it, and we hugged each other as we hadn't for ages.

"I'll miss you," she said. "But it's really time that you got to know your father."

Twelve

I FELT very sophisticated on the train, mainly because Mr. Forster and Aunt Celia came to see me off with Mother and brought me gardenias to pin on my new blue dress and a *New Yorker* to read. Also, I was wearing silk instead of lisle stockings, and a pair of high heels Aunt Celia said some deb had left by mistake and never turned up for. I can't believe that deb left Aunt Celia's apartment in stocking feet, and the shoes are my size and obviously new. I love Aunt Celia's white lies.

She took me aside while we waited for the train and warned me not to talk to men of whatever age and then slitted her eyes up and added, "And if a woman looks blowsy or overpainted, don't talk to *her*." I said I knew all about the white slave business from the *Graphic* and not to worry. Then she said, very softly, "Write me just what you find in Tucson—and if you want to come home ahead of time, send me a telegram and I'll wire the fare." I've no idea why she worries about nothing at all, and, after all, I'm visiting my own father, her own brother, but she's never happier than when she's imagining something sinister.

Mother clung to me and cried a little and said to wire as soon as I arrived in Tucson and to write at least twice a week. Then they put me into a coach, and Mr. Forster slipped an envelope into my hand, and then somebody outside called, "All aboard," and the train was off.

Can you imagine, when I opened that envelope a note said, "To have fun with," and there was a fifty-dollar bill. I couldn't believe it wasn't a five at first. Of course he was a millionaire and probably wouldn't miss it, but it was sort of overwhelming.

Trains go *tuddledy-tuddledy, tuddledy-tuddledy*— such a soothing rhythm. But I was still upset about leaving Rick and about the Theatre Guild. I'm sure I fooled my friends in school (I even had to lie to Marge and Kitty because Dr. Matheson had said to keep the facts in strict confidence), except possibly Vera Jordan, who proved she'd never be a friend by saying, "I never believed you had a chance anyway." I hoped that up on her estate she'd have a summer full of mosquitoes and midges and poison ivy because even very rich people can't escape the cruelty of nature.

At first the trip was fun, the porters so awfully nice, telling me what we were passing after Baltimore and Washington. I loved the dining car where a waiter said "native food" was served—crab cakes and Potomac oyster patties. Later came corn, and for two days I really had enough corn—inside and out. From the window I saw cornfields through a heat haze, nothing but cornfields. It got so monotonous that I was glad when finally Oklahoma came along, even though the plains looked like scorched toast. The scenery perked in New Mexico, with red sunsets and weird-looking trees and, at stations, cowboys sitting on fences. Finally Arizona, with those tall sentinel cacti that are called saguaro, and rock formations that looked as if giants had had a pillow fight with boulders. Most of the country was so lonely looking you wouldn't think it was settled.

We pulled into Tucson about three. Following Dad's order, I took a cab to the Santa Anita Hotel with my suitcases, remembering that the driver and the hotel bellboy must be tipped with a dime. Through a nice, cool lobby I hurried into a ladies' room to get off the dust and try to look pretty for Dad. I used my Tangee lipstick and pushed my hair over one eye. I wasn't too gruesome, considering the long trip.

Out in the lobby I sat down to wait. There were some cowboys there in blue jeans and boots, and a fat man smoking a cigar and reading a newspaper. He looked up and smiled, but I knew Dad couldn't have gone fat and gray. A few women sat waiting—that expectant look—and so I sat waiting. Every time the door opened, I felt a queer jerk where my heartbeat usually is.

After about ten minutes the desk clerk came over and asked if I was Miss Willis. My father was on the way, he said, and would be here in about twenty minutes. He'd been asked to bring me whatever I wanted. Would I please follow him into the lounge?

It was cooler than the lobby, with fans whirring, and I asked for a cold orangeade and did they possibly have a New York newspaper? He said the newspaper might be a few days old but he'd bring it.

So I drank and opened the *Graphic*. There on page two was a big headline: GANGSTER GETS IT. At the top of the page was a picture of that wonderful man who had helped me out of the speakeasy, looking a little younger than when I'd seen him. His name was Arcangelo Canello, aged 41, submachine-gunned by a rival gang on East 51st Street. Underneath was a photograph of him spewed all over the street—his head off—and I got sick.

Luckily, there was nobody else in the lounge, so I hurried over to a big plant and got sick in it. Back in my chair, I began to cry so that I couldn't read the print, since my eyes were so blurry. I tore out the page and folded it and put it in my purse, and then someone said, "Julie?" and I looked up.

Dad was blurry, too. I just knew that it was Dad, that he hadn't changed. I ran to him, and he held me tight, and then he drew back and said, "Darling, what's happened?" and patted at a tear.

But I couldn't talk just then for fear of being sick again. So he took me back to my table and sat me down and told me that heat sometimes bothered newcomers and to sip my orangeade slowly. He sat opposite me and pulled out a little flask and drank something from it—booze, I guess—and then replaced it in his hip pocket. He knew I couldn't talk, and he didn't babble, either. He just said, "Relax, darling," and lit a cigarette, and I noticed that he blew the smoke away from me.

Finally I said, "I'm sorry. But I just read in the newspaper a friend of mine died."

His voice was very gentle. "Oh."

"He was a—a guy with principles."

Dad nodded. "A schoolmate?"

I shook my head. "An older man."

"One of your teachers, then? Not Celia's new beau?"

"No." Dad offered me a handkerchief, and I wiped my eyes and blew my nose. "His name was Arcangelo Canello."

"But not your Italian boyfriend?"

"No. But he really was an archangel. He can't have been all bad. But he was a gangster."

I suppose most fathers would have leaped three feet, but mine just said, very quietly, "Well, tell me about him if you feel like it."

So I told him, and then I showed him the newspaper page. He read it, and then he said, "I don't think you should look at this again, Julie. You must remember him the way he was," and he put the page in his pocket.

I said, "I'm not at all sure I believe in heaven or all that, but if there's such a thing as a recording angel, don't you think Mr. Canello has a chance, being so good to me?"

"Certainly," Dad said. "I think you can leave hell out

of it. And don't ever sit in judgment on people. I've known as many good crooks as I have pious phonies."

Now that I'd stopped crying, I could see him. The same dark Heathcliffe good looks, the black eyes and heavy, tufty black brows. He was wearing a peculiar gray suit that I later learned was western, a gray shirt with tiny pearl buttons, and tight gray trousers and black boots. He looked at me at the same time and said, "I didn't expect quite such a young lady. You're prettier than your last photograph."

"With a red nose."

"Matches your lipstick."

"Mother doesn't approve of lipstick. Do you?"

"A little," he said, "just like you have it. How is your mother, Julie?"

I told him, and then he agreed that it would be nice if Aunt Celia married Mr. Forster. People were coming into the lounge now, so we went out into the lobby and collected my suitcases and got into a Model-T Ford and drove out of town.

Dad said that Tucson was sort of like a teacup in mountains. He pointed out the Santa Catalina Mountains and the Tucson Mountains and said there were pine trees up there, just as in Maine, but that he lived in the desert. After a few miles I could see the desert blooming, although he said it was past its peak.

We turned off a main road into a lot of dust that shimmered in the sun like gold spangles. He told me to scrounge around in the back seat—there was a palmetto fan—and I turned and leaned over and found it. Sweat was running down the back of my neck. He said the temperature was about 100 degrees, but that the nights were cool.

"I hope you like our house," he said, "although it's a little eccentric."

"Why?" I asked, fanning.

"Because it cost only a hundred and fifty dollars. It was abandoned last month, and I haven't had time to do much to fix it up. But it's a lot cheaper for me than hotels."

"I'll fix it up," I said. "I got an A in Household Arts. And I can clean and cook—"

"Certainly not," Dad said, avoiding a big floppy-eared rabbit in the road. "I didn't ask you here to drudge. We have a cook and a butler and, of course, a maid for you."

"A maid for *me?*"

"Her name is Concha. Her mother is Lupe, the cook. Her brother is Paco, the butler. You hire one Mexican and you acquire the family. You must help me train them, but you'll have to speak in sign language until you learn Spanish and they learn English."

A maid of my own! I'll bet even Vera Jordan didn't have that. "Do they live with us?"

Dad chuckled. "No, down the road. Our house isn't very big."

But when we came to it, I loved it on sight. It was small and white—adobe, Dad said—and partly covered by trumpet and bougainvillea vines. Strings of chilies hung outside the door, and up in the mesquite trees were earthen pots suspended from the branches which Dad said were *ollas* for holding water. Out in the yard was a mud oven, shaped like a beehive, and a rusty iron washtub. There were lots of wild flowers in cans and buckets. Back of the house, among greasewood bushes, I could see a sort of shed.

As we parked, three people came out, and the door fell off—not open, but off its hinges. Everybody laughed, and Dad helped me out of the car and lined up the people according to age, and then introduced them, very formally.

"Señora Guadalupe Delgado—Señorita Willis."

Lupe, who was very fat and wore a purple cotton dress trimmed with pink braid, made a kind of curtsy, and I shook her hand.

"Paco—Señorita Willis."

He was about sixteen, lanky, with a low forehead and huge brown eyes. He had outgrown his shirt and blue jeans; his wrists and ankles were bare.

Something told me it wouldn't be correct to shake

hands with a butler, so I just smiled and so did he, with a bow.

"Concha—Señorita Willis."

She couldn't have been any older than I. Big silver earrings looped from under a mane of black hair, and she'd have been pretty if she hadn't been as scrawny as her mother was fat. She wore a bright pink blouse with a drawstring neck, and a short black skirt with a pink ruffle up the side. Her feet were bare. She made the same sort of curtsy as her mother had.

Then Dad began to speak in rapid Spanish, and a lot of things happened fast. Paco took my suitcases. Lupe beckoned me inside the house, Concha trailing shyly. It was cool and dim, the shutters of the little sitting room–kitchen closed against the sun. They led me into another small room where Paco had just placed the suitcases on the floor near a small bed with a brass bedstead under some bright unframed pictures of saints. There was a rickety white chair and a small table with an earthen pot of wild flowers on it. The one window was shuttered, and I noticed that the walls were very thick.

They left me, smiling, and I thought I'd better hang up a few dresses, but there wasn't any closet, so I went into the other room. Paco was placing a pitcher of something and two glasses on a table. I was glad to see ice in that pitcher. Paco bowed again and left. Outside I could hear the door being hammered and Dad cursing, but not too badly. Mother might have been shocked, but I wasn't.

The room would have shocked her, too. The floor was of dirt, though very clean. The only furniture was a narrow bed, spread with a Mexican rug, the table, and two chairs. The white fireplace, which was arched, had a little shelf above with carved wooden saints.

Dad came in. "Damn that door!" and sat down on one of the chairs.

Paco came in, and Dad said something in Spanish, and Paco said, "Si, señor," and went out again.

"Have you ever drunk gin?" Dad asked me.

"No," I said. "I mean not seriously."

"Well, you may as well learn how. And this cocktail is very mild, mostly fruit juice." He looked up as Paco returned with a pitcher and glasses on a battered tin tray.

"Happy days," Dad said.

We drank. It tasted a little funny, but I liked it, and it was cold. Paco left us.

"How many rooms are there?" I asked.

"Two. I sleep in here."

"It's lovely," I said. "I love the white walls and the saints and everything. But where do I put my clothes?"

"In the woodshed," he said. "Concha will attend to that, and your laundry. There's an outhouse next to the shed."

"And where are the servants now?"

"In the yard. Are you hungry? Yes?" He called for Lupe.

I'd never had Mexican food before, and I adored it. Later I learned the names of what we'd had—chili and enchiladas. That night Lupe made us tamales, and we had the leftover chili on top of them.

About nine o'clock it grew suddenly cold, and after the servants had left, Dad made a fire of mesquite, and we sat down together on his bed-couch. "Tell me about this boy," he said.

So I told him all about Rick, except the kiss.

"Why doesn't your mother like him, then?"

"Because he's Italian and nineteen." I paused, remembering that Mr. Canello had been Italian, too. I think Dad must have read my mind because he took my hand and said, "You'll make all sorts of friends during your life, but you have to learn to evaluate them. Perhaps it's just as well you're here for a while. If it's just a crush, you'll get over it. If not—"

"If not?"

He lit a Piedmont. "We'll see. No rush about anything."

But I told him, in a rush, about Miss Vorse and the

Theatre Guild, and he said, "My poor baby," and suddenly the whole thing—the Guild and Rick and Mr. Canello—hit me right in the stomach on top of the tamales and chili, and I began to cry again, and Dad took me into his arms as if I *were* a baby, and then the bed collapsed flat on the floor.

It's strange to weep and laugh your head off within minutes. Dad was so funny, not being able to get the bed upright and cursing (I think) in Spanish. Every time he got half of the bed up, the other end went down. I tried to help, but I was laughing too much, and then I thought of the front door coming off and I got such giggles I was afraid he'd get mad.

But he didn't. He just looked at that bed, which was flat as a pancake, and kicked it and said, "Oh, the hell with it," and then he told me I'd better go to bed and sleep as late as I liked, but that he had to go to his mine early in the morning.

He'd told Lupe to bring me breakfast in bed when I called her, and he said I should give Concha anything to be washed or ironed. If I wanted a bath, Concha would show me how, in the woodshed.

I kissed him good night, thinking how wonderful he was, how wonderful he smelled—of something wild and deserty, of strong tobacco and garlic and gin and soap. He showed me into my room with a little kerosene lamp, and turned down the spread and the blankets, and said, "I love you."

Oh, and I loved him, too.

Someone had opened the shutters. There was no glass between me and the desert and the low stars. The sheets smelled of air and sun, not like those from a New York laundry. I should have fallen asleep right away.

But my train of thought puffed up to one station and wouldn't budge. Something worried me on the track, and it wasn't Rick or Mr. Canello or the Guild. And surely, I thought sleepily, it wasn't anything Dad had said.

Then I realized it was something he hadn't said. He

hadn't referred to Mother as "Emily," but as "your mother."

Like she never spoke of him as "Ruddell."

Strange they should be so Victorian. But I wasn't going to figure it out now. I pulled up the blankets and put my face into the cool pillow. It had a ripped case, and feathers tickled my nose, and I sneezed and fell asleep.

Thirteen

I AWAKENED to a rooster crowing and then fell asleep again and reawakened, drenched with perspiration. The heat shimmered outside like something you could almost touch. I threw back my blankets and shuttered the window and went to the door and called, "Lupe?" opening it just a slit. The doorknob fell off.

"Señorita?"

I hopped back into bed as she came in. She saw the doorknob and kicked it just as Dad had kicked the bed, and then made eating motions, and I nodded, and presently she brought me a tray. And I've never had such a marvelous breakfast in my life. Little ground-corn pancakes, which I learned were tortillas, and with lots of butter on them. A jelly made from prickly pear fruit. Orange juice and coffee.

Lupe kicked at the doorknob again, which rolled, and she said, "Paco fix." She smiled and I noticed a gold tooth that matched the tiny earrings she wore. My pillow was shedding feathers all over the dirt floor, and she said, "Me fix," and left me to eat.

When I'd finished, I opened the door again and called, "Concha?" and to my astonishment she said,

"Bath?" and I nodded and followed her in my robe and nightie to the shed next to the outhouse. Gallons of water stood on the floor, and soap in a dish, and towels in a basket. There wasn't any tub. You were just supposed to stand there and pour water over you, so I did.

On my way back to the house in my robe, I saw several scraggly chickens, and a little goat grazing near a collapsed fence. Lupe was sitting in the yard, mending my pillow, and Concha was kneeling in the shade, kneading bread on our cocktail tray. She jumped up as I came past, but I smiled and waved and went inside to dress.

The thinnest thing I had was the new blue dress, so I put it on over just my bra and step-ins. Shoes and stockings would be too hot, so I didn't wear them. Despite what Rick had said, I'd forgotten to buy suntan oil, but above the stove I found a jar of olive oil and put it all over my face and arms and went outside and lay down near Lupe.

She said something in Spanish and went inside and brought out a ragged little rug, so I lay on that. While she worked on the pillow and Concha baked bread in the mud oven, they began to sing. And it was beautiful. Of course I didn't understand the words, but I knew it was a love song. But too sad, somehow.

I must have been more tired from the trip than I'd thought, for I fell asleep until the noon sun became so fierce that it woke me. Inside, Lupe gave me a wonderful fruit salad and more tortillas and then brought me a book and said, "Señor, *padre*," and I gathered Dad wanted me to read it; it was an English-Spanish dictionary. I studied it all afternoon, lying in my cool bedroom, making notes of key words and phrases.

There was a big, cracked mirror hanging in the room, and I saw that I was getting a hideous red from the sun, although I didn't feel uncomfortable. When I went out through the yard, Concha pointed to my face and said something and brought me a big sombrero and tied it under my chin and motioned me into the shade. I watched her bring out round loaves from the oven and set them to cool on a flat rock. The goat and the chickens had disappeared.

With the dictionary, I managed to find out that she was fourteen, that Paco was seventeen, that Lupe was thirty-one, and that their father had been killed in the war. Then Concha pulled a little crucifix on a chain from her blouse; I think it was tin. She touched me with it and smiled, and I knew we were friends and that I could never think of her as a maid.

When Dad came home, about seven, Paco brought our drinks in with a flourish and deep bows and then re-entered with a little plate of crispy, broken tortillas that were a lot better than potato chips. Dad had brought home a bottle of gin, some of which he added to his drink. He said it was cool enough to go outside.

"You're awfully sunburned," he said as we sat under the vines.

"My own fault," I told him. "But I don't blister. Tomorrow I've got to get some suntan oil. I don't want to use up Lupe's cooking oil."

"I'll bring you some from town. What else do you need?"

I'd forgotten to tell him about the fifty dollars Mr. Forster had given me—and was upset when I remembered I hadn't even thought of sending a telegram to Mother. But he said he already had. As for the fifty dollars, I should save it.

"Are you—I mean, are we very broke right now?" I asked. I wanted to spend some of that fifty dollars on a blouse and skirt like Concha's and on little gifts for them, and when Dad took his boots off, I could see that he had a big hole in his sock.

"I don't discuss money," he said. "Your grandfather Willis used to say, 'A gentleman never mentions money to a lady. He gives it to her.'"

"I still have five dollars from the expense money you sent."

"Julie." Those black brows came together. "We do not *discuss* money. What else do you need besides suntan oil?"

"Something cool, like Concha's blouse and skirt."

"Okay. What size?"

"Ten."

"You should have sandals. What size?"

"Four."

He was silent for a moment, and then he said, "I used to buy your mother's clothes—shoes, too. She wore a four. Does she still?"

"Four and a half," I said. "I guess being on her feet at work maybe made them bigger."

I wished I hadn't said that because suddenly he looked so sad. Those luminous big eyes were looking off across the desert, not at me, and I didn't think he was seeing those flat, endless miles of the slow beginning of sunset. Then he said, very softly, "We spent our honeymoon in St. Louis, at the World's Fair. There were Lobster Palaces then—and red carpets. One night she wore a red velvet ball gown I'd bought her, with a long train. It had short puff sleeves. Her waist—"

He paused and poured a little more gin into his glass of juice.

"Yes?" I wanted him to go on. But he didn't. Paco came to say something, and Dad helped me to my feet, and we went in for a wonderful chicken and tomato stew.

Afterwards we sat outside again, with iced coffee. The tall cacti, the saguaros, were black against a dark gold sun that didn't want to go to bed. I didn't either, but pretty soon it got cold and we went inside, where Paco had made a fire. But Dad seemed awfully quiet, and I thought perhaps he wanted to be alone, so I said I'd go to my room and write Mother and Rick and Marge and Mr. Forster.

He kissed me good night. What's that word—abstractedly? Then he said that he would take me to one of his mines in Mexico the day after tomorrow if I wouldn't be bored. And on Saturday night we would have a party here.

I did write Mother and Mr. Forster, sitting in bed, with the kerosene lamp on. But I didn't write anyone

(172)

else. I felt peculiar. First hot and then cold. Probably the sunburn. I pushed my letters under the door so Dad would see them in the morning and mail them. Then I got back into bed.

It was a long time before I got to sleep, pushing off blankets and then pulling them up again. I heard something howling way off in the distance, like a mourning dog. Moonlight was so bright that I couldn't face the window.

In the morning, when I called Lupe for my breakfast, she took one look at me and said, *"Dios!"* Pretty soon she and Concha had my nightgown off and were patting me all over with cotton soaked in strong tea. It soaked into the bottom sheet, but they indicated I should just lie there, and I dozed off again.

When I awakened, Concha was sitting beside me on a chair, fanning me with the palmetto. I felt a lot better. Then I remembered the mourning of the dog and imitated it with a question mark.

"Coyote," Concha said.

I dressed but I stayed inside that afternoon. First, I wrote Marge and then I took a lot of trouble writing Rick, but remembering how Mr. Skinner sneered at prose being too poetic, I didn't really try to describe the desert and the sunsets and the way the mountains change from gray to blue to dark red to purple to black. Then for fifteen minutes I pondered how to sign it. "With love"? No. "Sincerely" was too formal. So I just said, "Miss you," at the end.

Dad brought me a white blouse and red skirt with a ruffle up the side like Concha's, and red sandals and a pair of silver earrings that don't screw on but loop through your ear. I decided to let my hair grow long just for the summer. Then he gave me a pint bottle of something with no label on it.

"I could buy you the fanciest suntan oil from Paris," he said, "but it wouldn't work like this does. It stains you brown, at the same time it keeps you from blistering."

It was medium-grade car oil from a gas station, and

it didn't smell like lilacs. When I rubbed a little on my arm, I could see it soak in, darkening the red a little. "Oh," he said, sitting down on the flattened bed-couch, "I met a friend in town, Mrs. Patterson. She told me to be sure to tell you to put a scarf on your hair or it'll dry up. She gave me this for you."

A lovely red chiffon scarf that matched the red skirt.

After dinner he said he hoped I wouldn't be bored here but that I'd meet a lot of people Saturday night, as many as we could cram in. Then he said, "I wonder if you'll really want to go to the mine tomorrow?"

"But I'll feel fine by then."

"What I mean is, I haven't taken a woman to the mines yet who enjoyed it. That old car can't manage the climb up the trail, which is pretty rough. Then there's the narrow elevator going down into the mine shaft that gives some people claustrophobia—"

"That's enough for me," I said, and told him about once getting stuck in an elevator in school which was wide enough for more than a dozen people but I'd felt smothered and always used the staircases afterwards. So it was decided that he'd drive Concha and me to Nogales across the border and leave us there a few hours to explore the town, and then we'd meet at a restaurant called the Cavern at six. Concha would eat with relatives.

We set out early the next day, mailed my letters in Tucson, and drove for miles and miles. I'd never imagined so much space—you could look so far and not see a living thing or meet another car. The sky was a harsh, cloudless blue.

We crossed the border from Nogales, Arizona, to Nogales, Mexico. There wasn't any fuss with passports. Dad said something to Concha and then translated to me. "I asked her to take you past the tourist traps and not let you buy any trash."

But I still had Mr. Forster's fifty dollars, and I did want to shop. When Dad left us, Concha took me into several little stores. While she waited, I bought her and

Lupe little Taxco crosses and a silver belt for Paco. Then I found some beautiful silver-and-amethyst earrings for Mother. I remembered the way she had of rejecting gifts as being too expensive, but I bought them just the same.

I'd never had so much money in my life. I suppose it does burn a hole in your pocket (cliché).

When I showed Concha the earrings and said, "*Madre!*" she grabbed the little box from my hand and went to the clerk and fumed and spit, and then $1.50 was put back into my hand. But I didn't want her bargaining for the other gifts, so I told the clerk to mail the earrings to Mother and got a receipt, and we went out into the heat.

After ice cream at a shady little stand, we went to more shops, but Concha didn't seem to approve of them and there wasn't anything I wanted anyway. So many toys and souvenirs—little burros pulling carts and miniature sombreros and pictures of saints and penny postcards and tin ashtrays. You see the same kind of thing in New York, on 42nd Street, where tourists buy tiny Woolworth Buildings and Brooklyn Bridges and trays marked "Whoopee, New York, 1928." I felt rather world-weary, although the smells were interesting—garlic and oil and some perfume the women used, or maybe it was the smell of the desert.

I bought a string bag for my purchases—Concha got it for twenty cents instead of fifty. And then we separated outside the Cavern and I went in.

It was so dark at first I couldn't see, for it really was a cave. Then a waiter came forward and led me to a table where Dad sat, or rather stood, as I came up. And then I had a real shock, for at first I thought Mother sat opposite him.

Later I realized it was because of the peculiar lighting—the stalagmites and stalactites of the cave, and candles. For though she was slender like Mother, with the same kind of straight little nose, her eyes were a deep green and her hair not as dark as Mother's, cut about like mine but fluffier. And Mother would never have worn a Mexican blouse partly off one shoulder.

"Julie," Dad said, "this is Mrs. Patterson. Lisa, this is my daughter."

Mrs. Patterson smiled, and we shook hands. Then I remembered she had given me the red scarf, and I thanked her, and she said she hoped it matched the skirt, and what had I been doing today?

Now I realized she wasn't as young as I'd thought, perhaps just a little younger than Mother but certainly very pretty. I told her I'd bought gifts, and then the waiter came with a cold pitcher of something and a bottle that he opened. And I had my very first tequila cocktail, in a small glass, while Dad and Mrs. Patterson drank taller ones.

"I'm teaching Julie how to drink sensibly," Dad said. "She's sure to drink anyway."

Just at that moment an orchestra started up and a man singer began "Button Up Your Overcoat," and then the words came, advising us to stay away from bootleg booze, and we all laughed, and Dad led Mrs. Patterson out onto the dance floor.

I loved watching them dance, just as I hate watching people who are awkward together. Now I could see that she was wearing a full dark blue skirt that matched some of the embroidery on her white blouse. Her shoes were flat blue sandals crisscrossed at the ankles. Dad was much taller, but they seemed to float together.

They came back, and we all ordered avocado first and then steak, and Dad and I danced to "S'Wonderful." Then it changed into a tango and we kept on dancing—I think he could dance better than Valentino—and somebody in the orchestra clicked castanets. Suddenly I felt that I was really in Mexico and on top of the world, especially when Dad let go of one of my hands and pranced around behind me, and I joined him with my other hand and we dipped. We hadn't even practiced, and the other people on the floor stood aside and watched us, and then they all clapped when it was over.

Over coffee, a guitarist played a Spanish song, and the whole room listened quietly. I remembered how the Empress Carlota had gone insane to some tune like that and decided she must have been a nut to begin with. I thought about poor Miss Vorse, but it didn't depress me, except that I was sorry for her. I'd be an actress someday, no matter what.

After Dad had danced with Mrs. Patterson again, we left and picked up Concha and then drove about twenty miles toward home, where we left Mrs. Patterson at a little adobe house about the size of ours. She said to me, "You must call me Lisa," and kissed my cheek and said she'd see us Saturday night.

Concha was asleep in the back seat as we drove on. Dad said, "How do you like Lisa?"

"Very much," I said. "Where's her husband?"

"Killed in the war. She's a painter, and good. Most people who say they're painters just talk it."

"Does she sell her work?"

"Sometimes. She did a beautiful mural for the Old Mission in the Catalinas. Some of her paintings are on exhibition in Phoenix—now dammit-to-hell!"

He had to swerve to avoid something in the road that he said was a jackrabbit, like the one we'd seen by daylight, only dazed by the car lights. It just stood there. So he stopped the car and carried it over to a ditch and dropped it behind a cattle fence. And though I didn't say so, all the way home I thought of his gallantry toward that rabbit. It made me love him more than ever.

All day Saturday Lupe and Concha cooked and swept and sprinkled the dirt floors until they were glistening hard. Dad came home with a carton of bottles.

"Are there bootleggers out here?" I asked.

"Home brew," he said. "You have to know who makes it, though. I'd do it myself if I had the time."

Paco and Dad repaired his bed, and Lupe and Concha lit candles in tin holders, and the two rooms looked very nice by the time the guests arrived. It was amazing to me that eighteen people fitted into such a small space. Lisa Patterson was there, and a Mr. and Mrs. Reede who had a big house in Tucson. Priscilla Reede was my age, and her brother Paul was at the university; otherwise everybody was older, but such fun. It was the first time I'd ever really felt natural and at ease with middle-aged people; they treated me as a grown-up.

I had two tequilas that Dad mixed for me, and food later, most of us sitting on the floor. Then Mrs. Patterson brought out a guitar and sang Mexican songs. The only one I knew was "La Golondrina." Afterwards I said, "Dad says you're a good painter, but I could listen to your singing forever."

She smiled and asked if there was anything special I wanted her to sing, and I said, "Do you know 'I'll Get By'?"

She did. And she knew just how to do it. But since the song, to me, was about Dad, and he was here, it didn't make me sad. Then Paul Reede said wasn't it hot by the fire, and would I like a little walk out into the desert?

He wasn't nearly as tall as Rick, or very good looking, but terribly nice. We walked out about a quarter of a mile past some queer rocks and saguaros, and then I heard the coyote and we stopped to listen in the moonlight.

I said, "It's the loneliest thing I ever heard."

"It shouldn't be—a mating thing."

But perhaps love was basically lonely, since no one ever loves to the same degree. I loved Rick more than he loved me. Marge had loved Dick more. Mother and Dad I wasn't sure about at all—but when he'd talked about her wearing the red velvet dress, as if she were framed in his mind in gold, I suspected he was more in love than she was. And for the first time, I wondered if she had sent him away and if it wasn't his business that kept them apart but her feelings, or lack of them.

"It's very hard being young sometimes," Paul said. "I

imagine that coyote is young, too. I thought when I got to be eighteen it would all be okay and straighten out, but it hasn't."

If it hadn't been for the desert, I don't think we'd have talked so personally right off. But it was as if there weren't any other world around, just the sound of that coyote and the wind. He told me about a girl named Joanne who cared about him one day and hated him the next. He wondered if she didn't respect him for not having tried to go the limit. I said most girls I knew would appreciate not being pushed into anything but that perhaps he should try being masterful just once. And I was just about to start telling him about Rick when we heard a whisper from behind a cholla bush, and Concha came out and said, "Meese!"

We turned and there was Dad walking toward us. Concha, my faithful maid, had followed us, apparently, and now was warning me. I wanted to giggle as she disappeared.

"Taking some air?" Dad asked casually.

"Yes, sir," Paul said, and was offered a cigarette. Maybe Dad thought he was being subtle, but he looked at the drawstring of my Mexican blouse, which I guess is where all southwestern fathers look first. "It was pretty hot in there."

"But a wonderful party," I said.

"You'd better go in," Dad said. "You shouldn't change temperatures fast in this climate," and the three of us walked back together.

I danced with Mr. Reede and then with Paul until it got too cold and windy and we all went inside to eat some wonderful things Lupe had made that tasted a little like waffles in syrup.

Pris sat down on the floor next to me. "You're getting a catsy tan," she said. "I wish I could."

She had pale, delicate skin, fair hair looped back of her ears like Norma Shearer's. She said she'd be out of high school next year and wanted to be a social worker.

Since I was guest of honor, I figured I ought to circulate and talk to everybody, but it wasn't too easy, stepping over and around people on the floor. Finally I came to Lisa Patterson, who said she was having a wonderful time but really ought to be getting home—a long drive.

Dad said, "I won't have you driving alone at this time of night. I thought you'd be staying with the Reedes."

She shook her head. "It means another bed to make up, and you just can't do that to people at the last minute. Besides, I'm not at all afraid of driving home."

"If you insist, then I'll follow you in my car," Dad said. "You know what Saturday nights are—bottles strewn in the roads. A puncture, and you've had it."

"It's kind of you to worry, but I'm not a child and I can take care of myself," Lisa said.

People were beginning to leave now, so they broke off the argument and Dad and I went to the door to say good-bye. The cars drove off, sounding very loud in the silence. Lisa was the last to leave, and Dad saw her out to her car.

Lupe and Concha and Paco were tidying up when Dad came in again. Before I could thank him for the wonderful party, he said, "I'm giving her five minutes' head start," and we both laughed.

"How long before you're back?" I asked.

"Two or three hours. You won't be afraid, baby?"

I didn't think I would, with the Delgados just down the road. "Coyotes don't come into houses, do they?"

"Hell, no. You don't even need to lock up, but if you'd feel safer, do, and I'll take my key."

He left, and I wondered if the door would fall off, but it didn't. The Delgados were still working, and I thought how tired they must be, and I looked up in the dictionary, "Go, rest," but the three of them were singing and simply shrugged and smiled at me.

Now was the time to bring out my gifts for them— and I've never seen such excitement. Both the women kissed their crosses and then touched me with them. Paco made such a deep bow for his belt that he nearly fell over, and then he brought me a cold drink which I *think* had tequila or gin in it. And after they'd left, I undressed and sipped a little for courage. It wasn't that I was afraid of burglars or coyotes; it was the silence that scared me. In bed, my window open, I couldn't hear a thing. The kerosene lamp cast peculiar shadows, and I wasn't sure I liked the way the painted saints sort of shivered and moved. I blew out the lamp and lay for a while in the darkness.

The next thing I knew it was sunrise and I heard Dad moving about in the next room. It couldn't be anybody else because I heard him say, "Hell," and I supposed the bed had collapsed again. Then I went back to sleep.

Fourteen

NEXT DAY I had a long letter from Mother, and it made me sad for her—just about nothing but bridge and what she had served her friends and what they had served her, like jellied cherry salad. I guess she hadn't received the earrings yet because she didn't mention them. But she did say that she thought Aunt Celia and Mr. Forster would probably get married, except that Aunt Celia was checking him up in Dun & Bradstreet because she wasn't at all sure that a mere display of money actually meant money. "Of course, she wouldn't marry for that alone, but she told me she was afraid of being lied to and didn't want to end up supporting him."

"Dad," I said when he came home that night, "why is Aunt Celia so suspicious?" and I told him why I asked.

"No idea," he said. "But even as a child, I remember she never wanted to play a princess or a captive queen in games. She always wanted to be a detective."

"And what did you want to play?"

"A general," he said. "That's why," he added bitterly, "it was decided by the fates that I should spend the war at a desk in Washington."

"Were we there?"

"Of course."

"And how long had you been married before I was born?"

He thought for a moment. "Nearly nine years."

I opened my mouth to say that seemed an awfully long time, then closed it again.

"Your mother," he said, tossing a cigarette stub into the fireplace, "was very fragile. The doctors thought she had TB and sent her up to Saranac Lake. That's why, until we knew she was all right, we couldn't have you."

"Sometimes," I said, "I've had the feeling that she didn't want me."

"But you've been the greatest thing in her life, darling."

"A baby, I mean. Oh, she loves babies, but she told me once that she'd had a nurse for me because she couldn't stand changing the diapers and all that—that it was disgusting."

"Oh, we had a nurse, all right," Dad said quickly. "We had a whole staff of servants until the bank crash. Then, as you know, it was ups and downs. Now it'll be the ups again just as soon as the mine gets into production."

"And where will we live? You'll have to stay in Arizona, won't you?"

Paco came in with my eleven o'clock lemonade and Dad's highball and then bowed good night. "I won't have to be tied here," Dad said. "I want to take you to Europe—you'll love it. But I'm afraid we'll have to wait until next summer."

I didn't care. And I knew by now that wherever he was, I had to be with him. For some reason, I had a loyalty toward him that I didn't have toward Mother —in fact, I'd been careful not to tell her that we had servants; she wouldn't understand. I decided that it was because Dad and I were adventurous and she was timid that I felt closer to him.

"Do you mind if I go on the stage?" I asked Dad.

"Not if you're as good as Madge Kennedy and Maude Adams," he said. "And don't you worry about the Theatre Guild. We'll get you to the best dramatic school in New York."

"And you'll be in New York?"

"When I get this mine going," he said. "New York is the place to triple the money—but you know how I feel about discussing that."

It would be wonderful.

But I didn't feel so wonderful next morning. I had a short letter from Rick—only about a paragraph—saying he was deep in exams. That New York was hot. That he hoped I was having a wonderful time. And he signed it, "Hastily, Rick."

Not "Miss you."

Well, I wouldn't miss him. Unless I had a proper letter from him later, I wouldn't even write to him again. I told Dad so, and he said, "Well, maybe he is deep in exams, baby. When I used to have to cram in college, I wasn't thinking about anything else."

There was also a letter from Marge:

Kitty says she misses Bob Lee, but she moons around over a soda jerk in Hyannis, and she thinks he's mad about her because he gives her extra scoops. As for me, I'm more sure than ever that I'll never marry. Dick was the last fling of my life. Are you still in love with Rick?

Of course I was, but he was an ache now instead of a pain. I wondered if I was shallow, fickle. Except that there wasn't another boy to be fickle for. Queer, though, I couldn't quite remember Rick's kiss. Now that I knew Dad better I decided to tell him about that kiss and ask him what was wrong with me, so after dinner that night I did.

"The last thing you want me to tell you," he said, "is the truth."

But I said I could take the truth. What was it?

"That you're so young. You'll have dozens of crushes before you finally marry."

"Did you?"

"Of course. It's part of growing up."

I was relieved that he didn't carry on about that kiss, as Mother would have. Instead he said I should meet more young men, and very casually he said he'd order a dozen from a Highway Patrol pal to come on Saturday night—golly, just like you'd order a dozen eggs from the grocer. "Ask Pris to bring a few girl friends and we'll have a party."

But something happened to me during the night, and we never did have that party.

It was still dark when I awakened, terribly hot, and pushed off the blankets. Then I began to shiver. The stars were bright and for some reason I wanted to know what time it was, but I lacked the energy to light the lamp. So I went back to sleep.

A little later something came and sat down on my chest. I thought it was a nightmare, but when I opened my eyes to the darkness, it was still there. I touched my chest and felt nothing, but the weight was still there.

It was a horrible feeling, but I was sure it would go if I got out of bed. And although I could feel the cool of the night through the windows, I couldn't seem to get any air. It was like smothering.

From then on, it was all rather hazy. I didn't want to awaken Dad because he left so early for the mine. But I had to get outside. I believe I put on my slippers but not my robe.

Then I was outside, trying to breathe, but it was even worse than in my room. The desert was too small. I raised my arms to push up the stars because they were too low. They kept closing in on me. I ran farther out into the desert, desperately needing space, but there wasn't any. And the stars were coming down, down, no matter how hard I tried to push them up. Then I must have run up against thorns or a prickly bush, but that wasn't what made me scream and scream—it was because the world wasn't big enough.

The next thing I remember is some man sitting beside me and placing something cold on my chest, like metal. I believe Dad was there, too, standing at the end of the bed. Outside, I could hear someone crying, and I wondered why.

I thought about dying, and I just didn't care. This was more a feeling than a real thought. I wasn't in any pain. I sort of floated. And I didn't mind at all where I floated to. The only person I knew who had died was Mr. Canello. If there was any heaven, probably neither of us would get in, but I certainly didn't believe in hell.

After a while I woke up and said, "Hello, Lisa," since she was sitting on the foot of my bed.

"Darling," she said. "Don't you know me?"

"You look so much like Mother," I said.

She came close. "Oh, darling, don't you *know me?*" To please her, I said, "Yes."

It was after the next day—I wasn't sure about time —after taking a pill from her, that I realized it really was Mother and that I wasn't going to die but that I'd had pneumonia.

I was in bed about a week more and I slept a lot. Dr. Bunnie—imagine, what a name for a dignified M.D.— said I could get up part of each day. But those days were very strange.

For one thing, Dad moved his things to the Reedes' and gave Mother his room. She had said the bed was too small for them and that they'd both be uncomfortable. He came to dinner each night almost like a visitor and left about eleven. Lupe and Concha stopped singing at their work. And Mother, who didn't think Mexican food was good for me, took over the cooking.

She didn't complain about the little house, but I knew she hated it, especially the outhouse and the baths in the woodshed. I felt trapped with her there, having to be in bed so much. Then Dad suggested that Mother might like to go on a business trip to Los Alamos with him—I'd be perfectly safe here—but she made all sorts of excuses, mainly that I might get pneumonia again and walk out into the desert and not be heard.

"Emily," Dad said, and very firmly, "if you want to take the trip, you don't have to worry about Julie. Priscilla Reede can stay with her."

"But she's only Julie's age."

"She's not a cretin."

She put up every possible objection, and he knocked them all down. The final thing was she appealed to Dr. Bunnie. "I really shouldn't leave Julie, should I?" and he said, "Why not? She's convalescing very well, and I'll stop by each afternoon."

I wonder if Mother had what Freud called a martyr complex—not wanting to have fun. After they did leave together, Pris told me that Los Alamos was terrifically romantic and if she ever got married she wanted to spend her honeymoon there.

Funny, as soon as Mother and Dad were gone, Lupe and Concha began singing again. They had learned how Mother scrambled eggs, but they looked the other way when I sneaked chili or a tamale. Pris and I got along fine, and one evening Paul and Bert O'Neill came by. There wasn't any whoopee—we just sat and talked by the fire, toasted marshmallows, and they told lovely, gory stories about the early settlers here and Indian raids and the ghosts that people think they see in the canyons.

Mr. and Mrs. Reede came by just once to see that we were okay, and Dr. Bunnie let me stay up all day and said I could eat whatever I liked.

Mother and Dad came home next day at noon. I thought she looked prettier than usual, with a light tan and her hair all piled up—she said it was to keep the heat off her neck but I thought it becoming. They had lunch with Pris and me, and then a car drove up and a man asked for Dad, looking very angry.

"Excuse me," Dad said, and walked outside with him.

He was gone about twenty minutes, his coffee cooling, and then he came back and said, "Sorry," and went on talking—about folklore.

"Who was that?" Mother asked.

"Just someone on business."

It happened again about two hours later—another man—and he looked angry, too; Dad went out again. Then Pris said she really should go and Dad drove her home.

"Did you have a nice trip?" I asked Mother, who was unpacking her suitcase.

"Yes."

"What was Los Alamos like?"

She didn't reply. She shook out a dress and hung it on the door. "Those men," she said, and began to cry, but so softly that if I hadn't seen tears I might have thought she just had the sniffles. "Those men."

"What about them?"

She turned. "He's been living on credit—nothing but promises—running up bills with tradesmen—"

"Oh, he'll pay them," I said. I mean, what a fuss about nothing.

"—signing things at the hotels, charging everywhere, even the gas stations. I can't live like that. I won't."

"But he'll pay when the mine starts—you know that."

"You mean *if*. This shed we're living in—do you suppose it's paid for? Or the servants? Or that tacky dress you're wearing?"

"It isn't! It's Mexican—"

"If your father wants to go native, that's *his* privilege. We're leaving here just as soon as I write Celia to send for us.

"Yes!" she said as I stared at her. "I'm in debt, too,

(189)

for this trip and for the tickets home. Heaven knows when I'll be able to repay her—I'll have to get right back to my job. And do you think he's given me one single dime for the rent? I had to borrow that from Celia, too."

I couldn't think of anything to say; I was too miserable. The trouble was, though I didn't love her as I did Dad, I was starting to see both sides.

"Couldn't we stay just a little longer? Please."

"No," she said. "I'm phoning Celia this afternoon, as soon as your father comes back to drive me to town."

There was no way to persuade her.

As soon as Dad came back, she went out to the car and got in and they were gone for two hours. I suppose he was trying to argue her into faith and she was being cynical. It was a bad time for me, wondering who would win, but I think I knew she would.

Then Dad came in and said, "Mail," and gave me a letter. Mother was behind him. They both looked very sad, so that I wasn't even curious about my letter. Dad called for Paco—he had to call twice, down the road— to bring drinks. I went into my room and took just a minute to see that the letter was from Rick. It ended, "Hope all is well."

I joined Mother and Dad in the little room that we called a living room and Paco offered us drinks from a tray and bowed out. Mother said, tasting her drink, "Julie, you're not having this, are you?"

"Oh, I'm used to it," I said.

"Better she learns to drink at home than in some speakeasy," he said, smiling at me.

"But gin at her age!"

"I'm nearly sixteen."

She has such a pretty mouth, but it doesn't look nice when she prims it up.

"I can assure you," Dad said, "that Julie has been a perfect lady since she's been here."

I think he was being a little sarcastic, but I couldn't blame her. That prim mouth, and the way she hitched down her skirt, which nobody does any more.

"Your mother wants to go home next week," Dad said.

He looked at me over the rim of his glass, and his eyes were so bleak, almost dead-dark, and his voice without any tone at all. It's a terrible thing, but at that moment, like perhaps I always do, I said to myself: Remember this. Keep every memory to use later. Eyes, voices, mouths. It will all go into what Mrs. Curran calls "the storeroom of the unconscious" that someday I'll draw on when I'm an actress. A lot better to have people's expressions and voices than just costumes and makeup. And when Mother put down her drink, I noticed the way she pleaded with her hand, held out to nothing in particular.

I didn't have any choice, of course; I had to go with her. They didn't bring up the matter of Aunt Celia's sending the money, but I assumed we would leave as soon as it came.

Then Mother said she thought she'd take a little walk before the sun went down, and when she left, I said, "Dad, I've still got most of Mr. Forster's fifty dollars. If you'd let me stay on a few weeks, I could take the bus home."

But he shook his head.

I wished I could talk to him as I usually did, but it was as if Mother were still in the room. I tried to get back to normal.

"I have absolute faith in your mine," I said.

"Good," he said, and he turned away and shuttered the window.

On the last night before we left, while Mother packed, Dad suggested a walk and put his jacket over me.

"Your mother thought I sent the amethyst earrings," he said. "I told her you had and she was pretty upset." He stopped and lit a cigarette, cupping his hand against the wind. "She insisted on leaving them here and having me return them and send you the money."

It was the same old thing—surely wanting them but being a martyr. After all, they'd cost only $3.50. You couldn't pay much rent with that.

"She thinks I'm a—"

He didn't say anything more. But he meant "a failure," and I didn't want to hear him say it, because it wasn't true—just because he owed bills.

"Dad," I said, "you know I'd stay with you if I could, don't you?"

He mashed out the cigarette with his foot and then dug his heel into it.

"I'm happier here," I said. Then I thought of Rick, who seemed closer now that I was going back. "Have you talked to Mother about Rick?"

"Does he mean so much now?"

"I won't have much of anything else," I said. "All my friends will be out of town. Besides, I do like him."

"Then I'll talk to her."

"But please don't tell her about the kiss?"

"I won't," he said. "It's a three-way secret. But, Julie —make sure it doesn't go beyond a kiss."

I promised it wouldn't.

"Will it be terribly long before you come to New York?" I asked.

He said he hoped not. But he didn't sound like himself, and I thought, Mother has taken the certainty out of him, and who's going to put it back? And maybe it was the way the moonlight, touched his face, but he looked strained and older, and I couldn't help it, I began to cry.

He held me very tightly, and then he said, "It will all work out, darling. It's only a damned shame that you have to be in the middle of—financial problems."

Oh, I'd have stayed with him and lived on plain beans and slept in the woodshed, but I thought of a word that Mr. Skinner had said was the ugliest four-letter word in the English language—duty. I couldn't let Mother go back alone.

Fifteen

IT WAS a long, awful, monotonous trip because we didn't sleep well sitting up in the coach. I insisted that we eat at least once in the dining car because I had the money, but she said we would be needing it for the light and gas bills. So we had snacks at station stops.

Heat and wailing babies and more heat. When we got off, finally, Pennsylvania Station was a big gray oven. But waiting at the gate was Aunt Celia, and she had a porter whisk us out into Mr. Forster's limousine, where the chauffeur stowed our luggage and drove us uptown to our house.

Almost immediately the two of them went into Mother's bedroom, and I suppose they were talking about money, because when I passed by to go into the bathroom, I heard Aunt Celia say, "But I don't need it, dear. Just stop worrying."

Then they came out, and Aunt Celia said she had stocked our icebox yesterday, and she certainly had— so we had chicken salad and cake and iced tea. It seemed very strange to be home—the apartment

(193)

looked so much smaller, although it was bigger than Dad's house. I suppose the desert creates a mirage of things, making them seem bigger than they really are.

Mother said, "What Julie must have is a job, until school starts."

I liked the idea. "But what can I do?"

"Help me," Aunt Celia said, and explained that she needed someone to help sell clothes and tidy up things like basting threads and be at her apartment when she had to go out. So it was decided that I'd start work Monday at twelve dollars a week, with lunches and subway fares.

After she left, Mother said, "I suppose charity begins at home," and all of a sudden I wasn't excited about the job any more. Aunt Celia was just doing me a favor.

"Why do you ruin things so?" I said.

"What do you mean?"

"People are thrilled about something—my first job—and then you spoil it all!"

"And I spoiled Arizona for you, too?"

"I didn't say that."

"Well, you and your father made it fairly clear that you could have gotten along very well without me. And don't think I'd have intruded, but even you would have come to me if you'd believed I was dying."

She was sitting on the couch, and I went over and knelt beside her. "I never said you spoiled Arizona."

"But I know I did. You two are just alike—I'm the different one, and I can't—I can't help it."

She put her face in her hands, and I tried to take one of her hands but she pulled it away. "Go and phone your boyfriend," she said. "Go on."

But I sat there waiting for her to stop that awful, silent sobbing.

"Please," I begged her. "Tell me what's the matter."

But she shook her head.

"If it's money, I'll be working soon. And then Dad will—"

She put her hands down and threw back her head and laughed. "'Dad will.' Oh, God, when will you ever wake up? Or are you going to be the Sleeping Beauty for the rest of your life?"

I pitied her, but at the same time I felt a kind of revulsion that anybody could sneer at somebody else's dream. And I didn't think Dad was just dreaming; he was working at something that he had faith in and that she didn't.

Then she got up and went into her room.

I was too depressed to call Rick, so I went downstairs to see if Mac was in, but Dan said he was on vacation for two weeks. I think he was the only person in the world I could have talked to.

Upstairs, I unpacked my suitcases and hung things up and then tiptoed into the bathroom to take a shower. There wasn't a sound from Mother's room, and I hoped she was asleep.

She seemed normal enough the next day, and then, the day after, she went back to work.

That evening she asked me, "Well, did you phone him? That boy?"

She knew perfectly well his name was Rick, or maybe she had what Mrs. Curran called a mental block about his name. It seems when you don't like somebody or something your mind instructs you to forget the name.

"Rick," I said. "Ricci Innocente. No, I haven't called him."

"Why not?"

Partly because she had me so depressed and partly because his two letters had been so unromantic. And what would I say to him? "My father approves of you"? And suppose he said, "Well, that's very nice, see you sometime"?

"I haven't had time," I told her.

The truth was, I was afraid to.

I liked working for Aunt Celia, but there wasn't much to do. Most of her customers were in Europe or Southampton. She said one thing I could learn, to help her, was to type. A big glossy machine came from Mr. Forster's office, and after about a week I got the knack of it and could make out a bill so people could read it. And, of course, I wrote Marge and Dad when there was nothing else to do.

And then, at the end of that week, I called Rick.

He sounded terribly surprised, but pleased, too. Yes, he had passed his exams, but just barely in Biology, and he was studying it at night. By day he worked in his father's store—he'd just come home for lunch.

"I hope I can see you?" he asked.

Thank Heaven for that. I said, "Yes," and he said he'd take me to the movies tomorrow night.

But we didn't go to the movies—we had a lot to talk about. We walked over to the Drive and sat on the grass, and I told him all that had happened. I think the pneumonia really interested him and, just like Dad, he took off his jacket and put it around me.

As it grew darker, the lights of Palisades Amusement Park came on across the Hudson. He reached for my hand. And I wondered how on earth I could have imagined I was forgetting him in Tucson—I'd been fooling myself.

Around us, behind the bushes, other couples lay on rugs and necked. But he didn't try to kiss me. And it didn't worry me because I knew he wanted to, but not here.

When I'd dated Robert and Everett, long silences had always upset me and I'd chatter to fill them in. But with Rick not saying anything was perfectly comfortable, although the way he held my hand was exciting.

"I'm sorry you got sick," he said finally, "but I'm glad you came home early. This summer's been hell."

"Why?"

"My parents quarreling. Mother wants me to go on with medicine, but my father wants to expand—not just one Italian store, but a chain of them, and put me in to learn the business and take over later."

"He should have told you that before you went into medicine."

"Oh," he said, sounding exasperated. "I've refused to stop medicine. I've got a scholarship, and it's not costing him anything but secondhand books. Not even that this term, with the money I've saved from clerking."

Parents, I thought, absolutely try to upset a person's youth. I told him I thought I agreed about experiments in Russia, where families gave their children to the state or something, and he said yes, but the state might force something worse than the parents. On the other hand, the state wouldn't be sentimental about grocery stores and carrying on the same business just because your father did.

"One thing about my father," I said, "he doesn't mind if I go on the stage. It's Mother I'll have to convince. I think she's just saving her ammunition till next year."

"I'm on your side," he said. Then from behind the bushes somebody with a ukulele began "I'll Get By." All around us, softly, people began to sing. We did too.

"Would you rather have gone to a movie?" he asked.

"No." Because movies are fake and this was real.

It was getting dark and cold, so we got up off the grass and walked, hand in hand, up the Drive a little way. There was the Claremont Inn, lit up like a ship on shore, and he said, "Let's go in."

But I knew it was terribly expensive and said so. And I'd given Mother all my money.

"Never mind," Rick said.

We sat on the terrace and had coffee and sandwiches and then we danced, his cheek against my hair, and he said something softly in Italian. I don't know if it was a love word or not, but I believe it was. We'd have stayed on and on, except people in evening clothes were coming in, and the waiter brought our bill in that suave way they have of indicating "Get out," very politely.

Besides, I had to get home by eleven, and it was nearly that.

Rick insisted on coming upstairs with me. Mother, who was in her dressing gown, started to go to her room. But I said, "Please stay a minute. Rick just wanted to say hello."

She had a cup of tea in her hand and smiled and sat down, making sure the dressing gown covered her nightgown. Did we want tea? No, we'd had coffee at the Claremont.

I can always tell when she's impressed. The mayor and movie stars go to the Claremont, and it was the site of the first steamboat sailing way back. She asked if we'd seen any celebrities.

To tell the truth, we hadn't seen anybody; we'd been too busy with each other until that waiter came. "And how have you been?" she asked Rick. I was almost certain she didn't remember his name.

He told her he had passed his exams, and he offered her a cigarette. She said no, thanks, but not coldly. Then he said, "May I take Julie to Palisades Park Saturday night?"

She nodded. "But she must be home by midnight."

There wasn't any chance for a kiss at the door—she saw us down the hall. As I paused to go into my room, she said, "It's odd. He looks a little bit like your father."

"Yes," I said.

"Like a much younger brother."

"Yes."

She fiddled with my bed light, and then she kissed me good night, but as if she were thinking of something else, and she left me.

Instead of being able to fall asleep thinking of Rick, I thought of her. Nothing to look forward to—no faith in Dad, as I had. I think that some people just naturally want to be unhappy. If Mother didn't have the excuse of no money, she'd be sure to find something else.

She had a very good excuse next day when I came home to tell her that Aunt Celia had to go to Paris to select new clothes. Obviously, I couldn't work in that apartment alone. Why not? There was a doorman and a desk clerk downstairs. I could perfect my typing, and if any customers came, I knew the stock.

She phoned Aunt Celia, and for the first time I think they had a fight, but of course all I could hear was Mother's end of it:

"I don't want Julie alone there," and then, "But *I'd* be nervous," and finally, "She doesn't know enough about the business yet.

"I am *not* being an alarmist," Mother said. Then she paused. "Well, we'll get along somehow, but I am not risking it. You'll be away a whole six weeks. You don't realize what a child Julie is. She'd probably forget to lock the door."

Mother made such a fuss about my working there alone that it meant either hiring someone else or closing the apartment, and so Aunt Celia closed the apartment. But she told me I could have the typewriter until she came back in late August. And she convinced Mother that, by practicing typing until school started, I would have a much better chance in life than just filling in somewhere for a summer job.

I began to pick and peck quite well, but, of course, this gave Mother the idea that I could become a secretary after school was finished, if I took a business course. I wrote to Dad in a hurry, that very day she said it, and told him my plans about being an actress would amount to nothing if he didn't move in fast and squelch her. "Thanks to you," I wrote, "I am seeing Rick, and tonight we're going to Palisades Park."

That was a funny, upside-down night. I'd sworn I'd never go on another roller coaster, but I did with him, hiding my head on his shoulder and screaming all the way down the terrible drop. Then I wondered why, on top of that, I went into those buckets with him that shake you to pieces so that you come out like Shredded Wheat. And the giant seesaw. But I didn't want to be shot out of a cannon, and he said my adrenaline had given out. We walked around eating salty, hot fried potatoes.

Rick was spending an awful lot, what with the rides and dance tickets and ice cream and hot dogs, but it was heavenly. Lots of pretty girls stared at him, and I wondered how many girls he had, remembering that his sister hadn't been able to keep track. I suppose most of them were out of town or he wouldn't be dating me on a Saturday night.

Rick offered me a cigarette. "No," I said. "I was only trying to smoke to be smart. I don't really like the taste."

"I do," he said, and lit a Camel. "Are you usually so honest with yourself?"

"I don't know. It's just that I tell the truth to myself sometimes. But it's hard to face the truth about other people—older people. Especially when you're not sure what's true. My parents, for instance," and I told him how Mother had said she wasn't like us, but left it all as a question mark. "She doesn't seem to approve of Dad, but I'm sure she loves him. It's almost as if she said to herself, 'I mustn't do this because it would make me happy.'"

"Ah, Julie," he said, and he sounded so sad you'd have thought it was *his* mother. But I was afraid he was sorry for me, so I pulled out my compact and powdered my nose and we walked around for a while before we took the ferryboat home.

All these opportunities tonight, and he didn't kiss me. Somebody played an accordion aboard, and a lot of people had their arms around each other, but Rick just stood beside me, and we watched the moon cruise over New York and the black water rushing by. When we got to my house, he tipped up my face and gave it a little stroke with his hand and said, "I'll phone you."

I think Mr. Forster must have missed Aunt Celia terribly because he began doing so many nice things for us. First came a white wicker hamper of fruit—the kind that looks false because it's so big and perfect—and after Mother had written him a thank-you note for that, along came his chauffeur with another wicker hamper, tied with a big yellow bow and containing brandied figs, anchovies, caviar, cheeses, watermelon

...vage basket for people who weren't
...ter he'd been thanked for that, up
...of white and purple asters and

..." Mother said, "but I wonder
...way into this family."

...horrid. "He just loves Aunt Celia,
...onely. Why don't we ask him to din-

...

But it wasn't really shabby, and after all, he'd been
here before. "Why not?"

"Well," she said, "I guess it would be all right. Celia
looked him up in Dun & Bradstreet."

"I don't care how much money he has," I said. "I like
him."

"It isn't money," Mother said, "it's credit. A credit
rating. Those things he sent aren't necessarily paid
for."

"If Aunt Celia isn't suspicious of him," I said, "I don't
see why you should be. I'm not."

"Oh, you," she said. "You'd trust anyone."

Not just anyone, but I really couldn't see what was
wrong in asking Mr. Forster to dinner. When he said
he'd like to come, we remembered that he was probably accustomed to very fancy foods and might like a
change.

So it was baked ham and corn pudding and green
beans, and I never saw a man eat so much. I think he'd
gotten thinner—perhaps because he missed Aunt
Celia. But he still had those protuberant eyes, like blue
grapes about to pop out. Not that he could help it, but I
just wondered if they'd stay in. Then I forgot about
them because he was so nice, telling me how good I'd
been as Queen Elizabeth and asking what I planned to
do next.

I'd almost forgotten about *Ichabod Crane,* then said
it would be lots easier writing that play on his typewriter and I could even make carbon copies. And he
said it wasn't his typewriter, but mine.

"How kind of you," Mother said, servin
shortcake. "But we can't accept it."

"But there are a dozen typewriters in the of
Forster said.

"Just the same," Mother said with that thin-
look, "it's far too much."

But Mr. Forster wasn't going to be intimidat
"Julie," he said, "it's your typewriter."

After he left, thanking us for a wonderful evening, and I'd washed all the dishes, Mother said, "Well, he *seems* quite nice."

And I blew up. "Seems? He *is*!"

"Don't you raise your voice to me!"

But I couldn't say I was wrong for defending Mr. Forster. I just used the cold technique and said, "I'm sorry," and went to my room.

There was this terrible wave of homesickness for Dad that made disappointment about Rick's not calling for four days just nothing. Rereading Dad's last two letters didn't help any, either. He didn't sound as optimistic as usual—perhaps Mother had taken that out of him. Not a word about the mine or prospects of his coming here—just hoping I was okay and sending me greetings from the Delgados and Pris and Lisa. And ending, "Remember how much I love you."

I was so depressed, sitting there on my bed, that I thought, She didn't want me, or she wouldn't have found me "disgusting" as a baby. I shouldn't have been born.

Life without Dad would be awfully dreary, and I had only another year before Mother was sure to wreck my dream of going on the stage. Now that I was beginning to type, she'd send me to some office job.

Tears can be a relief, but I was beyond them, in a dark gray misery.

Sixteen

NEXT MORNING I woke up late and was surprised to find Mother still in her dressing gown. Her cheeks were so pink that at first I thought she had a fever. Then she smiled and said, "I'm taking the day off, Julie—look!"

And she waved a check in front of me for three thousand dollars.

Then I read Dad's letter. The mine was in production. This was just a token payment "for rent and essentials" until he came home.

My first thought was, He'll be with us soon, and my second, I won't have to type for a living. My third was that Mother was absolutely a changed person. She hugged me, she wanted to dress up and go somewhere for lunch, but first—naturally—she began making out checks for rent and electricity even though the new electric bill was only two days old.

I had always believed in Dad, but this had come so unexpectedly. And Mother was behaving so *young*. She tried on two old hats and finally chose another one and perked it up with a little veil. She said that we would both buy new hats and silk stockings after lunch.

But she hadn't changed so very much. Instead of a taxi we took the bus downtown and went to Mary Elizabeth's tearoom, not the Waldorf. Not that I cared. This was like an episode in a movie series, although, as I recall, Pearl White was always left teetering on a cliff or tied to rails. What I mean is, it didn't seem real.

We deposited the check in a bank and then bought shoes and hats and stockings. And window blinds at Woolworth's. Mother seemed almost like a girl friend, but I wasn't stupid enough to confide in her about Rick. I suppose there were lots of good reasons he hadn't called. I saw them all as girls—older, prettier, with no reason to be home by midnight.

We both wrote Dad that night, and I took the letters down to the mail slot in the lobby, and there was Mac. Between switchboard calls we talked about our vacations, and then I told him about Rick not calling. He said, "Don't worry."

"But if he really cared about me—"

"What could he do? You're just a very young lady."

He paused, taking a call, and then said, "What's the rush, Julie?"

"It's not that I want to get married yet, but I do think Rick could sort of reserve me—like an engagement. I'll be sixteen next week."

"And next week how do you know you won't meet somebody else?" He sounded like Dad now. "Maybe it's just an episode. Plenty of time to tell. You all seem to be going too fast, like a roller coaster. What to? I'm not talking about you, Julie, but some kids, you'd think it was their last day on earth. And older people just as bad. Worse, maybe. Something too hectic about the way things are I don't like. Odessa and me, we're saving what we've got—all our friends are spending. I make home brew; our friends, they've got to have scotch off the boat. Nightclubs. We dance at home. I'm not cheap, but to spend five dollars for just setups and shoving around a little floor the size of a nickel—is that dancing?"

"I guess not."

"You just be glad your father's coming home and leave it all to him."

Dad telephoned the next night and asked Mother to look for a bigger apartment. I heard her say, "Oh, not Park Avenue—it's too expensive and far away from Julie's school and my job." Then evidently he told her to give up her job because she said, "But I'll need it, in case anything happens."

He must have said, "Put Julie on," because she called to me, and he told me he would be home in about two weeks and was sorry to miss my birthday but he'd make up for it. "We can't live in that tiny little apartment," he said. "You help your mother look for something bigger and don't let her worry about money."

I expected her to put up a fight about that, but maybe she was just tired of fighting, because next day we found an apartment on Fifth Avenue and 82nd Street—with two baths and three bedrooms and a study, besides the big living room and kitchen and dining room. She wandered around it, trying to find things wrong with it, but there weren't any; it even faced Central Park. So the next day she went to the real estate agent to put a deposit on it.

That day Rick called and said he was going to visit a friend in Atlantic City for two weeks. No excuses about why he hadn't phoned before, just the kind of talk a big brother might make, like hoping I was looking forward to school. I told him school was a whole month away—and I felt years away from him, he was so cool. I couldn't think what I'd done at Palisades Park to cause that, but since he seemed to be getting rid of me, I didn't tell him about Dad or moving or anything. I just wished him a happy vacation. I felt like a sponge that somebody'd squeezed.

Dad sent another check, this time for six thousand dollars, and I think Mother was finally convinced that it wasn't one of his daydreams. We moved—what a mess *that* was—and our furniture didn't half fill the new apartment. Except for dinner out at a little French place, my birthday passed without any excitement except a telegram and flowers from Dad and a vanity case and Coty lipstick from Mother, who said I could use it now—within reason.

I felt as if I were on a desert island. Marge didn't write, and I missed Mac, who, with Dan, forwarded mail and gave people our new phone number. We were on the tenth floor, and it seemed very high and removed and cold—not in temperature, but because of the ice-blue wallpaper and steel-gray tapestry sort of stuff. Mother quit her job and spent the next few days fiddling around with the furniture, but saying she wasn't going to buy new curtain material or anything until Aunt Celia came back from Europe—she was so artistic and could get materials at cost. The only visitors we had were Mother's women friends, who came up to coo about how gorgeous it all was. And one night Mr. Forster asked us out to dinner at the Central Park Casino. When the dance music started, I began missing Rick terribly and wondered if I'd ever see him again.

I've been trying very hard to avoid a cliché that Mr. Skinner would scalp me for: luxury does not bring happiness. Not even one's very own bathroom and a doorman downstairs to bow and say, "Good morning, Miss Willis." So I was even glad when Robert returned from Lake George and took me to a movie, and gladder when Marge and Kitty came back and I spent the night at their house.

"I'm sorry I didn't write," Marge said, "but for the past three weeks I've been dating this marvelous boy—"

"She's had three since July," Kitty said.

"Shut up. But he'll be a freshmen at Princeton and I won't see him except—"

"Proms," Kitty said.

"Shut *up*. Why don't you go out and roll a hoop or something?"

Kitty left, offended, while we talked over our love lives. Or rather Marge's, because nobody took Kitty seriously and I didn't have any. But Marge said Norman would have lots of friends at Princeton, and we could go to proms together, and just to forget about Rick, as she had forgotten about Dick. And wasn't the main thing having Dad back and money for dramatic school next year?

After dinner Kitty took Trixie out and Marge said, "I'm afraid it's the same old thing—boy-chasing. Only she doesn't throw things at them any more or whistle —what's the matter, Julie?"

I suddenly felt so old. If Rick had phoned at that very moment, I don't think I'd have been thrilled. I suppose it was world-weariness. A certain spring had ended and the autumn was coming on.

I tried to explain.

"Boys are a dime a dozen," Marge said, not meaning her Norman. "What you always wanted was your father back, and now he's coming."

"Of course," I said.

"Dramatic school."

"Yes."

"Europe next summer. It'll be marvelous."

I wondered.

You can't imagine what Aunt Celia did to our new apartment in one week. Suddenly there were no ice-blues or steel-grays, but pale primrose and crimson draperies against white walls in the living room and I was all set up in a pink ruffled bedroom.

And then Dad came home.

Mother had said that he should have the third bedroom, which I thought was a pity since it could have been used as a guest room. Anyway, Aunt Celia found a bed and chest at an auction. On the very first night, we had a celebration—just the family, which now seemed to include Mr. Forster.

It was about 2 A.M. when Mr. Forster and Aunt

Celia left, and Mother said that we must be tired, but Dad and I said no. We were sitting together on a love seat facing the big window, and he was smoking a very plump cigar.

"Well then," Mother said, and kissed us both and left us.

Dad got up and went to the champagne bucket. "Have the rest of it, Julie—it will only go flat." He poured me about half a glass, which finished it.

"But what about you?" I asked.

"Brandy," he said, and poured some from a decanter. "I'm glad you persuaded your mother to move. I was afraid she wouldn't."

"Oh, she likes it here now."

He was silent for a while. Then he said, "Well, we should get to sleep. I've an appointment on Wall Street at ten. Would you like to come along?"

"I'd love to."

He started to stub out his cigar, and then he said, extending his glass, "Good dog."

I woofed and brought him more brandy. Oh, it was so marvelous having him here. I realized it was hours since I'd thought of Rick. Just a crush.

"Tomorrow," he said, "we must buy a radio. And we'll have lunch at Ye Olde Chop House—remember?"

Did I! Now that I was older I could appreciate it more.

We separated out in the hall and kissed good night, but I lay awake for some reason. His room was next to mine and I heard him in there and in the connecting bathroom and then his footsteps along the hall toward Mother's room.

The apartment was very quiet except for the purr of traffic far below. I shut my eyes and wondered if I should wear the blue or the rose-colored dress tomorrow; it was sure to be hot.

I had just turned over, my face in the pillow, when I heard Dad come back into his room again. Then I slept.

Wall Street may be exciting to men, but to me it was

just a bore, sitting in what Dad said was a broker's office. He left me to go off somewhere with a man, but a lot of people were sitting near me, watching a silvery kind of tape moving along on a wall that said: *American Can* 77, *General Motors* 139½, *US Steel* 138⅛, and a whole lot of other companies. Some women sitting near me seemed as bored as I was, but a few had little gold pencils out, taking notes on bits of paper pressed onto their purses. Somebody said, "If Hoover gets in, it'll all go up," and the woman next to me sniffed. And then I was rescued by a young woman who said to come with her, and she took me into a quiet separate room and gave me coffee and told me that my father would be here soon.

"It"s a kind of gambling, isn't it?" I asked her.

"Not with the right advice," she said, and smiled at me. "Millions can be made on the stock market. We consider it investment."

Dad came in with a very elegant old man whom he introduced as Mr. Friar. Mr. Friar must have thought I was from Arizona because he asked me how I liked New York. He acted like a servant to Dad, almost, bowing us out. We walked toward Cedar Street.

"Wow!" I said. "You must have bought a lot."

"Oh, not so much. General Electric, General Motors, Montgomery Ward—and if radio will go up, I'll buy AT&T. Let's have lunch and then go and buy a radio."

Ye Olde Chop House hadn't changed—I hope it never will. Darkish oak and no tablecloths. We had wild duck and stuffed potatoes and Stilton cheese. Then we took a taxi uptown and bought a radio at Macy's. They said they would send it, but Dad said we wanted it right away, so we took it with us in another cab.

"I didn't know you cared much about music," I said as the cab started up Fifth Avenue.

"But you do. And I never gave you a proper birthday present. Now, before we go any farther uptown—what do you think your mother might like?"

I had to think. It would be awful to say, "Just money."

"What would you think?" I asked.

"Clothes?"

But Aunt Celia hadn't even unpacked trunks full of things from Paris, and Mother liked getting bargains. Anyway, we decided to consider it later.

During dinner at home Dad suggested we should have a housewarming and invite my young friends, too, and I thought it was a dignified way of asking Rick up. But Mother had the habit of poverty. We couldn't afford to have a lot of people in, not until we were sure that the mine wouldn't fail.

"Fail!" he said. "It won't, Emily. It's doing better than I'd even dreamed it would. When I called Tucson this afternoon—"

"You *telephoned?*" Mother asked.

"Of course I did. I have to keep in touch."

"You could have written."

She had a headache that night and went to bed early. And the same thing happened the next night. But Dad and I had wonderful evenings. We walked in Central Park, which is lovely just before it gets dark. We listened to Rudy's radio program, and although I'm not sure Dad was wild about it, he was respectful and didn't talk. And while he read the stock market reports, I worked on my play, but in the same room—I didn't want to be far from him. I suppose I was so accustomed to his being away that I was afraid this couldn't be real.

I hadn't quite forgotten about Rick, although it really didn't hurt. Dad said, "He's probably got good reasons, baby. After all, he's older than you—"

"Maybe he was just a father image?"

I explained Freud to Dad, and he chuckled. "I'd say he was caught between several considerations. His career, being pressured into the family business—and your mother. Oh, I'm sure she was polite, but the main point is, you're just at the wrong ages. He's in no position to ask you not to date other boys, and he's probably proud."

There's Dad for you—always trying to boost one's ego. What I thought was, Rick had another girl—or two or three.

"The funny thing is, it doesn't matter much—now that you're here."

Each day he went down to Wall Street and came home looking very happy, although, of course, he didn't talk about business. And nearly every day he called someone in Tucson, and Mother turned cool; she really had a thing about using long distance except for life-and-death calls. Marge and Kitty came for dinner one night, and I could tell they were terribly impressed by Dad because, when he put them into a cab, Marge whispered, "You never said he looked like an old movie star."

I didn't mind that "old"; I knew what she meant.

Mother's headaches, which always came at night, began to worry me, but she refused even to consider seeing a doctor. She urged Dad and me to go out in the evenings with Aunt Celia and Mr. Forster, so we saw *The Trial of Mary Dugan* on Broadway and *Funny Face* and *Showboat*. In the ladies' room at the Astor Aunt Celia told me that she was probably going to marry Mr. Forster in the winter, but to keep it a secret because her mind wasn't quite made up.

"Don't you trust him?" I asked.

She twirled her silvery cape at the mirror. It had an emerald-green lining that matched her dress. "Well, yes. I think I do. I'm sure I do."

"But don't you love him?"

She stopped twirling and stared at me as if I'd used a word she'd never heard before. "I keep forgetting you're so young," and dropped a quarter into the attendant's pin tray. Imagine, all that money for one tiny towel and the use of the mirror. "Come along," she said, and poked my hair off my eye. I poked it back before we joined the men.

Dad and Mr. Forster stopped a conversation about stocks, and we danced. Dad can really Charleston without making any effort at all, better than most of the college boys on the floor, who looked as if they'd just learned. Dad and I didn't get home until around one, but we were still wide-awake. Quietly, so as not to disturb Mother, we had coffee in the living room.

"I've thought of a gift for your mother," Dad said.

"What?"

"I could give her a personal savings account and the rate of interest—oh, this will bore you, darling."

"Go on," I said.

"A hundred shares of New York Central and a hundred shares of Westinghouse."

And of some other things. I was sure she'd be thrilled. I came over and sat on the floor by his chair and put my head against his knee.

"More than anything in the world," Dad said, "she wants security—and she deserves it. So do you."

"I don't care about it," I said.

"But dramatic school?"

"That's not security. I don't think of acting as making money."

"Someday you might. I think we ought to investigate dramatic schools right now, for next year."

So the next day Dad made some phone calls—I'd no idea he had friends in the theater—and said he was getting information, and he finally came up with what everyone he'd talked to agreed upon—a school named Encore. It had produced so many stars that you couldn't believe it, but it wouldn't accept just any student.

"Of course not," Mother said at dinner. "It's got to be a rich one."

"It's not cheap," Dad said, "but even if she doesn't get a scholarship who cares?"

"Well," Mother said, "it seems I haven't been consulted—as usual."

"Mother," I said, "don't you believe I'm a good actress?"

She hesitated. Maybe she had been just bragging to her friends that time. Then she said, "I think it would be a lot safer if you mastered touch-typing and then took shorthand."

"No," Dad said quietly. "Julie isn't going to be a stenographer. She's going to do what she does best."

What I loved about that, he took me on faith—he didn't even know whether I was any good. Mother said, "Very well," as if she were an aristocrat going to the guillotine. I think she wanted to skip coffee and go in and have a headache, but she and Dad were going to see *The Road to Rome* and then to a party at Mr. Forster's, and she was all dressed up in one of the dresses she'd bought from Aunt Celia—amber-colored crepe with amber beads on it—and she couldn't back out.

While they were gone, Rick called. He sounded very embarrassed, and no wonder. "I wish I could say I'd had the flu or something. But, Julie—it was the measles."

I didn't laugh.

"They stuck me in Willard Parker, that isolation hospital. The next-to-oldest patient in our ward was eleven. I ate prunes and strained spinach. I've probably picked up some baby talk."

You think you've gotten over someone, but his voice was It all over again. He wanted to know where we'd moved to—Mac just gave him the phone number—and I told him about Dad's being here. But when he asked for a date, I was smart, for a change; I said I wasn't sure what Dad had planned ahead, but I'd phone him soon.

So next day, when Dad and I took a cab down to Encore, I said, "Please persuade Mother that we should have a party. It would be easier for you to meet Rick that way." I added, "He's been having the measles."

He didn't laugh either. "Okay—we'll have a party."

The director of Encore was a large gray man with flappy jowls and a magnificent voice; his name was Mr.

Eden. He didn't audition me or anything; he outlined the school's program. He said that in the first term all attention was directed to proper breathing and diction. "Students who aren't very serious find it incredibly dull and drop out. They want to start acting right away without any basics."

"I'd want the basics," I said.

He asked me a lot of questions and said as long as I understood the hard work involved, I could be entered for next year. I signed a couple of things that Dad looked at first. Then they went off together and, I suppose, talked about money, while I stared at photographs of stars on the wall.

Then Dad came back and said, "It's all settled for your first term, paid up from June until October 1929. I was going to offer money for the second term, but he said they granted scholarships, and by then they'd know if you deserved one. Quite an honest guy," he added, as though surprised.

"I'm so happy," I said. "So *happy*."

And Mother agreed to the party. It would be the Saturday night before school started.

Seventeen

I ONCE heard somewhere that the best ingredients for a party are people of different ages, too much smoke, lots of booze, and a separate room for dancing. We cleared out the study for dancing and put the radio in there. Aunt Celia helped with the food, and we hired two maids and a man to mix drinks. And there certainly were people of different ages.

All of Mother's women friends came, including that awful Marie Jeans. She had the nerve to take me aside and say that I should wear a tighter bra, when I was practically in an Iron Maiden. I wondered what she thought of Kitty (who came without a boy—her own fault—once she has one, she doesn't want him), because Kitty looked kind of like a blooming milkmaid. Marge came with Norman (a nice-looking Dick) and, of course, Professor and Mrs. Craig. I'd asked Rick to bring his seventeen-year-old brother, Tony, who was adorable and went right for Kitty like steel to a magnet. And then there was Enid Rosenblum and her date, and Bernice Yellin and her date.

But the surprise was that Dad had so many friends. I'm sure it surprised Mother, too, because she couldn't remember half their names. They all came late, being mostly theater people. Mother kept whispering to Dad, "Where did you meet *her?* Am I supposed to know *him?*" It occurred to me that Dad had had a life in New York that Mother hadn't wanted to share and, even from Arizona, he had kept up these old friendships.

Rick looked just great, not a measle on him. I liked the way he followed me around unless I was dancing with somebody else. Then, around twelve-thirty, I saw him and Dad leave the room together and thought maybe they'd just needed a bathroom at the same time, but they were gone about thirty minutes.

"Well!" Mr. Forster said, bringing me a tiny hot cheese pie on a toothpick. "Are you having fun?"

"S'wonderful," I said.

We went into the study and danced to that, or tried to, since the room was so crowded. "Your Aunt Celia has agreed to marry me," he said.

All those toothpicks would be in the family now, and of course he was probably papered in stocks. But I honestly liked him and congratulated him. "Are you going to announce it tonight?"

"No," he said. "She wants another six months. She says she has some business to tidy up."

"And will you live here in New York?"

"Yes. And Greenwich in the summer."

I adore happy endings because, when you come to think of it, there aren't many. It was hot in that room, and we went back into the living room, and he raised the window a little higher. Looking down on the park, I could see two men on a park bench, and they were Dad and Rick, smoking. So that's where they were. I wondered if they were talking about me, or what. And though Dad was over forty and Rick nineteen they did look alike—older and younger brother.

"Julie." Tony came up. "Dance?"

We did, but I teased him. "How could you leave Kitty Craig?"

"That's a wild one," he said. "Why doesn't she have a date?"

I decided to dignify Kitty. "Oh, she's rather mysterious. She doesn't tell us much. The last one probably jumped off the Brooklyn Bridge."

He laughed. "And what's the way to her cold, cold heart?"

"Ignore her," I said. "I mean, if you're serious."

"But I want to see her again."

"Then take her to the Passion Palace on 123rd Street for a double banana split, chocolate and marshmallow sauce—it's not called that, but she'll know. But remember, ignore her."

"But how can I—I mean if she'll date?"

"Just be remote. Don't phone her regularly. Keep her guessing."

He thanked me. He said that his father had given up on Rick's managing the grocery business someday and had latched on to him. "But I'm going to be a doctor. Or an architect. I'm not sure."

Then Rick cut in on us—I was surprised to find him back again—and I said, "Weren't you and Dad out in the Park?"

"Yeah," he said. "We felt like cigars, and he said your mother doesn't like them."

A tango started, and he twirled me into it. Oh, I tell you, it takes a Latin to dance—except that we didn't have much space. Some of Dad's theater friends were willing to sing, and ukuleles came out of cases, and pretty soon the whole party was in the living room, lots of us sitting on the floor.

A long thin brunette sang "Bill," not quite as well as Helen Morgan, but nearly, so that I could feel goose pimples. And then, a man, without accompaniment, sang "Ol' Man River." But it was a big, voluptuous blonde who really got me with the saddest version of "Can't Help Lovin' Dat Man" I'd ever heard. She wasn't much of a singer, but she was a great actress. Later I talked to her about Encore, and she said she had started there when she was seventeen. "Oh, you'll hate it," she said, "for a while. Is there someplace we can talk quietly?"

We went into my room.

"Do you have paper and a pencil?"

"There at the desk," I said, and she sat down and wrote something and then handed it to me.

"Say it as fast as you can," she said. "Don't study it, just say it fast."

I read aloud, "She stood at the door welcoming him in."

Boy, what a mess I made of that. I tried it four times until finally she said, "You have to take a deep breath on 'welcome' before the 'him in.' Ghastly, isn't it? Want some more?"

So I had, "Are you chary with a cherry in your sherry?" and "A boor in the Boer War was a bore." Much worse than "Peter Piper picked," etc. But I could see how all this practice created good diction, and she said they would help me with all kinds of tricks and that proper breathing was most of the secret. It became second nature to you. Also, the breathing kept you from having a tummy in later years—certainly she didn't, and she must have been thirty or even older.

"I saw *Showboat*," I said, "but I don't believe I saw you."

"I'm Helen Morgan's understudy," she said. "I have to have a dark wig when I'm on."

"Is she sick much?"

"Not very much. When she is, it doesn't last long."

She smiled and got up from the desk. "Well, we should get back to the whoopee, shouldn't we?"

The party broke up about four. Mother, very pale, went to bed, and the maids cleaned up. Dad and I were still wide-awake and sat by the window.

"Rick has asked me to a dance at Columbia on the fifteenth," I said.

"Good," Dad said.

"You like him, then?"

"Very much, baby."

"Did you talk about anything in particular?"

Meaning me, of course. "Oh, lots of things," he said.

"Like what?"

"His career. Your dramatic school. The European situation. Whether Hoover will get in."

"But, Dad, didn't he ask permission to date me?"

"Didn't have to," Dad said, blowing a round, perfect smoke ring. Then he said, "Well, I'd better get a taxi for those maids," and we separated and I went to bed.

But it's harder to sleep when you're happy than when you're miserable. I had everything in the world I wanted, so I didn't have to black out by sleeping. I saw the dawn come up, pink over the park, and then about seven I decided to take a shower. Mother's bathroom has one, mine just a tub, so I tiptoed in.

As I passed her door coming out, I heard her say, "But for her sake."

And Dad's voice: "Yes."

For my sake, what? Oh, dramatic school. Back in my room, I got dressed and then sat at the desk and practiced those phrases, but I couldn't manage, "She stood at the door welcoming him in." No matter how I breathed, it got no better. Then I decided it was about time I returned to *Ichabod Crane.* After a while Mother heard the typewriter and said breakfast was ready.

Dad went down to Wall Street afterwards. It seemed odd on a Sunday, but he said he was meeting some broker for lunch. I don't know why Mother looked so unhappy about that, but she did. To perk up her mood, I asked if she hadn't thought the party was catsy.

"Very nice," she said. "And I thought Rick and his brother were very nice, too."

So she even remembered Rick's name.

I turned on the radio and along came "I'll Get By."

Tho' there be rain and darkness, too.
I'll not complain, I'll see it through.
Poverty may come to me, that's true ...

(219)

"Oh, turn it off," she said.

I did, but I was puzzled. Then she said, "I'm sorry, it always seems to be that monotonous song. I just don't like music in the morning."

"Mother," I said, "what ever happened to a red velvet dress you wore at the World's Fair?"

"Why?" she asked.

"Dad mentioned it when we were in Tucson."

"Oh," she said. "Well, that was a very long time ago. I gave it to Celia and she sold it to Brooks."

"As a costume?"

"Yes. It brought five dollars. We needed the money."

"But we don't need money any more."

"No," she said. "I guess not."

"I wish we could buy back that ball gown."

"What for? To use in a play?"

"Just to keep. You keep other things—lace and buttons."

"Some things," she said, "you can't keep."

"But fashions change. I read in *Vogue* that long dresses are coming back in, and I'm sure you could still wear that—"

"I can't," she said, and got up. "Will you stop? *Will you?*" and then she came to me and hugged me very tightly. "I'm awfully sorry," she said. "I didn't mean to shout at you. I'm just not—too much party, perhaps. Why don't you go ahead and work on your play? Remember, school starts tomorrow."

Dad is so unexpected; I'd been trying to think of a way he could come to visit school, but there weren't any events for a while. And on that very first day he turned up at lunch in the cafeteria, and you should have seen the impact. All the girls who'd thought I didn't have a father turned to look—Vera Jordan positively sullen—and Marge and Kitty joined us at our table, and you could hear a buzz all around the room.

Because Julie Willis did have a father. I suppose most of them thought I'd lied or that he and Mother were divorced. Then later he and I went up to Dr.

Matheson's office, and they had a talk about my grades, which were all good except Biology. Dad told him that when I was graduated next June, I'd be entering Encore, which Dr. Matheson said was fine. Dad attended History (more buzz), and then we went to the Passion Palace for orangeades.

"Baby," he said, "I'm sorry, but I've got to leave tonight."

"Oh!"

"Tucson. But, of course, I'll be back."

"When?"

"I'm not sure. Not long, though."

It seems you can't have a gold mine without attending to it. But although I understood that, I felt awful. "Will you be back in time for *Ichabod Crane?*"

"Next month? Oh, sure."

"I haven't talked to Mr. Skinner yet, but I think Halloween would be a good time for it."

"Yes. Jolly autumn. Baby, don't look so tragic."

"Does Mother know?"

"Yes."

Mr. Forster was busy somewhere, but at six Aunt Celia picked us up in his Rolls. Pennsylvania Station had the same smell—perfume, smoke, and cinders. It was the old smell of saying good-bye and then the old business of swallowing back tears. But Mother didn't cry; she stood very straight as we waved the train off.

Back in the car, Aunt Celia said, "Julie, here's a handkerchief. Emily, I thought we might dine at my place—"

"No," Mother said. "Thank you, but I think Julie and I will just have a snack at home."

But at home neither of us wanted anything.

In bed by eight, I tried to read. Then I thought, If Mother is asleep I might phone Rick just for comfort, but somehow I didn't want to, and I couldn't think of anything Marge would be able to say to help. That room next to mine so terribly empty, nobody sharing the bath. Not for more than a month.

Finally I got to sleep, but I awakened about five—it

was still dark—and when I switched on the light it was five-twenty. I went into the bathroom and then, for some reason, into the living room, where I sat by the window, waiting for the dawn.

Mother came in, in her robe.

"Can't you sleep?" she asked.

"No."

"I can't either."

We sat together on a love seat and looked down. The park was just beginning to show. A few yellow leaves fell.

"Darling," she said, "you know, I like Rick. I even think dramatic school will be good next year."

"Yes," I said. "If I do well."

"Oh, you will. Now, what kind of costume will you need for Katrina Van Tassel?"

"Eighteenth century," I said. "But nothing fancy. She was a country belle. I think a blond wig, curly. I see her in yellow."

"Silk?"

"Sateen would do. With russet panniers."

And I began to cry.

Oh, I knew Dad would be back in time, but it was something I can't explain—those leaves falling and being up at such a peculiar hour.

"Never mind," Mother said. "People are just—and things can be—"

"I know," I said. I wanted to comfort *her* now. "But things are a lot better than they were. I mean, we have money—all those stocks."

"Yes," she said. "And going up all the time."

"Security," I said.

"Yes."

We looked down at the falling leaves, and a wind rose, and more of them tore off the trees, like confetti.

"Well," Mother said, "some coffee?"